**Starcrossed Lovers—
In Outer Space,
And Down-to-Earth...**

He: Virile, vigilant, fearless . . .

She: Beautiful, innocent, outer-worldly . . .

In Space: They tackle unknown planets, challenging danger, adventure, even death. Meanwhile their families, vying for control of interstellar industry, scheme to keep the lovers light years apart . . .

In T.V. Land: The network mogul, producer, director, writer, sexy lady assistant, engineer, actors, and production staff struggle to get "The Starcrossed" series off the ground, in 3-D no less.

Or is it the other way around? Will "The Starcrossed" itself direct the fate of its creators, the future of T.V., and—most important of all —the ratings?

THE STARCROSSED

BEN BOVA

PYRAMID BOOKS NEW YORK

THE STARCROSSED

A PYRAMID BOOK

Published by arrangement with Chilton Book Company

Copyright © 1975 by Ben Bova

Pyramid edition published December 1976

Library of Congress Catalog Card Number: 75-23092

Printed in the United States of America

Pyramid Books are published by Pyramid Publications (Harcourt Brace Jovanovich, Inc.). Its trademarks, consisting of the
word "Pyramid" and the portrayal of a pyramid, are registered
in the United States Patent Office.

PYRAMID PUBLICATIONS
(Harcourt Brace Jovanovich, Inc.)
757 Third Avenue, New York, N.Y. 10017

To Cordwainer Bird...
may he fly high and strike terror
in the hearts of the unjust.

CONTENTS

1: THE BANKERS

"American ingenuity licked the pollution problem," said Bernard Finger, glowingly. "And the energy crisis too, by damn."

Tanned and golden in his new Vitaform Process body, Finger was impeccably dressed in the latest neo-Victorian style Bengal Lancer business suit, complete with epaulets and an authentic brigadier's insignia. He stood at the floor-to-ceiling windows of his sumptuous, spacious office and gazed fondly out at the lovely pink clouds that blanketed the San Fernando Valley.

The late morning sun blazed out of a perfect blue sky. As far as the eye could see, the entire Greater Los Angeles area—from sparkling sea to the San Berdoo Mountains—was swathed in perfumed, tinted clouds. Except for a few hilltops poking up here and there, it all looked like one enormous dollop of pink cotton candy.

"American ingenuity," Bernard Finger repeated. "And American know-how! That's how we beat those A-rabs and those bleeding heart conservationists."

Bill Oxnard watched Finger with some astonishment from his utterly comfortable position, sunk deep into a warmly plush waterchair. Surrounded by pleasantly yielding artificial hides, his loafers all but invisible in the thick pile of the office's carpet, he still kept his attention on Finger.

It was uncanny. Oxnard had met the man eighteen months earlier, before he had gone in for the Vitaform Process. Then he had been a short, pudgy, bald, cigar-chewing loudmouth approaching sixty years of age. Now he looked like Cary Grant in costume for *Gunga Din*. But he still sounded like a short, pudgy, bald, cigar-chewing loudmouth.

The lovely pink clouds that Finger was admiring were smog, of course. Oxnard had driven from his lab in the Malibu Hills through thirty miles of the gunk to get to Finger's lofty office. Sure, the smog was tinted and even perfumed, but you still needed noseplugs to survive fifty yards of the stuff and the price of them had gone up to eighteen-fifty a set. They only lasted a couple of weeks, at most. *The cost of breathing keeps going up*, he told himself.

Oxnard's mind was wandering off into the equations that governed photochemical smog when Finger turned from the window and strode to his airport-sized desk.

"It makes me proud," he pronounced, "to think of all the hard work that American men and women have put out to conquer the problems we faced when I was a kid."

As Finger sat in the imposing chrome and black leather chair behind his desk, Oxnard glanced at the two others in the room: Finger's assistants. The man was lean and athletic looking, with a carefully trimmed red beard. The woman was also slim; she hid much of her face behind old-fashioned bombardier's glasses. Her longish hair was also red, the same shade as the man's. Red hair was *in* this week.

They both stared fixedly at their boss, eager for every word.

"A hundred and sixty-seven floors below us," Finger went on, "down in that perfumed pink environment we've created for them, ordinary American men and women are hard at work. You can't see them from up here, but they're working, believe me. I know. I can *feel* them working. They're the backbone of America . . . the spinal column of our nation."

They're working, all right, Oxnard thought. Every morning he stared with dismay at the black waves of the Pacific turgidly lapping the blacker beaches, while the oil rigs lining the ocean shore busily sucked up more black gold.

"Men and women hard at work," Finger went on, almost reverently. "And when they come home from their labors, they want to be entertained. They demand to be entertained. And they deserve the best we can give them."

The woman dabbed at her eyes. The man, Les Something-or-Other, nodded and muttered, "With it, B.F."

Finger smiled. He carefully placed his palms down on the immaculately glistening, bare desktop. Leaning forward ever so slightly he suddenly bellowed:

"So how come we don't have one single top-rated series on The Tube? *How come?*"

Les actually leaned back in his chair. The woman looked startled, but never wavered from staring straight at Finger. Oxnard almost thought he could feel a shock wave blow across the room.

With the touch of a button, Finger projected a column of names and numbers on a wall where a Schoenheer had been hanging.

"Look at the top ten!" he roared. "Do you see a Titanic Productions series? No! Look at the top twenty. . . ." The list grew longer. "The top *fifty*. . . ." And longer.

Les Montpelier, that's his name, Oxnard remembered. He seemed to be trying to sink deeper into his waterchair. He slumped further and further into its luxurious folds, pulling in his chin until his beard scraped his chest. The woman was just the opposite: she perched on the edge of her chair, all nerves, fists knotted on knees. *Nice legs.*

Finger flashed more lists on the screen. And pictures. *All two-dimensional,* Oxnard noted. Everything about the room was two-dimensional. Flat paintings on the walls. Flat desktop dominating the decor. The waterchairs were sort of three-dimensional, but only to the tactile sense.

They looked just as flat as everything else. All planes and angles. Nothing holographic. Even the woman wasn't as three-dimensional as she should be, despite her legs.

It was a pleasant enough office, though. Brightly colored carpeting and draperies. Everything soft looking, even the padded walls. Up here on the one hundred and sixty-seventh floor of the Titanic Tower they never had to worry about smog or noise or dust. The air was pristine, cool, urged smoothly through the sealed offices by gently whispering machinery hidden behind the walls. Very much the same way that people were moved through Titanic's offices: quietly, efficiently, politely, relentlessly.

Oxnard remembered how nice everyone had been to him the first time he had visited Titanic, eighteen months earlier. They had all been very polite, very enthusiastic, had even pronounced *laser* and *holographic* correctly, although they never quite seemed to grasp the difference between a hologram and a holograph. He had first met Les Montpelier then, and had been ushered into Finger's lofty sanctuary, right here in this same room. Finger wasn't looking like Cary Grant in those days and his comment on Oxnard's invention was:

"Stop wasting my time with dumb gadgets! What we need is a show with growth potential. Spinoffs, repeats, byproducts. This thing's a pipedream!"

That was eighteen months ago. Now Finger was saying:

"Every major network has three-dee shows on the air! All top ten series are three-dees! People are standing in line all over the country to buy three-dee sets. And what have you and the other flunkies and drones working for me produced? *Nothing!* No-thing. Not a goddamned thing."

Finger was perspiring now. The sculptured planes of his face were glistening and somehow looked as if they might be beginning to melt. He touched another button on his desk and the faint whir of an extra air blower sounded from somewhere in the padded ceiling.

"*I* had to go out *myself* and find the *inventor* of the three-dee process and *personally* coax him to come here and consult with us," Finger said, his voice sounding at once hurt and outraged.

It was almost true. The woman, whose name Oxnard still couldn't recall, had called him and said Mr. Finger would like to meet with him. When Oxnard reminded her that they had met eighteen months earlier, the woman had merely smiled on the phone screen and suggested that the future of her career depended on getting him into Finger's office. Oxnard reluctantly agreed to a date and time.

"All right, then," Finger went on. "A less *loyal* man would make some heads roll in a situation like this. I haven't fired anybody. I haven't panicked. You still have your jobs. I hope you appreciate that."

They both bobbed their heads.

"After lunch, the New York people will want to see what we've got. Take him," Finger barely glanced in Oxnard's direction, "back to the studio and make sure all this fancy gadgetry is working when I arrive there."

"With it, B.F.," Montpelier said as he struggled up out of his waterchair.

The woman got to her feet and Oxnard did the same. Finger swivelled his chair slightly and started talking into the phone screen. They were dismissed.

It took exactly twenty-eight paces through the foot-smothering carpet to get to the office door. Les Montpelier swung it open gingerly and they stepped into the receptionist's area.

"One good thing about flightweight doors," Montpelier muttered. "You can't slam them."

The Titanic Tower was built to earthquake specifications, of course. Which meant that it was constructed like an oversized rocket booster, all aluminum or lighter metals, with a good deal of plastics. If the sensors in the subbasement detected an earth movement beyond the designed tolerances, rocket engines built into the pods along the building's sides roared to life and hurtled the entire tower, along with its occupants, safely out to a splashdown in the Pacific, beyond the line of oil rigs.

The whole system had been thoroughly tested by NASA;

even though a few diehard conservative engineers thought
that the tests weren't extensive enough, the City of Los
Angeles decided that it couldn't grow laterally any more—
all the land had been used up. So skyscrapers were the
next step. Earthquake-proof skyscrapers.

There hadn't been an earthquake severe enough to really
test the rocket towers, although the Tishman Tower had
been blasted off by a gang of pranksters who tinkered with
the seismographic equipment in its basement. The building
arched beautifully out to sea, with no injuries to its occupants beyond the sorts of bruises and broken bones you'd
expect from bouncing off the foam plastic walls, floors
and ceilings. A few heart attacks, of course, but that was
to be expected. The pedestrians who happened to be stroll-
ing on the walkways around the Tower were, unfortunately,
rather badly singed by the rocket exhaust. A few of them
eventually died, including eighty-four in a sightseeing bus
that was illegally parked in front of the Tower. Most of
them were foreign visitors, though, and Korean mission-
aries at that.

As they walked down the corridor toward the studio,
Oxnard noted how the foam plastic flooring absorbed the
sounds of their footfalls, even without carpeting. It was a
great building for sneaking up behind people.

"Why did you let Finger yell at you like that?" Oxnard
wondered aloud. "Les, you brought me up here to see him
a year and a half ago."

Montpelier glanced at the woman, who answered:
"We've learned that it's best to let B.F. have his little tantrums, Dr. Oxnard. It's a survival technique."

Her voice was low, throaty, the kind that would be un-
bearably exotic if it had just the faintest trace of a foreign
accent. But her pronunciation was flat Southern California
uninspired. Over the phone she had managed to sound
warm and inviting. But not now.

"I don't have a Doctorate, Miz . . . uh. . . ." Oxnard
grimaced inwardly. He could remember equations, but
not names.

"Impanema." She flashed a meaningless smile, like a

reflex that went along with stating her name. "Brenda Impanema."

"Oh." For the first time, Oxnard consciously overrode his inherent shyness and really looked at her. Something about her name reminded him of an old song and a girl in an old-fashioned covered-top swimsuit. But Brenda didn't look like that at all. She seemed to be that indeterminate age between twenty and forty, when women used style and cosmetics before resorting to surgery and Vitaform Processing. She had the slight, slim body of the standard corporate executive female who spent most of her money on whatever style of clothing was fashionable that week and got most of her nutrition on dates with over-eager young stallions. Good legs, though. Flat chested, probably: it was difficult to tell through all the ribbons and flouncy stuff on her blouse. But she had good legs and the good sense to wear a miniskirt, even though it wasn't in style this week.

Behind those overlarge green glasses, her face was knotted into a frown of concentrated worry.

"Don't get upset," Oxnard said generously. "The laser system works like a charm. Finger and his New York bankers will be completely impressed. You won't lose your jobs."

Montpelier laughed nasally. "Oh, B.F. could never fire us. We've been too close for too many years."

"What he means," Brenda said, "is that we know too much about him."

Pointing a lean finger at her, Montpelier added, "And *he* knows too much about *us*. We're married to him—for better or for worse."

Oxnard wondered how far the marriage went. But he kept silent as they reached the elevator, stepped in and dropped downward.

"It must make for a nerve-wracking life," Oxnard said.

"Oh, no . . . the elevator's completely safe," Montpelier said over the whistling of the slipstream outside their shuddering, plummeting compartment.

"I didn't mean that," Oxnard said. "I mean . . . well,

working for a man like Finger. He treats you like dirt."

Brenda shrugged. "It only hurts if you let him get to you."

Montpelier scratched at his beard. "Listen. I'll tell you about B.F. There's a lot more to him than you think. Like that time he kicked me down the elevator shaft. . . ."

"He *what?*"

"It was an accident," Brenda said quickly.

"Sure," Montpelier agreed. "We were discussing something in the hallway; my memory's a little hazy. . . ."

"The chess show," said Brenda.

"Oh, yes." Montpelier's eyes gleamed with the memory of his idea. "I had this *terrific* idea for a chess show. With real people—contestants, you know, from the audience—on each square. We'd dress them in armor and all and let them fight it out when they got moved onto the same square. . . ."

"And the final survivor gets a million dollars," Brenda said.

"And the Hospital Trust gets the losers . . . which we would then use on our 'Medical Miracles' show!"

Oxnard felt a little dizzy. "But chess isn't. . . ."

Brenda touched him with the fingertips of one hand. "It doesn't matter. Listen to what happened." She was smiling. Oxnard felt himself grin back at her.

Montpelier went on, "Well, B.F. and I went round and round on this idea. He didn't like it, for some reason. The more I argued for it, the madder he got. Finally we were at the end of the hallway, waiting for the elevator and he got so mad he *kicked* me! He actually kicked me. He was taking Aikido lessons in those days and he kicked me right through the goddamned elevator door!"

"You know how flimsy the doors around here are," Brenda quipped.

Before Oxnard could say anything, Montpelier resumed:

"I went bum-over-teakettle right down the elevator shaft!"

"Geez. . . ."

"Luckily, the elevator was on its way *up* the shaft, so I

only fell twenty or thirty floors. They had me fixed up in less than a year."

"Les was the star of 'Medical Miracles' for a whole week . . . although he didn't know it at the time."

"And Bernard Finger," said Montpelier, his voice almost trembling, "personally paid every quarter of my expenses, over and above the company insurance. When I finally regained consciousness, he was right there, crying over me like he was my father."

Oxnard thought he saw the glint of a tear in Montpelier's right eye.

"*That's* the kind of man B.F. is," Montpelier concluded.

"Cruel but fair," Brenda said, trying to keep a straight face.

Just then the elevator stopped with a sickening lurch and the flimsy doors opened with a sound like aluminum foil crinkling.

Everything here happens on cue, Oxnard thought as they stepped out into the studio.

The laser system was indeed working quite well. Montpelier clapped his hands in childish glee and pronounced it "Perfect!" as they ran through the demonstration tapes, although Oxnard noted, from his perch alongside the chief engineer's seat in the control booth, that the output voltage on the secondary demodulator was down a fraction. Nothing to worry about, but he tapped the dial with a fingernail and the engineer nodded knowingly.

No sense scaring them, Oxnard thought. He went down the hall to the cafeteria and munched a sandwich with Brenda and Montpelier. There wasn't much conversation. Oxnard put on the abstracted air of a preoccupied scientist: his protective camouflage, whenever he didn't know what to say and was afraid of making a fool of himself.

Finger and his New York bankers glowed with the aura of *haute cuisine* and fine brandy when they entered the studio. Despite the NO SMOKING signs everywhere, they all had long black Havanas clamped in their teeth. Finger had changed his costume; now he wore a somber, stylish

Pickwick business suit, just as the bankers wore. *Protective coloration,* Oxnard thought. *I'm not the only one who uses camouflage.*

The men from New York were old; no Vitaform Processing for them. Their faces were lined, their mouths tight, their eyes suspicious. Three of them were lean and flinty. The fourth outweighed his three partners and Finger combined. He looked hard, not fat, like an overaged football lineman. Oxnard had seen his type in Las Vegas, watching over their casinos through dark glasses.

"And this is the *inventor* of the three-dee system," Finger said, smiling and waving Oxnard over to him. "Dr. William Oxnard. Come on over, Bill. Don't be shy. I want you to meet my friends here . . . they can be *very* helpful to a brilliant young scientist looking for capital."

Oxnard shook hands with each of them in turn. Their hands were cold and dry, but their grips were tight, as if they seldom let go easily.

Then Finger led them to the plush chairs that had been lined up for them around the receiver console. Ashstands were hurriedly set up at each elbow, while Finger stood in front of the bankers, scowling and shouting orders to his aides with a great flourish of armwaving. Montpelier and Brenda sat off to one side in plain folding chairs. Oxnard went back to the control consoles, got a fully confident nod from the chief engineer and then walked toward the cameras.

The lights in the studio went down, slowly at first, almost imperceptibly—then very suddenly dwindled to total darkness, except for a single overhead spot on Finger, who was still standing in front of the bankers.

"Everything seems to be in readiness," Finger said at last. "Gentlemen . . . once again may I present to you Dr. William Oxnard, the genius who invented the holographic home entertainment system."

Bill Oxnard stepped into the spotlight. Finger scuttled to the seat beside the beefy New Yorker, who had—sure enough—put on dark eyeglasses.

"Thank you, Mr. Finger. Gentlemen . . . as you very

well know, three-dimensional holographic entertainment systems are the biggest thing to sweep the industry since the original inception of the old black-and-white television broadcasting, about a half-century ago.

"For the first time, fully three-dimensional projections can be shown in the home, using receiving equipment that is cheap enough for the average householder to buy, while low enough in manufacturing cost to provide an equitable profit to the manufacturers and distributors. . . ."

"We are neither manufacturers nor distributors, young man," rasped one of the frail-looking bankers. "We are here to see if Titanic has anything worth investing in. Spare us the preliminaries."

Bill nodded and suppressed a grin. "Yessir. What Titanic has, in brief, is a new and improved holographic photography system, as you know, the three-dimensional images now received over home sets are spotty, grainy, and streaked with quantum scintillations. . . ."

"Looks like the actors're always standin' in a pile of sequins," said the beefy one, with a voice like a cement truck shifting gears.

"You mean confetti," one of the flinty ones corrected.

Beefy turned slowly, making his chair creak under his bulk. "Naw. I mean sequins."

"I call it snow!" Finger broke in brightly. "But whatever you call it, the effect's the same. Watching three-dee gives you a headache after a while."

Beefy muttered something about headaches and Flinty returned his attention to Oxnard.

"Very well, young man," he said. "What are you leading up to?"

"Simply this," Oxnard replied, smiling to himself. "My laboratory. . . ."

"*Your* laboratory?" one of the bankers snapped. "I thought you worked for the RHB-General Combine?"

"I was Director of Research for their Western Labs, sir," Oxnard said, feeling the old acid seething in his guts. "I resigned when we had a difference of opinion about the royalties from my original holographic system inventions."

"Ahh," wheezed the oldest of the quartet of bankers. "They squeezed you out, eh?" He cackled to himself without waiting for Oxnard's answer.

"At any rate," Oxnard went on, feeling his face burn, "I now own my own modest laboratory and we've developed a much improved holographic projection system. The patents have come through on the new system and Titanic Productions has taken an option on the exclusive use of the new system for home entertainment purposes."

"What difference does the new system make?" Beefy asked. "Three-dee is three-dee."

"Not quite correct, sir," Oxnard replied. "The old system *is* very grainy. It does give viewers headaches after an hour or so. You see, the impedance matching of the primary. . . ."

"Skip the technical details," Finger called out. "Show us the results."

Oxnard blinked. For a moment he was terribly conscious of where he was, of the cold light streaming down over him, of the people he was speaking to. He longed for the safety of his familiar laboratory.

But he pressed onward. "All right. Basically, my new system gives an absolutely perfect image. No distortions, no scintillations, no visible graininess or snow. Unless you're an engineer and you know precisely what to look for, you can't tell a projected image apart from someone actually standing in front of you."

"And that's what you're going to demonstrate to us?" Flinty asked.

"Yes, sir. With the help of one of you gentlemen. Would one of you care to step up here in the spotlight with me?"

They all looked at each other questioningly, but no one moved from his chair. After a few seconds, Bernard Finger said, "Well I'll do it, if nobody else. . . ."

Beefy pushed him back down into his seat. Finger landed on the padding with an audible *thwunk!*

"I'll do it," Beefy said, with a grin that was almost boyish "Always wanted t'be in show business . . . like my *cumpar'* Frankie. . . ."

He lumbered into the spotlight, glanced around, suddenly self-conscious.

Oxnard stretched out his right hand. "Thank you for volunteering," he said. His palms were suddenly sweaty.

Beefy reached for Oxnard's hand. His own heavy paw went *through* Oxnard's.

The other bankers gasped. Beefy stared at his own hand, then grabbed at Oxnard's image. He got nothing but air.

"Actually I'm 'way over here," Oxnard said, as a couple of technicians pushed aside the screen that had hidden him from their view. He looked up from the tiny monitor he had been watching and saw the bankers, more than fifty yards across the huge empty studio. Beefy was standing under the spotlight, gaping at Oxnard's three-dimensional image; the others were half out of their chairs, craning for a view of where Oxnard *really* was standing.

"How about that?" Finger crowed and started pounding his palms together. The bankers took up the applause. Even Beefy clapped, grudgingly.

Turning back to the camera, Oxnard said, "If you gentlemen will forgive my little deception, we can proceed with the show. I think you'll find it entertaining.

It was.

For twenty minutes, the bankers saw strange and wonderful worlds taking shape not more than ten feet before their eyes. Birds flew, mermaids swam, elephants charged at them, all with flawless three-dimensional solidity. They visited the top of Mt. Everest (a faked set from the old MCA-Universal studios), watched a cobra fight a mongoose, then went on a whirlwind tour of all the continents and major seas of the world. A beautiful chanteuse sang to them in French, a Minnesota sexual athletics class competed for originality and style. The windup was a glider flight through the Grand Canyon, while the Mormon Tabernacle Choir sang "America the Beautiful."

"Breathtaking!"

"Perfect!"

"Awe-inspiring!"

"Terrific!"

As the lights came back up, Bernard Finger took the floor again, beaming at the four bedazzled banke s.

"Well," he asked, "what do you think? Do we have something here, or do we have something?"

"I liked the Balinese broad," said Beefy. "*She* had something, all right."

"She's right here. We flew her in from Ft. Worth, where she was working. Also a few members of the Minnesota team. I was planning to introduce you gentlemen to them all at a little cocktail party this evening."

Oxnard, walking across the studio toward them, could see that they were impressed with Finger's foresight and generosity.

All except Flinty. "That's well and good," he said, steepling his bony fingers as he sat back in his chair. He cocked an eye at Finger, standing poised before him. "But we haven't come to Titanic for technical products; your business, Bernie, is show business. What have you got that will get Titanic to the top of the ratings?"

Finger's teeth clicked shut. It was the only sign of distress he showed. Immediately they parted again in a cheery smile.

"Listen," he said, "shows are a dime a dozen. We're planning a whole raft of 'em . . . every kind of show, from quizzes to really deep drama—Simon and Allen, stuff like that. It's the *technical* side that we wanted to show you today."

Oxnard stopped a few feet behind their chairs. He could see the sort of desperate look on Finger's face. Beefy and the other two bankers seemed anxious to move on to the cocktail party. Montpelier and Brenda both had disappeared. Glancing over his shoulder, Oxnard saw that the engineers and technicians had cleared out, too. There was no one in the studio except Finger, the four bankers and himself.

The studio looked like a gaunt framework: big, mostly empty, skeletal girders showing where other rooms have walls and ceiling panels. It reminded Oxnard of an astronomical observatory, although it wasn't domed. *An un-*

finished chamber, he thought. *Full of sound and fury; signifying nothing.* He felt a little surprised at his sudden burst of literary pretension.

"I'll admit the technical side is impressive," Flinty was saying adamantly. "But nobody's going to watch travelogues very long, no matter how perfectly they're broadcast. You need *shows,* Bernie. Come up with good shows and we'll come up with money for you."

"But. . . ." Finger's composure broke down for the first time. "I need the money *now.*"

Flinty got slowly to his feet. Oxnard could see a crooked little grin forming on his granite-tight face. "Now? Really? You need the money now?"

He put a bony arm around Finger's shoulder and, trailed by the other bankers, they walked toward the red-glowing EXIT sign.

Oxnard stood there alone in the vast, empty studio, with nothing but the echo of Flinty's cackling laughter to keep him company. Just as he realized that he didn't know what to do, he heard a movement behind him.

Turning, he saw Brenda. She looked very serious.

"It's been a long day," she said.

"Yeah." He suddenly realized he was very tired.

"Come on; I'll buy you a drink."

"Thanks. But I suppose I should get along home." *Idiot!* he raged at himself. *Why'd you say that?*

Brenda pointed casually toward the exit and they started walking toward it.

"Wife and kids?" she asked.

Oxnard shook his head. "Worse. A fifty-person lab that needs me to make decisions and sign paychecks."

"You're there every day?"

"Bright and early."

"But you do eat and sleep, don't you?"

Why am I trying to run away? "Sure," he said. "Now and then."

They were at the exit door. She let him push it open for her.

"Well then," Brenda said as they stepped into the hallway, "why don't we have dinner together? I know B.F. will want to have a debriefing later tonight."

The debriefing came in the middle of dinner. Oxnard let Brenda drive him through the swirling pink smog—scented like rancid orchids, even through the noseplugs—to a small restaurant in the Valley. They had just finished the wine and asked for a second bottle when the owner trudged up to their table with a portable phone. He placed it on the edge of the table, so they could both see the screen.

Finger looked ominously unwell.

"They didn't put up the money?" Brenda asked.

Glowering from inside a rumpled Roman toga, Finger said, "They *wanted* the option on our new holosystem."

Oxnard was about to ask where the *our* came from, but Brenda preempted him. "What did you give them?"

"Sweet talk. Four solid hours of sweet talk and a horde of teeny-boppers from every part of the world."

"And?"

"They'll put up the money for one show. One series, that is. We can use the new system and see if the audience likes the series well enough to put us in the Top Ten. If not, they foreclose and take everything."

"Not my new system!" Oxnard blurted.

"The option," Finger answered tiredly. "They'll get the option. And sooner or later they'll get you too, if they really want you. Don't think you could fight 'em."

"But. . . ."

Again Brenda was quicker. "They'll put up the money for one new series? We've got that much?"

"Yeah."

"Then we'll have to make it a Top Ten series. We'll have to get the best writers and producers and. . . ."

Finger shook his head wearily. "They're not putting up *that* much money."

Oxnard was struck by the contrast in their two expressions. Finger looked utterly tired, on the verge of defeat and surrender. Brenda was bright, alive, thinking furiously.

"What we need first is an idea," she said.

"For the series?" Oxnard asked, almost under his breath.

"And I know just who to go to!" Brenda's eyes flashed with excitement. "Ron Gabriel!"

Finger's eyes flashed back. "No! I will not work with that punk! Never! I told you before, nobody calls me a lying sonofabitch and gets away with it. And he did it to my face! To my goddamned *face!* He'll never work for Titanic or anybody else in this town again. I swore it!"

"B.F.," Brenda cooed into the phone screen, "do you remember the first lesson you taught me about how to get along in this business?"

"No," he snapped.

"Well I do," she said. "It's an old Hollywood motto: 'Never let that sonofabitch back into this studio . . . unless we need him.' "

"I will *not*. . . ."

"B.F., we need him."

"No!"

"He's a great idea man."

"Never!"

"He works cheap."

"I'd sooner see Titanic sink! And the whole holographic project go down with it! Not Gabriel! Never!"

The image clicked off the screen.

Brenda looked up at Oxnard. "Better cancel the wine," she said.

"Why?"

"Because we're driving out to Ron Gabriel's place. Come on, it's not far."

2: THE WRITER

Oxnard and Brenda ran through cold, heavy sheets of rain to her car. Although it was only a few yards from the restaurant door, they were both gasping and drenched as they slid onto the plastic seats and slammed the car doors.

Brenda rubbed at her eyes. "At least it'll clear away the smog for a while."

Sucking in air through his mouth, Oxnard realized that for the first time in weeks there was no perfume smell pervading the environs. And he could breathe without noseplugs.

"Every cloud has a platinum catalytic filter for a lining," he said.

Brenda laughed as she gunned the car to life. In the dim light from the dashboard, Oxnard could see that her long red hair was glistening and plastered down around her face. It somehow looked incredibly sexy that way.

They roared off through the rain and soon were threading the torturous curves of Mulholland Drive, heading up into Sherman Oaks. The rain and sudden cold made the car's windshield steam up and it was impossible to see more than a few yards ahead. The headlights were drowned in gusting walls of rain.

Twice they found themselves on the shoulder of the road, with nothing between them and a sheer drop except a few inches of gravel. Once, on a hairpin curve, Brenda nearly steered into an oncoming set of headlights. Which car had drifted onto the wrong side of the road, it was impossible to tell.

Oxnard was just as drenched when the car finally glided to a stop as when he had first climbed in. But now he was soaked with clammy nervous sweat. Brenda seemed perfectly at ease, though.

"Here we are," she said cheerfully.

"Here" was a low-slung modernistic house perched on the shoulder of a hill, in the middle of a long winding street lined by similar houses. Brenda had pulled the car up on the driveway, so that by sliding out on the driver's side they could splash across one small puddle and dive directly under the protective overhang at the front door.

The door was more ornately carved than Queequeeg's sarcophagus, a really handsome piece of work. Hanging squarely in the middle of it, under the knocker, was a tiny hand-lettered sign that said:

TRY THE BELL

with a drawing of a hand pointing one finger toward an all-but-invisible button, hidden behind a flowering shrub.

Brenda touched the doorbell button and a speaker grill set above the door grated:

"Yeah?"

"Ron, it's Brenda."

"Brenda?"

"Brenda Impanema . . . from Bernard Finger's office."

"Oh, Brenda!"

"Can we come in?"

Oxnard was beginning to feel foolish, standing out there with the wind cutting through him, wet and chilled, all the rain in Southern California sluicing down around them, watching a girl he had just met talking to a door.

"Who's we?" the door asked.

Brenda seemed to be enjoying the fencing match; well,

maybe not enjoying it, but at least neither surprised nor dismayed by it.

"Someone you'll enjoy meeting," she said. "He invented the. . . ."

"He?" The voice sounded disappointed.

For the first time, Brenda frowned. "Come on, Ron. It's cold and wet out here."

"Okay. Okay. Come on in."

The door clicked. Brenda pushed on it and it swung open. They stepped inside.

Oxnard blinked. It was like the first time he had tried sky-diving. One minute you're safely strapped into the plane and the next you're out in the empty air, falling, disoriented, watching the blur of Earth spinning up to hit you.

The door slammed behind him. The entryway of the house was ablaze with lights. Oxnard and Brenda stood there dripping and disheveled, gaping at the cameras, people, props, chairs, lights.

"Smile!" a voice shouted. "You're on candid camera."

"What?"

Ron Gabriel pushed past a tripod-mounted camera directly in front of them, a huge grin on his face.

"Only kidding, *buhbula*. Don't panic."

He was wearing nothing but a bath towel draped around his middle. He was a smallish, compactly built man in his thirties, Oxnard guessed: dark straight hair cut in the latest neo-Victorian mode, blazing dark eyes, hairy chest, the beginnings of a pot belly.

He grabbed Brenda and kissed her mightily. Then turning casually to Oxnard, he asked, "You her husband or something?"

"Or something," Oxnard replied, feeling testy.

"Hey come on, I'm paying overtime already!"

A large, lumpy, bearded man stepped out from behind the cameras. He was swathed in a green and purple dashiki. Some sort of optical viewer hung from a silver cord around his neck.

Gabriel grabbed Brenda and Oxnard by the arms and walked them back behind the cameras.

"What's going on?" Brenda asked.

"I'm renting my foyer to Roscoe for filming his latest epic."

"Roscoe?" Oxnard was impressed. "The guy who did the underground film festival at Radio City Music Hall?"

"Who else?" Gabriel answered.

Now it all made sense to Oxnard. Two dozen girls of starlet dimensions stood around languidly, in various styles of undress. A couple of muscular, hairy guys were doing pushups over in a far corner of the foyer. Electricians, lighting women, camera persons of indeterminate gender, and a few other handymen were busily moving cameras and lights around the long, narrow foyer.

"All right already!" Roscoe bellowed in a voice four times too large for Grand Central Station. "Everybody take their places for the grope scene!"

Brenda said, "I'm awfully chilled. Could I borrow a hot shower?"

"Sure," Gabriel said. "Throw your clothes in the dryer and grab a couple of robes out of my closet. Brenda, you know where everything is. Show him around."

Oxnard stammered, "Uh . . . we're not . . . not together. I mean, not like that." *Dammit!* he raged to himself. *Why should I feel embarrassed?*

With a grin, Gabriel led him to the guest room and took a terryplastic robe from a drawer.

"Gotta get back to work now," he said.

"You're in the movie?"

Gabriel's grin broadened. "I'm an assistant groper."

Brenda looked good with a rich brown robe pulled snugly around her, Oxnard decided. One glance in a mirror after his steamshower had convinced him that wearing a robe two sizes too small was better than prancing around nude. But not much. His hairy legs showed to midcalf. He had to be careful how he sat.

Brenda, Gabriel and Ornard were sitting in the living

room. It was furnished in old-fashioned Nineteen Sixties style, with authetic green berets and protest posters artfully arranged here and there. The walls were covered with paintings, drawings, sketches—all from stories that Gabriel had written.

The camera crew was in the process of stowing gear into the truck they had parked outside. Roscoe himself had borrowed Brenda's keys to move her car out of the driveway. Now, as the three of them sat in the comfortable living room, they could hear the wind-whipped rain and the sounds of grunting people moving heavy pieces of equipment out into the wet.

Oxnard and Brenda had brandy snifters in their hands. Gabriel, still clad in only his bath towel, had graciously poured them the drinks while making dates with three of Roscoe's starlets. He refrained from drinking, himself.

"When did you become a movie actor?" Brenda asked, a quizzical smile on her lips.

"Always been an actor, sweetie," he replied. "You think sitting through a story conference with some of those assholes you call executives doesn't take thespic talents?"

"I've seen histrionics from you. . . ."

One of the starlets walked barefoot into the living room as far as Gabriel's slingback chair. She was wearing a knit sweater that barely reached her thighs. Her cascading blonde hair was slightly longer. Her eyes didn't seem to focus well.

"Hey Ron, honey, can I use your shower?"

"Sure, sure," he said.

"Thanks." She bent over and kissed him on the cheek. The sweater rode up and Oxnard found himself tugging at the hem of his borrowed robe, trying to make certain that he was covered adequately. The blonde plodded sleepily out of the room without rearranging her sweater.

"But I don't understand why you're performing in Roscoe's movie," Brenda resumed.

Gabriel made a sour face. "Money, kid. Why else? You have any idea how much it takes to keep this house going? My gardener makes more than that cutesy-poo does." He jerked a thumb in the general direction of the partially sweatered starlet.

"But you've got so many books and filmscripts . . . you must make plenty on royalties."

With a wave of his hand that took in all the illustrations on the walls, Gabriel said, "What books? You know what you get from books? Nickels and dimes. Unless you write a book about a veterinarian's carnal lust for his customers. Nobody reads about *people* anymore. I write about people."

Oxnard felt puzzled. "Aren't you the Ron Gabriel who writes science fiction? I've read some of your stuff."

Gabriel's eyebrows went up a centimeter. "Yeah? Like what?"

"Let's see now. . . ." Oxnard concentrated. "It was . . . oh yes, 'The Beast That Had No Mouth' and 'Repent . . .' something about a watchmaker."

Nodding furiously, Gabriel said, "Yeah. And you know how much money I made from those two books? Peanuts! The goddam publishers give you peanuts for an advance, then they sell a zillion copies and claim that they haven't made enough money to start paying royalties yet!"

"I didn't know. . . ."

Gabriel leaped out of his chair. "Those humpers! You don't know the half of it!"

He stomped out of the room. Confused, Oxnard got up and watched Gabriel duck down the house's central atrium and into a doorway. He slammed the door behind him.

"That's his office," Brenda said.

"What's he. . . ."

The muffled sound of Gabriel's voice floated back to them. "Sue the bastards . . . I don't care what it costs . . . get them for every nickel they owe me. . . ."

Brenda stood up beside Oxnard "He must be calling his lawyer."

"At this hour?" Oxnard glanced at his watch. It was after midnight.

"Ron's friends and associates are accustomed to his late hours. He starts working when the sun goes down."

"Must be part vampire."

"It's been suggested."

Abruptly, the office door opened and Gabriel came stamping back into the living room. "We'll get those mothers," he was muttering.

As they all sat down again, Brenda asked, "What about the TV series you were doing? I thought. . . ."

"Don't mention it!" Gabriel snapped. "The less said about that, the better."

For an instant the room was silent, except for the rain drumming on the roof.

Then Gabriel said, "We had the whole goddam series set up. Worked my tail off for six months; fights with the producers, fights with the network, the director, the actors. Finally they began to see the light. It's all starting to go right. I could *feel* it! We had it all in the groove. . . ."

"What was the show about?" Oxnard asked.

"Huh? Oh, it was going to be a series based on a short story of mine, about a giant pterodactyl that attacks New York City."

"I heard about it," Brenda said. "And then it was cancelled, just before shooting began. What happened?"

"What happened?" Gabriel's voice went up several notches. "Those lumpheaded brain-damage cases that run the network decided they couldn't do the show because it wasn't in three-dee!"

"No!"

"Oh no? Those maggotheads are turning everything into three-dee shows. Everything! I thought, great. The series will be even more spectacular in three-dee. But we'd need a bigger budget and a couple weeks to work out some of the technical problems. *Wham!* Nothing doing. They cut us off. Done. Finished."

Oxnard felt vaguely guilty about it. He stirred uneasily in his chair, started to cross his legs, but remembered just in time and stopped himself.

"Know what they put into our timeslot?" Gabriel was still fuming. "A cops-and-robbers show. Some idiot thing about a robot and a Polack cop. Ever see an animated fireplug doing Polish jokes? Arrgghhh."

Roscoe suddenly called from the front doorway. "Hey superstar! We're leaving!"

Without moving from his chair, Gabriel bellowed, "So leave already! Just make sure you send the check tomorrow morning!"

"Will do," Roscoe hollered back. "Oh, Rita and Dee-Dee said they're too tired for the drive back to Glendale. They flaked out in your guest room. Okay by you?"

"Yah, sure. I'll unflake 'em later on."

"Good luck, buddy."

"Break a leg, C.B."

The door slammed.

Oxnard cleared his throat. "Do you mean that they really cancelled your show because it wasn't going to be shown in holographic projection?"

"That was their excuse," Gabriel answered. "They wanted to castrate me. I'm too honest for those Byzantine bronze nosers." He glowered at Brenda. "And I still say that Finger had something to do with it."

Brenda returned his gaze without flinching.

"But still," Gabriel grumbled, "I'd like to meet the jerk who started this three-dee crap and. . . ."

"What about that other project you were talking about?" Brenda broke in. "The historical thing. Was it going to be a musical?"

Gabriel scratched at his stubbly chin. "*That* thing! I got the shaft on that, too."

"What was it going to be?"

"I was going to do 'Romeo and Juliet' in modern terms. You know, instead of Italy in the old times, make it L.A., here, today. Make the two feuding families a pair of TV networks that are fighting it out for the ratings." He grew more animated, expressive. Getting to his feet, gesticulating: "Then the star from one show on the first network falls in love with a girl from a show on the other network. Their shows are on the air at the same time . . . they love each other, but their networks are enemies. Then when the executive producers find out about them. . . ."

It took nearly an hour before Gabriel calmed down enough to sit in his chair again. He ended his monologue with:

"Then some jerk says that it's just like some old opera called 'West Side Story.' I looked it up . . . wasn't anything like that at all."

"So that's fallen through, too?" Brenda asked.

"That's right," Gabriel said, slumping back in his soft chair, looking exhausted. "Every goddam thing I've touched for the past year has turned to shit. Every goddam thing." He sat bolt upright. "It's gotta be Finger! He swore I'd never work for anybody in this town again. He's living up to his name, that no-good. . . ."

"That's not true, Ron," Brenda said. "He wants you to work for him. He needs you. He's desperate."

Gabriel stopped in midsentence and stared at her.

"He needs me?"

Brenda nodded gravely.

"Good! Tell him to go engage reflexively in sexual intercourse."

It took Oxnard a moment to interpret that one, although Brenda giggled immediately.

"No, Ron. I'm serious. B.F.'s really in a bind and you're the only one who can pull him out."

"Got any rocks? Heavy ones?"

"Wait a minute," Oxnard heard himself say. They both turned toward him. "Before we go any further, you ought to know . . . I invented the holographic projection system."

Half expecting Gabriel to leap for his throat, Oxnard sat tensed in his chair, ready to defend himself verbally or physically.

"You invented it?" asked Gabriel incredulously.

"I'm Bill Oxnard. The jerk who started this three-dee stuff."

They talked. They sat in the comfortably furnished living room, draped with towel and robes while the rain made background music for them, and talked for hours. One of the girls from further back in the house wandered sleepily into the room, naked, looking for the kitchen and murmuring about a midnight snack. The phone next to Gabriel's chair rang a couple of times and he snarled into it briefly. Oxnard told him about the exciting days when he was perfecting the first holographic system, how the corporate executives had beamed at him and given him bonuses. And then how they tossed him out of the corporation when he asked for a share of the royalties they were reaping.

"They screwed you out of your own invention," Gabriel said, with real pain in his voice. "Just like they've screwed me out of my royalties."

"It was my own stupid fault," Oxnard said. "I was so wrapped up in the technical work that I didn't pay any attention to the legal side."

"Why the hell should you have to?" Gabriel demanded. "If those pricks were honest men you wouldn't have to worry about them sticking it to you. They wear clean clothes, but their skins are slimy. The bastards."

Gabriel showed Oxnard his own three-dee set and they turned it on. The Kier Dullea similacrum appeared in miniature, hovering in the far corner of the living room, riding a model spacecraft across a simulated Martian crater. The images looked solid, but they sparkled and shimmered.

"Most of that's in the transmission system," Oxnard said, squinting at the scintillations in the images. "But I think I can improve the picture quality a little, if you have a toolkit handy."

Gabriel produced a toolkit. Oxnard went happily to work on the mahogany-like plastic console that housed the three-dee receiver, tinkering with the controls in the back.

Brenda, meanwhile, outlined Titantic Productions' precarious fiscal situation. By the time Oxnard rejoined the conversation, she was saying:

"Of course, he's screaming that he'll never deal with you again. Repeat, never. But he knows that he needs a good show right away and you've got the imagination and talent to create it for him."

Gabriel was lying flat on the Rya carpet, stretched out in front of the sofa on which Brenda was sitting. She had her legs tucked demurely under her, Oxnard noticed. Kier Dullea had ridden off into the sunset, so Oxnard turned off the set.

"No, I won't work for Finger. That sonofabitch is just too slimy to deal with. He'd sell his own mother to the cannibals."

"But you wouldn't have to deal with Finger," Brenda urged. "You could work with Les. . . ."

"That turd!"

"And me."

Gabriel heaved a deep sigh, making the towel around his middle flutter slightly. "It would be nice, baby. I'd really like to work with you. You're one of the few honest people left in this town. . . ."

"I'd enjoy working with you, too, Ron. You know that."

Oxnard found himself frowning at both of them.

"But. . . ." Gabriel said, his voice distant and small, "I've gotten so emotionally involved. . . ."

"You?"

"Yeah. With this 'Romeo and Juliet' project. I really wanted to tackle Shakespeare. Bring the Old Bard up to date. There's no greater challenge to a writer. I wanted to show them all that I could do it."

Brenda shook her head. "No, I don't think 'Romeo and Juliet' would be right for The Tube. Those New York bankers want something sound and safe . . . not Shakespeare. They need something much more conventional, like science fiction."

"Science fiction!" Gabriel complained. "Is that all those frogbrains can think of? I'm sick of science fiction; it's on every network, every show. Why can't we do something new, fresh, original?"

"Like 'Romeo and Juliet?' " Oxnard asked, sitting down beside Brenda.

"Yeah, why not?" Gabriel countered.

"Ron, Titanic won't go for a show that deals with the networks or the studios," Brenda said. "That's *realism!* You know how they steer clear of that. Why, even the news programs get permission before they put anything *real* on the air."

"Yeah, I know." Tiredly.

Oxnard said, "No starcrossed lovers, then."

Brenda started to reply, but Gabriel said, "What was that?"

"Huh? Oh, I said . . . no starcrossed lovers. You know, Romeo and Juliet."

Gabriel sat bolt upright. "Starcrossed lovers! Holy shit! That's *it!*" He leaped to his feet. "That's it! Wow, what an idea!"

The towel started sliding downward and Gabriel made an automatic grab for it as he pranced around the room. "That's it!" he said again. "That's it!"

Brenda was grinning but she looked just as befuddled as Oxnard felt. "What? Tell us."

Pouncing atop the three-dee console, Gabriel shouted: "They want science fiction and I want Shakespeare. We'll merge 'em. . . ." He stood on the console, stretched to his full height, flung his arms over his head and boomed:

"THE STARCROSSED!"

The towel fell to the floor.

Time lost its meaning. At some point the rain slackened, then died away altogether. The windows of the living room started to show the misty gray promise of a new day. Inside the room, Bill Oxnard felt himself being drawn into the chaotic vortex of creation. It was like being present at the creation of a new world.

"There're these two families, see," Gabriel was saying, oblivious of his nudity, "on two different spaceships. They're merchants . . . they go from planet to planet, trading goods. You know, spices, hardware. . . ."

"With a gambling casino in the back," Brenda suggested.

Gabriel eyed her. "Maybe . . . maybe it would work. Well, anyway. One family has this guy, the youngest son of the head of the family. . . ."

"And the other family has a daughter."

"Right! The two families land on the same planet at the same time, see?"

Brenda nodded vigorously. "We could have a different planet every week . . . and the same major characters. That's just what a good series needs!"

"Sure," Gabriel agreed. "Good guest stars and the same regulars each week."

"So the boy and girl fall in love," Brenda said.

Gabriel was rubbing his hands together anxiously. "Right. But their families don't like it. They compete with each other, see, for the interstellar trade. They don't. . . ."

"Wait a minute," Oxnard said. "If these are interstellar ships there's going to be a time factor involved. You know, the twin paradox."

"The what?" Gabriel looked blank.

"If you travel at almost the speed of light, there's a time dilation. The two families wouldn't age at the same rate. The boy will get older than the girl or *vice versa.*"

"Oh that," Gabriel said. "Don't worry about it. We'll just make the ships go faster than light."

"But you can't do that. It's physically impos. . . ."

Gabriel flapped a hand at him. "We'll use a space warp. Been doing that for years."

"But it's not. . . ."

"It's dramatic license," Brenda said.

Oxnard shook his head but kept silent.

"Okay," Gabriel said. "Every week the kids are trying to get together and every week the families try to keep 'em apart. We can have them stowing away on each other's ships, captured by the natives on the planets, lost in space . . . zowie, there's a *million* storylines in this!"

"And we can have subplots every week," Brenda said eagerly. "With all sorts of different characters and cultures on each planet they visit. It's terrific!"

On and on they went, as the sky brightened outside and birds began to welcome the not-quite-risen sun. Gabriel pranced into his office and Brenda and Oxnard followed him into the cramped, cluttered little room. With an unlit pipe clamped between his teeth, Gabriel turned on his voicewriter; their free-for-all conversation began clattering out of the machine in black and white.

They sketched out the major characters while Gabriel ransacked the bookshelves lining the walls to find his *Asimov's Guide to Shakespeare*. The voicewriter dutifully typed up a summary of the series' basic theme and outline, plus outlines for the first three hour-long segments. Then they went into details of characterizations, the types of actors needed, the costuming. Oxnard found himself doing most of the talking when it came to describing the spaceships and their equipment.

Finally it got uproariously funny. They began giggling at every line coming out of the voicewriter. When the machine obediently began typing, "Ha-Ha-Ha," they broke up completely. Gabriel fell out of his desk chair onto the floor. Brenda had tears streaming down her cheeks. Oxnard felt as if his insides would burst. And they couldn't stop laughing. Not until the machine ran out of paper and shut itself off. Seventeen sheets of "Ha-Ha-Ha" littered the office floor.

They staggered into the kitchen, breathless and squinting at the morning light. As coffee perked and orange juice defrosted, the blonde in the knit sweater came along. She was wearing stretch slacks and jewelry now, as well as the sweater.

"You guys sure were having a good time," she said.

"Stay for breakfast," Gabriel told her.

She smiled sweetly and kissed him on the nose. "Can't, honey. Got to get back to the studio. I'm a working girl, you know. Not like you writers. 'Bye!"

And off she flounced.

Sobering, Oxnard mumbled, "I ought to get back to my lab, too."

"They can do without you for one day," Brenda said.

"They did. Yesterday."

"Grab a couple hours' sleep first," Gabriel said. "You can use the guest room."

"Might be a good idea at that," Oxnard let himself yawn. His eyes felt very heavy.

He was about to push himself up from the kitchen table when Gabriel put a steaming mug of coffee down in front of him and said:

"Listen, I appreciate all the advice you gave me about the spaceships and all. I want you to be my technical advisor for the series."

"The series?"

"Yeah. 'The Starcrossed.' Remember?"

"I'm no technical advisor. I run a laboratory. . . ."

Brenda was sitting across the table from him, with a curious expression on her sleepy face.

Gabriel said, "You know this science stuff. I'm going to need somebody I can trust, if we're going to do this series right. Right, Brenda?"

She nodded and murmured, "Aye-aye, master."

"But my responsibility's to the lab. That's. . . ."

Gabriel wagged a finger at him. "You don't have to leave the lab. All I'll need is some advice now and then. Probably handle most of it on the phone. Maybe read the scripts when they've gotten to second draft."

"My big chance in show biz," Oxnard said.

"It'll be a helluva help," Gabriel said. "To me personally."

Brenda nodded. "Finger will want you on the scene as a consultant anyway, on your new holographic process."

"I suppose so," Oxnard admitted.

Gabriel grasped him by the shoulder. "Go on, get some sleep. We can talk about it later."

Oxnard nodded and got up wearily from the table. Padding down the hall toward the guest room, he wondered what Gabriel and Brenda were going to do while he slept. *Hell, you know what they're going to do.* The thought irked him. Greatly.

The guest room was midnight dark. Oxnard was completely blind the instant he let the door snap shut behind him. He took two cautious steps forward, hoping to make a less-than-shincracking contact with the bed, and stumbled against something soft.

It squirmed and he fell on top of it.

"Hey, whatcha . . . oh, Ron, it's you," a sleepy voice murmured.

They were sprawled on a sea of pillows that the girl had evidently strewn across the guest room floor.

"No, it's not Ron." Oxnard whispered, feeling rather flustered. He wished he had pockets to put his hands into.

"Oh? Who're you?"

"Uh . . . Bill," he said into the darkness. He still couldn't see anything, but he felt her soft body and breathed in a tawny scent.

"What's goin' on?" another lissome voice whispered.

"It's Bill," said the first girl.

"Oh, gee, that's nice."

Oxnard felt another soft, warm body snuggle close to him. Four hands began fumbling with his robe. He thought furiously about the lab and his responsibilities. And about Brenda. He tried to remind himself that he was, after all, an adult who could take care of himself. He didn't need . . . didn't want . . . maybe they . . . but. . . .

Finally, he said to himself: *So this is show business.*

3: THE AGENT

Jerry Morgan had two hysterical unemployed actresses in his waiting room, one tightlipped producer who was trying to break into comedy writing, and a receptionist who had just given two days' notice. The actresses and producer were all formerly employed by Titanic Productions: a significant phenomenon, as Sherlock Holmes would have said if he'd been a theatrical and literary agent with an office off the Strip.

At the moment Morgan had a worse problem on his hands: a morose Ron Gabriel. It wasn't like Gabriel to be downcast: ebullient, brassy, argumentative, noisy, egregious, foolhardy, irreverent—all those yes. Morgan was accustomed to seeing Gabriel in those moods. But morose? And—fearful?

Morgan studied his client's face on the big view screen set into the wall of his private office. He had considered getting the phone company to put in a three-dee viewer, but so far hadn't gotten around to it.

"So it's been more than a week since Brenda brought the idea to Titanic," Gabriel was saying, his voice low, "and I haven't heard a word from her or anybody else."

"Neither have I, Ron," said Morgan as pleasantly as he could manage. "But, hell, you know Finger. He never moves all that quickly."

"Yeah, but Brenda would've gotten back to me if there'd been some good news. . . ."

Morgan glanced at the outline and fact sheet for "The Starcrossed" that rested on a corner of his desk.

"Did you give her the same poopsheet you gave me?" he asked.

Gabriel nodded. "We did it that morning, right on the voicewriter. Haven't seen her since. She just took off. . . ."

"She's probably waiting for Finger to finish reading it. You know he can't get through more than one page a day. His lips get tired."

Not even the joke stirred Gabriel. "They've torn it up," he said miserably. "I know they have. Finger took one look at my name on the cover and tore it into little pieces. Then he must've fired Brenda and she's too sore at me to even let me know about it."

"Nonsense, Ron. You know. . . ."

"Call him!" Gabriel said, his face suddenly intense, his voice urgent. "Call Finger and find out what he did with it! Make a personal pitch for the show. I'm broke, Jerry. Flat busted. I need *something!* That show. . . ."

With a sigh, Morgan said, "I'll call Les Montpelier. He'll know what's happened."

Morosely, Gabriel nodded and shut off the connection.

Three hours later, Morgan took off his sunglasses and peered into the dimly lit bar. Vague shapes of men and women were sitting on barstools; beyond them, the narrow room widened and brightened into a decent restaurant.

The hostess was dressed in the very latest Colonial high-necked, long-sleeved, floor-skirted outfit with the bosom cut out to show her bobbing breasts.

"Lookin' for somebody?" she said in her most cultured tones.

"Mr. Montpelier was supposed to meet me here," Morgan said, still trying to make out the faces of the men at the bar.

"Oh yeah, he was here, but he went on back into the restaurant. Said he couldn't wait and you could find him at his table. Big tipper."

Silently grumbling at the Freeway traffic jams that had made him late, Morgan worked past the executives and bar girls and quickly found Montpelier sitting alone at a booth near a window.

He waved and put on his heartiest smile at he approached the booth. The slim, redbearded Montpelier smiled back and Morgan saw a mirror image of his own phony graciousness.

"Hi, Les! How the hell are ya?" Morgan said as he slid into the booth.

"Just great, Jerry! And you? Geez, it's been a helluva long time since we've seen each other."

As Montpelier motioned for a waiter, Morgan said: "Well, you know how this town is. You can be in bed with the same guy for months and then never see him again for years."

"Yeah. Sure."

The waiter was professionally icy. "Cocktail, m'seur?"

"A Virgin Mary for me, please," Morgan said.

Montpelier grinned at him. "Off the toxics?"

Morgan grinned back. *The Game,* he sighed to himself. *The everlasting Game.* "I was never on it, Les. I drink a little wine with a meal, that's all. The hard stuff never appealed to me. I prefer smoking."

"Then why the camouflage?"

"The Virgin Mary? I like tomato juice . . . and besides, there are people in this town who don't trust an agent that doesn't drink."

"Hell," Montpelier said, "I've seen it just the opposite. I know an agent who drinks nothing but milk in public. Says, 'What kind of an agent would people think I am if I didn't have an ulcer?' One of the biggest juicers in town, in private."

You got that from an old TV show, Morgan replied silently.

The waiter brought Morgan's drink. Montpelier clinked his own half-finished rum sour with it and they began the serious business of inspecting the menus.

It wasn't until the salads had been served that the conversation got to the subject. Morgan deliberately avoided an opening gambit, which in itself was one of The Game's most frequently used opening gambits: let the other guy bring up the subject, makes him appear to be more anxious than you are.

"What's this brilliant new idea Gabriel's got? Brenda seems very impressed with it."

"I thought you knew about it," Morgan said.

"Yeah—in general. B.F.'s got it tucked under his arm, though. Hasn't let anybody see any details yet."

Morgan munched a lettuce leaf thoughtfully, then said, "It's the kind of idea that could save Titanic from the wolves."

"Wolves?" Montpelier looked startled. "There're no wolves at our doors."

With a shrug, Morgan said: "I must have heard wrong, then. Anyway, it's a powerful idea. It's got scope."

"What's it all about?"

Morgan leaned back and put his fork down. This was the part he liked best. It was like fishing. Only instead of standing hips-deep in an Alpine stream, he was sitting in a plush restaurant, wearing last year's zipsuit, trying to hook a wary young executive who was dressed like Buffalo Bill Cody. *Trout are fairer game,* Morgan told himself.

"It's got everything you could ever want in a successful series. Drama, action, love interest—a couple of attractive young central characters, lots of continuous characters and color. *Plus* exotic new settings every week, with plenty of scope for guest stars and in-depth characterizations. Plenty of spinoffs, too. And byproducts. . . ."

"What *is* it, for Chrissake?"

Morgan inwardly smiled. Montpelier had blown his cool: *Twenty points for our side.*

"It's called 'The Starcrossed.' "

Montpelier's anxious frown dissolved as he savored the title.

" 'The Starcrossed,' " he murmured.

"It draws its dramatic punch," Morgan quoted from Gabriel's poopsheet, tucked into his zipper pocket, "from the depths of the human heart in conflict with itself. The origins of this idea trace back through Shakespeare and the Renaissance, back into Medieval romance, and even. . . ."

Montpelier's face went sour. "It's not that damned 'Romeo and Juliet' thing he was trying to peddle at Mercury, is it?"

"Of course not," Morgan snapped and immediately wished he hadn't. *Too quick, he sees through it. Lose ten points.*

"Well, what is it then?"

"It draws on some of the same material as the 'Romeo and Juliet' idea. . . ."

"Ah-hah!"

"But it's a completely new concept. Fully science fictional. No historical or contemporary parts to it at all."

"No realism?" Montpelier asked, with an expression that was close to a sneer.

"None."

"I know Gabriel. He's always trying to sneak some realism in."

With a grin, Morgan realized that Montpelier had suckered himself. He had set up a strawman; now all Morgan had to do was to knock it down.

"Let me tell you about this idea," Morgan said, hunching forward over the table conspiratorially. He hesitated just long enough to make Montpelier hold his breath, then started quoting again from the poopsheet:

"Picture a starship floating through space, just like any ordinary starship, like you see on all the shows, but this ship's been designed by the man who *invented* the three-dee process. Accurate. Technically detailed. A perfect jewel, shining in the black velvet of the infinite interstellar wilderness. Now, aboard that starship. . . ."

It was dark outside and people were starting to trickle in for dinner before Montpelier stopped asking questions about the show. Morgan was hoarse, as much from the nervous strain of improvising answers as from talking steadily for so many hours.

Montpelier was nodding. "It's got scope all right. I like the whole idea. It's got *depth.*"

"Uh-huh," Morgan grunted. Then, as noncommittally as possible, he asked, "How's B.F. reacting to it?"

Montpelier shook his head. "If it was anybody else except Gabriel, B.F. would've snapped it up."

"Oh. I see."

"As it is," Montpelier went on, "he's stuck *me* with the job of getting along with Gabriel and not letting Ron get to the top."

"Oh?" Morgan felt his head go light.

"It's a pretty shitty job." Montpelier complained. "I'll have to handle Gabriel and keep him away from B.F. We'll have to settle on a damned executive producer; maybe Sheldon Fad. He's hot right now."

"Yes," Morgan agreed, with a genuine smile. "I think he'd be fine."

When Montpelier finally left the restaurant, there were stars in his eyes. *Or dollar signs,* Morgan reflected as he bade the executive goodbye and promised to be in touch with him the next day for some "hard-nosed, eyeball-to-eyeball, tough-assed money talk."

Morgan went to the men's room, threw up as he always did after one of these extended bull-flinging lunches, cleaned himself up, then found a phonebooth out near the bar. He sat down, closed the door firmly, and punched out Ron Gabriel's number.

It was busy. With a sigh, Morgan punched Gabriel's

private number. Also busy. With a deeper sigh, he tried the writer's ultraprivate "hot line" number. *He can't be carrying on three conversations at once.* Morgan realized it was more a fond hope than a statement of fact.

A sultry brunette appeared on the tiny screen. "Mr. Gabriel's line," she moaned.

"Uh. . . ." With a distant part of his mind, Morgan was pleased that he could still be shaken up by apparitions such as this one. "Is, uh, Mr. Gabriel there? This is Jerry Morgan, his agent."

"I'll see, Mr. Morgan," she breathed.

The screen went gray for an instant, then Gabriel's hard-bitten features came on the tiny screen.

"Well? How'd it go?"

Morgan said, "I just finished having lunch with Les Montpelier. . . ."

"God, you sound awful!" Gabriel said.

"I did a lot of talking."

Gabriel's face fell. "They don't want the show. They hated the idea."

"I talked it all out with Montpelier," Morgan said. "Finger's read the poopsheet and. . . ." He hesitated.

"And?"

It was criminal to tease Gabriel, but Morgan got the chance so seldom.

"And what?" Gabriel demanded, his voice rising.

"And . . . well, I don't know how to say it, Ron, so I might as well make it straight from the shoulder."

Gabriel gritted his teeth.

"They're buying it. We talk money tomorrow."

For an instant, nothing happened. No change in Gabriel's facing-the-firing-squad expression. Then his jaw dropped open and his eyes popped.

"What?" he squawked. *"They bought it?"* He leaped out of view of the phone's fixed camera, then reappeared some ten meters further away. He jumped up and down. "They bought it! They bought it! Ha-*ha!* They bought it! Those birdbrains bought it!"

The sultry brunette, another girl whom Morgan vaguely remembered as Gabriel's typist and a third woman rushed into the room. Gabriel was still bounding all over the place, crowing with delight.

With the smile of a man who's put in a hard but successful day's work, Morgan clicked off the phone and started on his way home.

4: THE PRODUCER

Sheldon Fad lay awake, staring at the ceiling as the sun rose over the Santa Monica Hills. Gloria snored lightly beside him, a growing mountain of flesh.

The baby was due in another month or so and Gloria had been no fun at all since she had found herself pregnant. No fun at all. Zero. Sheldon wondered, at quiet times like this, if it was really his baby that she was carrying. After all, she got pregnant suspiciously fast after moving in with him.

He frowned to himself. It all seemed so *macho* at first. An actress and dancer, lithe and exciting, Gloria had attached herself to Sheldon's arm when she could have gone with any guy in Los Angeles. They were all after her. He had ignored the stories about the vast numbers who had succeeded in their quest. That was all finished, she had told him tearfully, the night she moved in. All she wanted was him.

Yeah, Sheldon told himself. *Just me.* And a roof over her head. And not having to go to work. And a two-pound box of chocolates every day. And her underwear dripping in the bathtub every time he tried to take a shower. And her makeup littered all over the bathroom, the bedroom, even in the refrigerator.

A bolt, as the song says, of fear went through him as he realized that in a month—probably less—there'd be an infant sharing this one-bedroom apartment with them. What did Shakespeare say about infants? Mewling and puking. Yeah. And dirty diapers. A crib in the corner next to the bed; Gloria had already mentioned that.

Shit! Sheldon knew he had to get out of it. He turned his head on the pillow and gazed sternly at Gloria's face, serene and deeply asleep. *It's not my kid,* he told himself savagely. *It's not!*

And what if it is? another part of his mind asked. You didn't want it. She told you she was fixed. You believe her? And her line about hemophilia, so she can't have an abortion? Even if it is your kid, you didn't ask for this.

He sat up in bed, fuming to himself. Gloria didn't move a muscle, execpt to breathe. Her belly made a giant mound in the bedsheet.

No sense trying to go back to sleep. He swung his legs out of the bed and got to his feet. Stretching, he felt his vertebrae pop and heard himself grunt with the pain-pleasure that goes with it. He padded into the bathroom.

Twenty minutes later he was booming down the Freeway, heading for the Titanic Tower, listening to the early morning news:

". . . and smog levels will be at their usual moderate to heavy concentrations, depending on location, as the morning traffic builds up. Today's smog scent will be jasmine. . . ."

It was still clear enough to see where you were driving. The automatic Freeway guidance system hadn't turned on yet. Music came on the radio and began to soothe Sheldon slightly. Then; he saw the Titanic Tower rising impressively from the Valley.

"I'll ask Murray what to do," Sheldon said to himself. "Murray will know."

It was still hours before most of the work force would stream into the Tower. Sheldon nodded grimly to the bored guards sitting at the surveillance station in the lobby. They were surrounded by an insect's eye of fifty TV screens showing every conceivable entryway into the building.

As Sheldon passed the guard, a solitary TV screen built into the wall alongside the main elevator bank flashed the words:

GOOD MORNING MR. FAD. YOU'RE IN QUITE EARLY.

"Good morning, Murray," said Sheldon Fad. Then he punched the button for an elevator.

The *Multi-Unit Reactive Reasoning and Analysis Yoke* was rather more than just another business computer. In an industry where insecurity is a major driving force and more money has been spent on psychoanalyses than scripts, *Murray* was inevitable. One small segment of the huge computer's capacity was devoted to mundane chores such as handling accounts and sorting out bills and paychecks. Most of the giant computer complex was devoted to helping executives make business decisions. It was inevitable that the feedback loops in the computer's basic programming—the "Reactive Reasoning" function—would eventually come to be used as a surrogate psychotechnician, advisor and father confessor by Titanic's haggard executives.

Sheldon Fad didn't think of Murray as a machine. Murray was someone you could talk to, just like he talked to so many other people on the phone without ever meeting them in the flesh. Murray was kindly, sympathetic, and damned smart. He had helped Sheldon over more than one business-emotional crisis.

Well, there was *one* machine-like quality to Murray that Sheldon recognized. And appreciated. His memory could be erased. And was, often. It made for a certain amount of repetition when you talked to Murray, but that was better than running the risk of having someone else "accidentally" listen to your conversations. Someone like Bernard Finger, who wasn't above such things, despite the privacy laws.

In all, talking to Murray was like talking to a wise and friendly old uncle. A forgetful uncle, because of the erasures. But somehow that made Murray seem all the more human. He even adapted his speech patterns to fit comfortably with the user's style of speaking.

At precisely 7:32 Sheldon plopped tiredly into his desk chair. He felt as if he'd been working nonstop for forty days and nights. He took a deep breath, held it for twenty heartbeats, then exhaled through his mouth. He punched buttons on his desk-side console for orange juice and vitamin supplements. A small wall panel slid open, a soft chime sounded and the cold cup and pills were waiting for him.

Sheldon swallowed and gulped, then touched the sequence of buttons on the keyboard that summoned Murray.

GOOD MORNING SHELDON, the desktop viewing screen flashed, chartreuse letters against a gray background. WHAT CAN I DO FOR YOU THIS MORNING?

"This conversation is strictly private," Sheldon said. He noticed that his voice was trembling a little.

OF COURSE. PLEASE GIVE ME THE CORRECT ERASURE CODE.

" 'Nobody knows the troubles I've seen,' " replied Sheldon.

THAT'S FINE, Murray printed. NOW WE CAN TALK IN PRIVATE AND THE TAPE WILL BE ERASED BETTER THAN THEY DO IN WASHINGTON.

Sheldon couldn't help grinning. He had told Murray all about Washington politics long ago.

"This is a personal problem," he began, "but I guess it affects my work, as well. . . ."

A PERSONAL PROBLEM IS A BUSINESS PROBLEM, Murray answered.

Sheldon outlined his feelings about Gloria, omitting nothing. Finally, feeling more exhausted than ever, he asked, "Well?"

Murray's screen stayed blank for a heartbeat—a long time for the computer to consider a problem. Then:

ABOUT THE SEX I DON'T KNOW. I'M BEYOND THAT SORT OF THING, YOU KNOW. BUT IF THE GIRL ISN'T MAKING YOU HAPPY AND YOU'RE NOT MARRIED TO HER, WHY DON'T YOU JUST TELL HER YOU WANT TO SPLIT.

"It's not that easy. She'd make a scene. It'd get into the news."

OH. SO. AND THAT WOULD BE BAD FOR BUSINESS.

"That's right. B.F. doesn't like to hear about rising young producers making messes of their personal lives."

BUT YOU'RE ONE OF HIS FAIR-HAIRED BOYS!

"That was last season. I had the only Titanic show to be renewed for this year."

FORTY-SIX SHOWS TITANIC PUTS ON LAST SEASON AND YOURS IS THE ONE RENEWED. GOOD WORK.

That came from Murray's general business memory bank, Sheldon realized. "That's about average for the industry," he said defensively. "Titanic didn't do any worse than Fox or Universal."

WE'RE GETTING SIDETRACKED, Murray pointed out.

"Right. Well . . . in addition to trying to figure out what to do with Gloria, I've got this new project on my hands . . . and it's a crucial one. The whole future of Titanic depends on it."

SEE? THEY'RE DEPENDING ON YOU!

"Yes, but. . . ." Sheldon felt miserable. "Look at it from my point of view. If I don't get rid of Gloria somehow, I'm not going to be able to give my best to this new show. If I do get rid of her and she raises a stink, *and the new show flops,* B.F. will blame it all on me."

YOU'RE IS A DOUBLE BIND, ALL RIGHT

"There's more," Sheldon said. "The shows' creator,

Ron Gabriel, doesn't get along with B.F. *at all*. I'm in the middle on that, too. And Gabriel wants to put on the most extravagant space opera you've ever seen, while I've got to stay within a budget that won't even buy peanut butter!"

AGAIN IN THE MIDDLE.

"Exactly."

SO? WHAT ELSE?

Sheldon pondered for several moments, while the sickly greenish letters glowed on the screen.

"I guess that's about all," he said at last. "I've got a meeting with Gabriel and his agent later this morning. I know Gabriel's going to make impossible demands . . . and he . . . he's so . . . *loud!* He shouts and screams. Sometimes he hits!"

SO SUE HIM.

"I don't *want* him to hit me!"

WHAT DO YOU WANT?

For the first time since he had become acquainted with Murray, Sheldon felt some slight impatience. "What do I want? I want to get rid of Gloria without a fight that'll ruin my career. I want to make a hit of this stupid idea of Gabriel's without driving the company broke. I want to get out of the middle!"

ALL RIGHT. ALL RIGHT, DON'T GET SO WORKED UP. HIGH BLOOD PRESSURE AND ULCERS NEVER SOLVED ANY PROBLEMS.

"But what can I *do?*"

I'M SEARCHING MY MEMORY BANKS FOR A CORROLATION. AND AT THE SAME TIME USING MY ANALYTICAL PROGRAMMING TO ATTACK THE PROBLEM. AHAH! THAT'S IT.

"What?" Sheldon leaned forward in his chair hopefully.

GET OUT OF THE COUNTRY

"Get out. . . ." He sagged back.

IF YOU PRODUCE THIS SHOW OUTSIDE THE U.S., YOU CAN TELL GLORIA THAT YOU'LL BE AWAY FOR SEVERAL MONTHS. CAN'T BE HELPED. BUSINESS. CAREER. ALL THAT SORT OF STUFF.

"But she'll see through. . . ."

CERTAINLY SHE WILL. SHE WILL UNDERSTAND WHAT YOU'RE REALLY TELLING HER. BUT SHE WON'T BE ABLE TO DO MUCH ABOUT IT. AND IF SHE'S THE SORT OF GIRL YOU TOLD ME SHE IS, SHE'LL SEE THE WISDOM IN PICKING UP SOME OTHER MAN TO SUPPORT HER.

Wearily, Sheldon asked, "But who in his right mind would let an eight-months-pregnant woman grab him....?"

YOU'D BE SURPRISED. THERE ARE LOTS OF MEN RIGHT HERE IN THIS COMPANY WITH ALL SORTS OF HANGUPS.

"You think she'd really find somebody else?"

CERTAINLY. IN THE MEANTIME, YOU CAN FIND A REALLY CHEAPO OUTFIT TO PRODUCE YOUR NEW SHOW AND GET OFF THE FISCAL HOOK THAT WAY. PRODUCTION COMPANIES OUTSIDE THE U.S. WORK MUCH MORE CHEAPLY THAN OUR OWN UNIONIZED PEOPLE.

"Where?" Sheldon asked, suddenly eager to travel. "Yugoslavia? Argentina? New Zealand?"

NONE OF THE ABOVE. YOU'VE GOT TO BALANCE YOUR TRAVEL EXPENSES AGAINST THE EXPENSES OF PRODUCTION. CALCULATIONS ARE THAT CANADA WILL BE THE CHEAPEST BET.

"Canada?" Sheldon felt his enthusiasm sinking.

CANADA. MEXICO LOOKS CHEAPER ON THE SURFACE, BUT MY SUBROUTINES TELL ME THAT YOU'VE GOT TO BRIBE EVERYBODY IN THE GOVERNMENT, FROM THE CUSTOMS INSPECTORS TO THE TRAFFIC COPS, IF YOU WANT TO DO BUSINESS DOWN THERE. RAISES THE COSTS BEYOND THOSE OF A CANADIAN OPERATION. THE CANADIANS ARE HONEST AS WELL AS PRETTY CHEAP.

"Canada?" Sheldon repeated. His mind filled with visions of snow, sled dogs, pine trees, Nelson Eddy in a red Mounties jacket.

"Canada," he said again.

Fad's office wasn't very large, considering he was an executive producer on the rise. Merely a couple of leatherite couches, a few deep chairs scattered here and there across the fakefur rug, his own desk and keyboard terminal and a few holographic pictures where windows would normally be. Sheldon preferred the holographic views of Mt. Shasta, San Francisco's Bay Bridge and Catalina Island to the view of a tinted smog that he could see through his window. He wasn't high enough in Titanic's hierarchy to be above the smog level.

When his secretary told him that Gabriel and Morgan had arrived, Sheldon carefully clicked on the *record* button on Murray's controls. A friendly blue light glowed steadily at him, from an angle that could be seen only from behind the desk. Sheldon felt as if he had a silent ally standing beside him.

His visitors were ushered into the office by his secretary, who discreetly went no further than the door. But Gabriel was already jotting down her phone number in the little book he always carried. She was giving him her most dazzling smile; he had apparently already turned the full force of his charisma on her.

Morgan was still wearing his same tired old red zipsuit; it had been out of style for a year or more. Gabriel, who was a style setter, wore tight black leather slacks and what looked like a genuine antique motorcycle jacket, complete with studs and chains.

Sheldon got up and came around the desk, arms outstretched. "Fellaaas . . . how *are* you?"

Morgan, who was tall enough to be a laughable contrast to the smaller, stockier Gabriel, backed away automatically. Gabriel aimed a mock punch at Sheldon's stomach. They ended up shaking hands.

"Isn't it great to be starting something new?" Sheldon enthused. "This is going to be the best series Titanic has ever done. I just know it!"

"Great. Great," said Gabriel, with something of a scowl on his face. "Where's Brenda? I thought she'd be here."

Retreating back to his desk chair, Sheldon answered, "Why no, she's not part of this project. She works directly for B.F., you know."

Morgan had taken the nearest deepchair and started to

say, "We got all the financial arrangements ironed out with Les Montpelier last week. He says the legal department is drawing up the contrasts."

Sheldon nodded. "That's entirely correct. Want some coffee? Juice? Anything?"

Gabriel was prowling around the room, still scowling. "I thought Brenda was going to be here. She was in on the beginning of this idea. . . ."

"Brenda," said Sheldon patiently, "is B.F.'s assistant. She does *not* get involved in preproduction planning for a specific show."

"Lemme use your phone," Gabriel said, heading for the desk.

Sheldon quickly swivelled the phone around so that Gabriel could see the screen without coming around the desk and noticing Murray's recording eye. Gabriel sat on a corner of the desk and started punching numbers on the phone's keyboard.

Sheldon had to push his chair over a bit and lean sidewise to see Morgan.

"You and Les settled all the financial matters?" he asked, while Gabriel was saying:

"Brenda Impanema . . . whattaya mean she's not at this number? What number is she at? Screw information! *You* look it up, why dontcha?"

Morgan seemed to be taking it all in stride, the eye of Gabriel's hurricane. "There are a few minor matters that we're not happy with, but I'll straighten those out once the contracts are drawn up. Nothing to worry about. It's not as much money as we expected, though."

Sheldon shrugged. "Money's tight all over."

"Brenda! How the hell are you? Where've you been keeping yourself?"

"If money's so tight, how will this affect the production values on 'The Starcrossed?'" Morgan asked.

"That's what I wanted to discuss with you. I know Ron thinks big and I agree with him, I really do—but. . . ."

"Whattaya mean you think it's best if we don't see each other? Is this Finger's idea of getting even with me?"

"You know," Morgan said, "I've seen a lot of shows with great potential fold up because the producers didn't put enough backing into them."

"Yes, I know. But I think I've worked out a way to get the best production values and still keep the costs down. . . ."

"I don't care if Finger cancels the whole season!" Gabriel yelled at the phone. "I don't want you pussyfooting around because you think it'll make him sore if you see me. He can stick it. . . ."

"How are you going to do that, Sheldon?"

"Well, after an *exhaustive* computer analysis of the situation. . . ."

"I know you're doing it for me," Gabriel was shouting now, "but I'd rather see you than win an Emmy. Yah, that's exactly what I said."

"You were saying?"

"Our analysis shows that the optimum choice for producing the show. . . ."

"This is just a stall, isn't it? What you're really saying is that you can't stand the sight of me! Right?"

". . . would be outside the U.S., away from the high rates that all the unions here charge."

"Okay, kid. Maybe you're protecting me. But I think it's a Pearl Harbor job and I don't like it!"

"And where do you want to put it?"

"Goodbye!"

"In Canada."

"Canada?"

"Canada!" Gabriel leaped off the desk corner. "Who the hell's going to Canada?"

"We are."

"You are?"

"No, *you* are."

Morgan said calmly, "He wants to shoot the show in Canada."

Gabriel looked as if he was ready to lead a bayonet attack. "Canada! I can't go to Canada! What in hell is there that you don't have more of here? And better?"

Sheldon sank back in his chair. It was going to be just as rough as he had feared. Only the friendly stare of Uncle Murray's steady blue eye gave him the courage to go on.

Two hours later, Sheldon was still in his desk chair. His jacket was crumpled on the floor and had Gabriel's bootprints all over it. His suppshirt was soaked with sweat. Morgan hadn't moved at all during that time, nor hardly spoken; he still looked calm, relaxed, almost asleep.

But the walls were still ringing with Gabriel's rhetoric. Two chairs were overturned. Both couches had been kicked out of shape. One of the holographic pictures was sputtering badly, for reasons unknown. The Bay Bridge kept winking and shimmering . . . or maybe, thought Sheldon, it was merely cringing.

"This is the dumbest asshole trick I've ever heard of!" Gabriel was screaming. "I don't want to go to Canada! There's nothing and nobody in Canada! All the good Canadian directors and actors are *here,* in California, for Chrissakes! We've got everything we need right here. Going to Canada is crazy! With a capital K!"

He was heading for the phone again when Morgan lifted one hand a few centimeters off the armrest of his chair. "Ron," he said quietly.

Gabriel stopped in midstride.

"Ron, the decision's already been made. It's a money decision and there's nothing you can do about it."

Gabriel frowned furiously at his agent.

"That's the way it is," Morgan said blandly.

"Then I want out," Gabriel said.

"Don't be silly," Morgan countered.

"I'm walking."

"You can't *do* that!" Sheldon protested.

"No? Watch me!"

Gabriel started for the door. Halfway there, he stopped

and turned back toward Sheldon. "Tell you what," he said. His face still looked like something that would stagger Attila the Hun. "If I have to go to Canada, I'm going first class."

Sheldon let his breath out a little. "Oh, of course. Top hotels. All the best."

"That's not what I mean."

"What then?"

"I'm not going to let this show get stuck out in the boondocks, with no pipeline back to the money and the decision makers."

"But *I'll* be there with you," Sheldon said.

Gabriel made as if to spit. "I want *personal* representation from top management, right there on the set every goddamned day. I want one of Finger's top assistants in Canada with us."

"Ohhh." The clouds began to dissipate and Sheldon could see a Canadian sunrise. "Maybe you're right. Maybe I could get Les Montpelier . . . or Brenda Impanema. . . ."

Gabriel pointed an index finger at him, pistol-like. "You've got the idea."

Nodding, Sheldon said, "I'll ask B.F. tonight, at the party. . . ."

"Party?"

That was a mistake! Sheldon knew. Backtracking, "Oh, nothing spectacular. B.F.'s just giving one of his little soirées . . . on the ship, you know . . . just a couple of hundred people. . . ." His voice trailed off weakly.

"Party, huh?" was all that Gabriel said.

After he and Morgan left the office, Sheldon went to his private john and took a quick needle shower. Toweling himself off, he yelled through the open door to Murray:

"Well, what do you think of our star writer and creator?"

The computer hummed to itself for a few moments, then the screen lit up:

SUCH A KVETCH!

5: THE DECISION MAKERS

Sheldon was dressing for the party. It had been a long, exhausting day. And it wasn't over yet. Bernard Finger's parties were always something of a cross between a long-distance marathon and being dropped out of an airplane.

After Gabriel and his agent had left, Sheldon spent the rest of the morning recuperating, popping tranquilizers and watching Murray run down lists of Canadian production companies. There weren't very many. Then the computer system started tracking down freelance Canadian directors, cameramen, electricians and other crew personnel. Distressingly, most of them lived in the States. Most of them, in fact, lived in *one* state: California, southern, Los Angeles County.

At a discreet lunch with Montpelier, Sheldon dropped the barest hint that it would have Titanic money to shoot the show in Canada. Montpelier scratched at his beard for a moment and then asked:

"What about Gabriel? What's he think of the idea?"

"Loves it," exaggerated Sheldon.

Montpelier's eyebrows went up. "He's willing to leave

that sex palace he's got in Sherman Oaks to go to the Frozen North?"

"He wants the show to be a success," Sheldon explained, crossing his ankles underneath the table. "When I explained that we'd be able to make our limited budget go much farther in Canada, he agreed. He was reluctant at first, I admit. But he's got a huge emotional commitment to this show. I know how to lever him around."

With a shrug, Montpelier said, "Fine by me. If Gabriel won't screw up the works. . . ."

"He, eh . . . he wants one favor from us."

"Oh."

"It's not back breaking; don't get worried."

"Tell me about it."

"He wants Brenda up there with him."

Grinning, Montpelier asked, "Does she know about it?"

"That Gabriel wants her?"

"No. The Canada part."

"Not yet."

"So if she doesn't go, Gabriel doesn't go."

Feeling somewhat annoyed at Montpelier's smirk, Sheldon replied, "Yes, I suppose that's so."

After a long silent moment, Montpelier finally said, "Well, I guess that means Brenda's going to Canada."

Sheldon let his breath out. It was going to work!

"I mean," Montpelier justified, "if it's vital to the company's interests, she'll just have to go to Canada."

"Right."

"Her relationship with Gabriel is her own business."

"Right," Sheldon said again.

"We're not responsible for her private life, after all. She's an adult. It's not like we're forcing her into Gabriel's clutches."

"Right." It was an important word to know.

Their lunch went on for several hours while they discussed serious matters over tasteful wines and a bit of anti-caloric food. Sheldon tried to suppress the nagging memory of a recent magazine article about the carcinogenic properties of anticaloric foods. Muckraking journalism, of course. Who could work in an industry where more business was conducted in restaurants and bars than in offices, without the calorie-destroying active enzyme artificial foods? Besides, the news from the National Institutes of Health was that a cure for cancer was due within another few years. For sure, this time.

By the time lunch was over, Sheldon was too exhausted to go back to the office. So he drove home for a short nap, before getting ready for the party. Gloria was out when he got home and he gratefully jumped into the unoccupied bed and was asleep in seconds.

She woke him when she returned, but it didn't matter. She was already beginning to look slightly fuzzy at the edges, becoming transparent to Sheldon's eyes. Not that he could see through her, so much as the fact that now he could look *past* her. Beyond her swollen belly and sarcastic mouth he could see lovely, pristine Canada.

She whined about not going to the party, of course. Sheldon just stared at her bloated body and said, "Now really!" Instead of starting one of her scenes, she cried and retreated to the already rumpled bed.

Sheldon didn't tell her about Canada. He wanted to be barricaded in his office, with Murray at his side, when he popped that surprise. On the phone he could handle almost anything.

Now he stood at the costumer's, being cleverly made over into his Party Personality. While the two makeup men were building up his new plastic face, the viewscreen in front of Sheldon's chair played a long series of film clips showing his Personality in action. It was an old film star named Gary Cooper and it seemed to Sheldon that all he had to do was to say "Yep" and "Nope" at the appropriate times. He concentrated on remembering those lines while the makeup men altered his face.

As the sun sank into the sea—sank into the smog bank hovering over the line of drilling platforms out there, actually—Sheldon drove toward the harbor, where the party was already in progress.

Bernard Finger almost always gave his parties on shipboard. It wasn't that he could cruise outside the limits of U.S. and/or California law enforcement. After all, the nation claimed territorial rights out to the limits of the continental shelf and there were a few California legislators who claimed the whole ocean out as far as Hawaii.

It's just that a cruise ship relaxes people, Sheldon realized as he drove up to the pier. You forget your landbound inhibitions once you pull away from the shore. And you can't walk home.

He parked his bubble-topped two seater in the lot on the pier and sprinted the fifty meters through smog to the air curtain that protected the main hatch of the ship. Out here, on the docks, the smog was neither perfumed nor tinted. It looked and smelled *dirty*.

The ship was called the *Adventurer*, a name that Bernard Finger apparently thought apt. Titanic had bought it as a mammoth set for an ocean liner series they made a few years back. They had gotten it cheaply after the old Cunard Line had collapsed in economic ruin. For a while, Finger wanted to rename the ship *Titanic*, but a team of PR people had finally dissuaded him.

Now Sheldon stepped through the curtain of blowing air that kept the shoreside smog out of the ship. He stood for a moment just inside the hatch, while the robot photographer—a stainless steel cylinder with optical lenses studding its knobby top—squeaked "Smile!" and clicked his picture.

Sheldon smiled at the camera. Gary Cooper smiled back at him, from the elaborate mirrors behind the photographer. Dressed in buckskins, with a pearl-handled sixgun on his hip, lean, tanned, full of woodsy lore, Sheldon actually felt that he could conquer the West single handedly.

John Wayne bumped into him from behind. "Well, move

it, fella," he snarled. "This here wagon train's gotta get through!"

Feeling a little sheepish and more than a little awkward in his platform boots, Sheldon made room for John Wayne. The cowboy was taller than Sheldon. "Wait 'til I get my hands on the costumers," he muttered to himself. They had promised him that nobody would be taller than Gary Cooper.

Maneuvering carefully up the stairway in his boots, Sheldon made his way up to the Main Lounge, It was decorated in authentic midcentury desperation: gummy-looking velvet couches and genuine formica cocktail tables. The windowless walls glittered with metal and imitation crystal.

The party was already well underway. As he took the usual set of greenies from one live waiter and a tall drink from another to wash them down, Sheldon saw a sea of old movie stars: Welches, Hepburns, Gables, Monroes, Redfords, a pair of Siamese twins that looked like Newman and Woodward, Marx Brothers scuttling through the crowd, a few showoff Weismullers, one stunning Loren and the usual gaggle of Bogarts.

No other Coopers. Good.

Up on the stage, surrounded by Harlows and Wests, stood Bernard Finger. He was instantly recognizable because he wore practically no makeup at all. He looked like Cary Grant all the time and now he merely looked slightly more so. Sheldon didn't have to look around to know that there were no other Cary Grants at the party.

He drank and let the greenies put a pleasant buzz in his head. After a dance with a petite Debbie Reynolds, the ship's whistle sounded and everybody rushed up to the main deck to watch them cast off.

As the oil-slicked dock slid away and the ship throbbed with the power of its engines, everyone started back to the various bars sprinkled around the lower decks. Or to the staterooms.

Sheldon turned from the glassed-in rail to go back to the

Main Lounge, but a tall smoldering Lauren Bacall was slouching insolently in his path.

She held a cigaret up in front of her face and asked casually, "Got a match?" Her voice was sultry enough to start a forest fire.

Trying to keep his hands from trembling, Sheldon said, "Yep." He rummaged through his buckskin outfit's pockets and finally found a lighter. Bacall watched him bemusedly. He finally got it out and touched the spot that started the lighter glowing.

"Good," said Bacall. She slowly drew on the cigaret, then puffed smoke in Sheldon's face. "Now stick it up your nose. And Canada too!"

"Brenda?" Sheldon gasped. "It that you?"

She angled a hip, Bacall-like, and retorted, "It's not Peter Lorre, Sheldon."

"How'd you know who I was? I mean. . . ."

"Never mind," she said; her voice became less sultry, more like Brenda Impanema's normal throatiness. "What I want to know is what gives you the right to decide 'The Starcrossed' is going to Canada. And me with it."

"Oh," Sheldon said. There didn't seem to be any Cooper lines to cover this situation. "Les told you about it."

"No he didn't," Brenda-Bacall said. "Les is as big a snake as you are. Bigger. He kept his mouth shut."

Sheldon glanced around for a possible escape route. None. He and Brenda were alone on the sealed-in weather deck. The rest of the crowd had gone inside. Brenda stood between him and the nearest hatch leading to the party. If he tried to run for another hatch in these damned platform boots, he'd either fall flat on his face or she would catch him in a few long-legged strides. Either way it would be too humiliating to bear. So he stood there and tried to look brave and unshaken.

"If you must know how I found out," Brenda went on, "I asked Murray what you were up to."

"Murray told you?" Sheldon heard his voice go up an octave with shock. Uncle Murray was a fink!

"Murray's everybody's friend. Knows all and tells all."

"But he's not supposed to tell about private conversations! Only business matters!"

"That's all he told me," Brenda said. "Your business conversation with Ron Gabriel."

Sheldon felt a wave of relief wash over him. Or maybe it was a swaying of the ship. At any rate, Murray could be trusted. At least one central fixture in the universe stayed in place.

Lauren Bacall grinned at him and Brenda's voice answered, "I called Les's secretary for a lunch appointment and she told me he'd already gone to lunch with you. When he got back, he was kinda smashed. As usual. I dropped into his office before his sober-up pills could grab hold of him. He leered at me and asked how I like cold winters. Which means he approves of your plans."

Sheldon shook his head in reluctant admiration. "You ought to be a detective."

"I ought to be a lot of things," she said, "but I'm not a call girl. I'm not going to Canada."

"But I thought you liked Gabriel."

"Whatever's between Ron and me is between Ron and me. I'm not going to become part of his harem just to suit you."

"It's not me," Sheldon protested. "It's for Titanic."

"Nope," Brenda stole Cooper's line.

"It's for B.F."

She shook her head, but Sheldon thought he noticed the barest little hesitation in her action.

"B.F. wants you to do it," Sheldon pressed the slight opening.

"B.F. doesn't know anything about it yet," Brenda said, "and when he does find out. . . ."

The roar of a powerful motor drowned out her words. Looking around, Sheldon saw that a small boat was racing alongside the ship, not more than twenty meters from the *Adventurer.* The cruise ship had cleared the line of off shore oil rigs and was out of the smog area. The sky above was clear and awash with moonlight. A few very bright stars twinkled here and there.

"That damned fool's going to get himself killed," Sheldon said.

The motorboat was edging closer to the *Adventurer*, churning up a white wake as it cleaved through the ocean swells.

"He's going to sideswipe us!" Brenda shouted. "Do something, Sheldon."

But there was nothing he could do. No emergency phone or fire alarm box in sight along this stretch of plastic-domed deck.

The motorboat disappeared from their view, it was getting so close to the liner. Brenda and Sheldon pressed their noses against the plastic, but they'd have to be able to lean over the railing to see the motorboat now.

They heard a thump.

"Oh my god!" Brenda's voice was strangely high and shrill.

More bumps.

"They must be breaking up against our hull," Sheldon said. He still couldn't think of anything to do about it.

Then something hit against the plastic wall not five meters away from Sheldon's face. He shrieked and leaped backwards.

"Giant squid!" Sheldon shouted.

It did have suction cups on it. But after that first wild flash of panic, he saw that it was a mechanical arm, not a tentacle.

"It looks like a ladder," Brenda said.

His stomach churning, Sheldon said, "I think we'd better get back inside and tell somebody. . . ."

Brenda blocked his way and took hold of his buckskin sleeve. "No. Wait a minute. . . ."

As Sheldon watched, firmly clutched by Brenda, a man's hand appeared on one of the rungs that extended from either side of the mechanical tentacle. A small man in a dark suit came into view. He was wearing a 1920s Fedora pulled down low over his forehead.

"He'll never get through the dome. It's airtight," Sheldon said.

The man ran a hand along the outside of the transparent plastic, seemingly searching for something. Twice he made a sudden grab for his hat, which was flapping wildly in the twenty-knot breeze. His hand finally stopped below the line of the railing, so Sheldon couldn't see what he was doing. But from the action of his shoulder, it looked as if he pushed hard against something. The section of the plastic dome in front of him popped open with a tiny sigh and slid backward. The wind suddenly swirled along the deck.

"Must be an emergency hatch," Brenda murmured.

The man hesitated a moment; then, looking downward, he reached below the level where Sheldon could see. He hauled up a strange-looking object: long and slim at one end, thicker at the other, with a round drum in the middle.

"A Tommygun!" Sheldon realized, in a frightened whisper. "Like they used on the 'Prohibition Blues' show!"

The dark-suited man threw a leg over the rail and clambered onto the deck. He clutched the Tommygun with both hands now, his left arm stretched out almost as far as it could go to reach the front handgrip.

He turned slowly in the shadows along the deck and saw Brenda and Sheldon frozen near the rail.

"Don't make a move," he whispered. In a voice that Sheldon somehow knew.

Leaning over the rail, the dark-suited man called, "Come on up, you guys. It's okay."

Sheldon *knew* that voice. But he couldn't place it. And the hat was still pulled too low over the man's face to recognize him.

"They're going to hijack the ship." Brenda whispered. "Do something!"

Sheldon didn't answer. He was busy staring at the Tommygun.

Two more dark-suited men climbed up to the deck. Each of them carried huge, ugly-looking pistols. Colt 45s, Sheldon realized. Named after the beer commercial.

The first man stepped up to Sheldon and Brenda, shifting the Tommygun to the crook of his arm.

"You dirty rats," he said. "You didn't invite me to your party. So I'm crashing it."

He was close enough for Sheldon to see his face now. And recognize it. They were being confronted by Jimmy Cagney.

Behind Cagney stood Alan Jenkins and Frank McHue, both grinning rather foolishly.

Cagney hitched at his pants with his free hand. "Where's Finger?" he demanded. "I wanna find that rat. He's the guy that gave it to my brother and now I'm gonna give it to him."

The voice finally clicked in Sheldon's memory. It was Ron Gabriel doing his Cagney imitation.

"Ron?" Sheldon asked, a little timidly. "It that you?"

Cagney's face fell. "You recognized me. Shit. I thought I had you fooled, Sheldon."

"You did. It's a *wonderful* costume."

Brenda said, "That's really you, Ron?"

"Yeah . . . who're y . . . Brenda? Wow, you look terrific!"

"Thanks."

"How did you recognize me?" Sheldon wanted to know.

Cagney-Gabriel shrugged with one shoulder. "Gary Cooper. You always use the Cooper costume. Every party."

"Once or twice," said Sheldon, defensively.

"Often enough."

Sheldon started thinking. Not about his costume, but about Gabriel crashing the party. When he thought that Cagney and his henchmen were hijackers or thieves, he had been scared. But the thought of Gabriel coming face to face with B.F. terrified him. *I've got to keep them separated,* he realized.

"Let's go up to the Sky Bar and have a drink," Sheldon said, pointing forward and up.

"I wanna see Finger," Gabriel replied, switching back to his Cagney voice. "I wanna show him my violin." He hefted the Tommygun.

Brenda stepped closer to him and slipped an arm inside Gabriel's arm. "Come on, tough guy," she said, doing Bacall perfectly. "Buy a girl a drink."

Gabriel couldn't resist that. "Okay sweetheart. Umm . . . they got any grapefruit up in that bar?"

"Never mind," Brenda-Bacall said. "You don't need a grapefruit. All you've got to do is whistle."

As the five of them headed down the swaying, rolling deck toward the bar perched atop the ship's bridge, Sheldon thought, *And all I've got to do is keep Brenda with him.*

They took over a corner table in the Sky Bar, ordered drinks and watched the moonlight on the waves. Gabriel parked his Tommygun behind the sofa that they sat on. A blocky-looking computer over by the dancefloor was belting out the new atonal electronic music and flashing its lights in numbered sequence for the dancing couples slinking along: one, two, one-two-three; one, two, one-two three. Every once in a while the computer would throw in an extra beat, just to keep the humans off balance. Most of the dancing couples were heterosexual.

As the waiter brought their drinks, Brenda leaned close enough to Sheldon to whisper in his ear, "Thanks, hero."

He looked askance at her. "For what?"

"For sticking me with. . . ." She made a tiny nod in Gabriel's direction. He was busy watching the dancers and arching his eyebrows at the prettiest of the girls.

"You volunteered," Sheldon protested.

"Sure. When it looked like you were going to faint. You're hiding behind a woman's skirts!"

"You can handle him," Sheldon assured her. "Don't be afraid. . . ."

Brenda was suddenly yanked up from the sofa.

"Come on, kid," said Gabriel-Cagney. "Let's show them how to do it."

He pulled Brenda onto the dancefloor. Sheldon watched them gyrate as he sipped his drink and watched Gabriel's henchmen surreptitiously. They were paying no attention to him; instead, they were ogling a table full of Rita Hayworths, Jill St. Johns and Tina Russells.

Carefully putting his drink down on the table. Sheldon slowly got to his feet. Alan Jenkins gave him a sour look.

"Men's room," Sheldon said. Jenkins shrugged as if to say, *What do I care?*

He edged past the dancefloor, trying not to trip over anybody in his clumsy platform boots. Thankfully, Gabriel's back was to him. But that meant that Brenda was facing him and the look she shot at him was pure venom.

Sheldon mouthed at her, "Relax and enjoy it," and scuttled out of the bar.

He raced down three flights of stairs, clutching madly at the railing to keep from falling. The ship tossed and swayed and the stairs seemed to be trying to deliberately move out from under Sheldon.

But finally he made it to the Main Lounge. B.F. was sitting at a table near the bandstand, surrounded by blondes of all description, from a Pickford to a pair of Monroes. Lassie, believe it or not, was lying on the carpeting at his side.

A George Jessel was on the bandstand singing the Marine Corps Hymn, while George Burns and Jack Benny argued quietly but with great animation, off at the far end of the lounge, over who would go on next.

Sheldon made his way around the outer perimeter of the once-plush Lounge, squirmed through a phalanx of blondes and finally managed to get close enough to Bernard Finger to lean over his shoulder and whisper:

"Trouble, B.F."

Finger raised his dimpled chin in Sheldon's direction. "So he sings off key. So did the original Jessel."

"That's not what I mean. Ron Gabriel's crashed the party."

"What?" Finger shouted loud enough to startle Jessel into almost a full bar on-key. "That little snot! Here? Uninvited?"

"What else?" Sheldon said.

"How'd he get here? Where is he? What's he want? Is he hitting anybody?"

If Sheldon weren't convinced that it was impossible, he'd have been tempted to speculate that B.F. was physically frightened of Ron Gabriel.

"He's in the Sky Bar. Brenda's got him in tow. . . ." And suddenly Sheldon realized that this was an opportunity straight out of the blue, a gift from Olympus. He had B.F.'s complete and undivided attention.

He took a quick breath, then suggested, "Maybe we'd better get you to a more protected location, B.F. You know how crazy Gabriel can be."

Finger pushed two blondes aside and stood up. He seemed almost dazed with fear. "Yeah . . . right. . . ."

"And there's a lot about this situation that I have to tell you about," Sheldon went on.

"Okay," Finger said. "Down in my stateroom."

Finger's stateroom was a suite, of course. And it was actually up on deck from the Main Lounge, not down. It wasn't until the steel doors of the luxurious suite were firmly locked behind them that Finger appeared to relax.

"That Gabriel," he muttered. "He's crazy. He hit Lucio Grinaldi once, just for adding two or three songs to one of his scripts."

"That was Gabriel's adaptation of *In Cold Blood*, wasn't it?"

"Yeah." Finger plopped down into an overstuffed chair. "Imagine punching a producer just for turning a show into a musical."

A butler appeared and took their order for drinks. Sheldon sat down. His chair accommodated itself to his body. The air was sweet and cool. The suite was dimly lit, quiet, tasteful, with the kind of silence and comfort that only a lot of money could buy.

"Who're you, anyway?" Finger said suddenly. "You work for me, don't you?"

"I'm Sheldon Fad."

"Oh?" No comprehension whatsoever dawned on Finger's Cary Grant face.

"I'm one of your producers. I did the 'Diet Quiz' show last year."

"Oh, *that* one!" Recognition beamed. "The one that got renewed."

The butler brought the drinks and Sheldon eased into a roundabout explanation of his problems with "The Starcrossed." How it was Gabriel's idea and the untrusting fink had immediately registered it with the Screen Writers Guild. How he, Sheldon, had hit on the money-saving idea of taking the show to Canada for production. (B.F. smiled again at that; Sheldon's heart did a flip-flop.) How Gabriel wanted Brenda as a hostage or harem girl.

"Probably both," Finger grunted.

Sheldon nodded and pressed on. He told Finger that only Brenda's body stood between him and a face-to-face confrontation with Gabriel.

"And he's carrying a Tommygun," Sheldon concluded.

"Now? Here?"

Sheldon nodded. "I think it's going to be very vital to us to have Brenda go with us to Canada."

"You're damned right," B.F. agreed.

"But she doesn't want to go."

"She'll go."

"I'm not sure. . . ."

"Don't worry about it. What I tell her to do, she does."

"She might quit."

B.F. shook his head, a knowing smile on his lips. Somehow, it didn't look pleasant. "She won't quit. She can't. She'll do what I tell her, no matter what it is."

6: THE CONFRONTATION

Ron Gabriel sipped a gingerale as he sat at one of the Sky Bar's tiny round tables. Brenda Impanema sat on the couch beside him, staring moodily out at the moonlit ocean. On his other side, Alan Jenkins and Frank McHue were playing poker on a little table of their own.

The crowd in the bar had thinned considerably. Many couples had drifted outside, now that the ship was clear of the L.A. smog and the moon could be seen. Others had gone down to their staterooms for some serious sexual therapy.

"It's like a movie scene," Brenda said, reaching for her Hawaiian Punch. "Moonlight on the water, the ship plowing through the waves, romantic music. . . ."

Gabriel scowled at the computer, which was now issuing a late 1970s rotrock wail. "Call that romantic?"

Brenda, still in Lauren Bacall's looks, made a small shrug. "It could be romantic."

"If it was different music."

"Right."

"Then all you'd need would be Fred Astaire tapdancing out on the deck."

"And sweeping me off my feet."

Gabriel looked in the mirror across the room and saw Jimmy Cagney. But he no longer felt like Cagney. *I should have come as Astaire,* he told himself. But Cagney fitted his personality better, he knew.

77

"How come I can't sweep you off your feet?" he asked Brenda.

Becall grinned back at him. "It's chemistry. We just don't react right."

"I'm crazy about you."

"You're crazy about every girl you meet. And I don't want to go to Canada with you."

Gabriel remembered why he had come aboard. He picked up his glass of gingerale. In the mirror, Cagney's face hardened.

"I don't want to go to Canada at all. Period."

"We can drink to that." Brenda touched her glass to Gabriel's.

Cagney scowled.

She tossed her head slightly, so that the long sweep of her hair flowed back over her bare shoulder. "Are you really after me or just my body? Or just a grip on B.F.?"

"That's a helluva question," he said.

"It's of more than passing interest to me."

Gabriel put his glass down firmly on the tabletop. Without looking up from it, he said, "I'm crazy about you. I don't know anything about your body. I've seen it clothed and it looks pretty good. But more than that I can't tell. And I don't go after girls for business reasons." He looked up at her. "What I have to settle with Finger I'll settle for myself. And it's time that I did."

Brenda put a hand on his arm. "If you confront B.F. you'll blow the whole series. He'll have you kicked off the ship and out of any connection with Titanic."

"So I'll take the idea someplace else. I don't need Titanic. He needs me."

"He'll make life miserable for you."

Gabriel pulled his arm free of her. With a light tap on her cheek, he went back to pure Cagney. "Don't you worry about me, kid. I know how to handle myself."

To his cronies, who looked up from their cardgame, Gabriel said, "Keep her out of trouble."

They nodded. Both unemployed, nonselling young

writers, they were looking forward to script assignments
on the series. If they could avoid starvation long enough
to wait for the series to go into production. At the moment they were avoiding starvation—and work—by living
in Gabriel's house.

The rest home for starveling writers, Gabriel thought
as he made his way around the dancefloor and toward the
Sky Bar's exit. But he remembered his own beginning
years, the struggle and the hollow-gutted days of hunger.
Somehow he seemed to have more fun in those days than
he did now. *Shit! You'd think there'd be a time when a
guy could relax and enjoy himself.*

He reached the exit and gave a final glance back.
Jenkins and McHue had resumed their cardgame. Bacall
had moved closer to them and started kibbitzing.

Gabriel hitched up his pants and made a Cagney
grimace. "Okay, Schemer," he whispered to himself.
"Here's where you get yours."

It took a while for Gabriel to figure out where Finger
had gone. He searched the Main Lounge, the pool area
and all the bars before realizing that Finger must have
retreated to his private suite.

Theoretically, the suite was impregnable. Only one entrance, through double-locked steel watertight doors. Nobody in or out without Finger's TV surveillance system
scanning him. Gabriel considered knocking off one of the
fire alarms, but rejected that idea. People might get hurt
or even jump overboard and drown. Besides, Finger had
his own motor launch just outside the emergency hatch of
his suite. That much Gabriel knew from studying the
ship's plans.

For a few moments he considered scrambling over the
ship's rail and down the outer hull to get to the emergency hatch. But then he realized that there would still
be no way for him to get inside.

With a frown of frustration, Gabriel paced down the
ship's central staircase, thinking hard but coming up with
no ideas.

He stopped on the deck where the ship's restaurant was. Looking inside the elaborately decorated cafeteria, where the walls and even the ceiling were plastered with photos from Titanic's myriad TV shows—all off the air now—Gabriel started on a chain of reasoning.

It was a short chain; the last link said that there must be some connection between the ship's galley, where the food was prepared, and Finger's suite on the deck above.

Gabriel made his way through the restaurant-turned-cafeteria, heading for the galley. A few couples and several singles were scroffing food hastily, as if they expected someone to tap them on the shoulder and put them off the ship. Gabriel noticed almost subliminally that they weren't the young hungry actors or writers or office workers; they were the older, middle-aged ones. The kind who dreaded the inevitable day when they were turned out to the *dolce vita* of forced retirement on fixed pensions and escalating cost of living.

Move up or move out, was the motto at Titanic and most other business establishments. The gold watch for a lifetime of service was a thing of ancient history. Nobody lasted that long unless they owned the company or were indispensable to it.

Gabriel walked like Cagney through the cafeteria: shoulders slightly forward, bouncing on the balls of his feet. He entered the galley, where a couple of cooks were loafing around a TV set.

"Hey, whatcha doin' back here?" one of them asked, a black tall enough for college basketball.

"City Health Inspector," Gabriel replied in his own voice.

The cook towered over Gabriel and waved a frozen dinner-sized fist at him. "What is this? We paid you guys off last week, on your regular collection day."

Gabriel shook his head. "Those guys are in jail. There's been a crackdown. Didn't anybody tell you?"

The cook's face fell.

"I ought to get your name and number," Gabriel bluffed, "so that you can be subpoenaed. . . ."

The other cooks had already backed away into the shadows. "Hey wait. . . ." The black man's voice softened.

Gabriel put on a smile. "Look, I don't want to make trouble for you guys. I got a job to do, that's all. Now, how many exits are there from this area . . . for emergency purposes. . . ."

Within seconds, Gabriel was riding alone up the tiny service elevator to the kitchen of Finger's suite.

The door slid open silently and he stepped into the darkened kitchen. He stopped there, waiting for his eyes to adjust to the darkness so he could move without bumping into anything. He heard voices from another room.

". . . and according to the computer analysis, doing the show in Canada will save us a bundle of money." Sheldon Fad's singsong.

"Whadda' the Canadians know about making a dramatic series? All they do is documentaries about Eskimos." The dulcet tones of Bernard Finger, part foghorn and part fishmonger.

"They have commercial networks in Canada," Fad replied, dripping with honey.

"You seen any of their shows?"

"Well. . . ."

"They stink! They're even worse than ours."

Gabriel smiled in the darkness, uncertain whether Finger's "ours" referred to all of American commercial TV or merely to Titanic's steady string of fiascoes.

"But we'll be using our own top staff to run things. The Canadians will be working under our supervision."

"And the writing? We're going to put up with Ron Gabriel? That loudmouth?"

"We'll handle him," Fad answered. "He'll be the top writer, but the scripts will actually be turned out by Canadians. They work cheaper and they listen to what you tell them."

Gabriel's smile faded. He started moving carefully

toward the voices. As he got out of the kitchen and into what looked like a dining area, he could see a doorway framed in light; the door was closed, but light from the next room was seeping through the poor fit between the door and its jamb.

"I've even got a start on the theme music," Fad was saying, with more than the usual amount of oil in his voice. "It's from Tchaikovsky. . . ."

Fad must have worked the computer terminal, because the opening strains of the *Romeo and Juliet Overture* wafted into the suite. Finger must have reached the volume control, because the music was immediately turned down to a barely audible hum.

"Now about the production values. . . ." Fad began.

Gabriel kicked the door open and strode into the living room, chin tucked down in his collar, right fist balled in his jacket pocket as if he had a gun.

Fad was standing beside the computer terminal, at one end of a long sofa. Finger was sitting on the sofa. He was so startled that he dropped the glass he'd been holding. Fad jumped back two steps, a frightened Gary Cooper, so scared that the fringes of his buckskin jacket were twitching.

"Okay you guys," Gabriel said, in his Cagney voice.

"Who the hell are you?" Finger demanded.

"Never mind that." Gabriel walked slowly toward the sofa.

Backing away from him, Fad squeaked, "Is that a gun in your pocket?"

"Does a bear shit in the woods?"

"What're you doing here?" Finger asked. His voice cracked just the tiniest bit.

"You guys have been making life tough for Ron Gabriel. Now I'm going to give you what's coming to you."

Fad looked as if he was going to collapse. But Finger stared intently at Cagney's face.

"Gabriel," he said. "Is that you?"

"Who else, buhbula?" Ron took his hand from his pocket and scratched his nose. "Now what's all this shit about going to Canada?"

"The show's going to be shot in Canada," Finger said testily. "*If* I decide to do the show, that is. And how the hell did you get in here?"

"Whattaya mean, if you decide to do it?" Gabriel shot back. "It's the best damned idea you've seen in years."

"Ideas don't make successful shows. People do."

"Which explains why you've got a string of flops on your hands."

"Goddammit Gabriel!" Finger's voice rose. "I'm not going to take any of your crap!"

"Go stuff yourself with it, bigshot! I'm a creative artist. I don't need your greasy paws on my ideas!"

Fad edged around the sofa and tried to interpose himself between the two men. "Now wait, fellas. Let's not. . . ."

"Where the hell's the phone?" Finger turned as he sat, searching the room. "I'll get the security guards up here so fast. . . ."

"You reach for that phone and I'll break your arm," Gabriel warned. "You're going to listen to me for a change."

"I'm gonna get you thrown overboard, is what I'm gonna do!"

"The hell you are!"

"Fellaaas . . . be reasonable."

"Loudmouth creep."

"Moneygrubbing asshole!"

"Fellaaas. . . ."

It was a cosmic coincidence that at precisely that moment the love theme from *Romeo and Juliet* started on the computer-directed stereo. Such moments are rare, but they happen.

And precisely at that moment, the most exquisitely beautiful girl Gabriel had ever seen stepped sleepily into the living room, rubbing her eyes. She wore nothing but a whiff of a pink nightgown, only long enough to reach to her thighs and utterly transparent. Her long golden hair was sleep tousled. Her face was all childish innocence, especially the sky-blue eyes, although her mouth was sensuous. Her body had everything the eternal woman possessed: the litheness of youth combined with the soft fullness of newly ripened maturity.

"What's all the shouting about?" she asked in a little girl voice. Petulantly: "You woke me up."

Finger scowled mightily and got up from the sofa. "See what you've done?" he grumbled at Gabriel. "You woke her up!" To the girl/woman he said soothingly, "It's all right, baby. We were just having a discussion. I'll be back with you in a few minutes. You just go back to sleep."

Gabriel remained rooted to the spot where he was standing. He couldn't move. He couldn't breathe. His blood seemed congealed in his veins. It was like being petrified, mummified, frozen into a cryogenic block of liquid helium. Yet his brain was whirling, feverish, spinning like a Fourth of July pinwheel shooting off sparks in every direction.

She made a little *moue* with her full, ripe lips and turned to head back to the bedroom.

"Wait!" Gabriel's voice sounded strained and desperate, even to himself.

She stopped and looked back at him, with those incredible blue eyes.

"Wha . . . I mean . . . who . . . what's your name? Who are you?"

"Never mind!" Finger urged the girl toward the bedroom with an impatient gesture.

"No, wait!" Gabriel shouted. He unfroze himself and moved toward her. "What's your name? I've got to know!"

"Rita," she said, almost shyly. "Rita Yearling. Why do you hafta know?"

"Because I'm in love with you," answered Gabriel, with absolute honesty.

7: THE AGREEMENT

Bernard Finger was not the kind of narrow-minded man to let his personal life interfere with business.

"Go on back to bed, Rita," he said in as fatherly a tone as he could produce.

She blinked once in Gabriel's direction. Finger could see the effect her long lashes had on the writer: the Cagney makeup seemed to be melting and Gabriel shuddered violently.

"Goodnight," she breathed.

Gabriel watched her go back into the bedroom. To Finger, he looked like a puppy watching its master take a train to Australia. Gabriel was no longer a free-swinging, independent, irreverent sonofabitch. He wanted something that Finger possessed. That was a basis for doing business.

"Ron," he said, as the bedroom door closed behind Rita Yearling.

Gabriel stared at the door. His eyes seemed to be unfocused.

"Ron!" Finger called more sharply.

The writer shook himself, as if suddenly awakening from an incredible dream.

"Who is she?" Gabriel asked. "Where did you find her?"

Finger indicated the sofa with a gesture and Gabriel obediently sat down. Pulling a chair close to him, Finger said to Fad, "Get us some brandy and cigars." The producer nodded once, briskly, and went to the phone.

"I've never seen anyone like her." Gabriel's voice was still awestruck. "Who is she?"

"Titanic's always searching for fresh talent," Finger said. "We have scouts everywhere. But we found Rita right here in L.A.; right under our noses." It was even the truth, Finger realized with an inward laugh.

"She's fantastic!"

Fad sat at the end of the sofa, close enough to be included in the conversation if Finger so chose, yet far enough away so that he could continue a private-seeming talk with Gabriel. *Kid's got some good sense,* Finger noted.

"What would you say," Finger asked Gabriel, "if I told you that Rita is one of the most accomplished actresses I've ever seen?"

"Who cares?" Gabriel said.

With a knowing grin, Finger added, "What would you say if I told you that I'm considering her for the female lead in 'The Starcrossed'?"

Gabriel actually gulped. Finger could see his Adam's Apple bob up and down. To a lesser man, what was about to happen would seem like taking milk away from an infant; but Bernard Finger was equal to the situation. False scruples had never intereferred with his business acumen—nor true scruples, for that matter.

"I think she's a natural for the part," Finger went on, enjoying the perspiration that was breaking out on Gabriel's Cagneyish face. "She's got looks, talent, exper . . . eh, youth."

"The show couldn't miss with her in it," Fad chimed in.

"Yeah," said Gabriel.

Finger slapped his palms on his thighs, a sharp cracking sound that startled the other two men. "Listen," he said. "Let's let bygones be bygones. I know you and I have had our differences in the past, Ron. But let's work to-gether to make 'The Starcrossed' a big hit. Titanic needs a hit and you need a hit. So let's work together, instead of against each other."

Gabriel nodded. He still seemed to be stunned. "Okay," he mumbled.

Looking over at Fad, Finger said: "Our producer's come up with the idea of doing the show in Canada. It'll let us stretch our money further. What we save in produc-tion costs we can add to production values: better sets, better scripts, better talent. . . ."

Gabriel was visibly trying to pull himself together, get his brain back in gear.

"This is going to be an expensive show to produce. Starships and exotic planets every week . . . expensive sets, expensive props, big-name guest stars every week . . . it's all very expensive."

"And costly," Fad echoed. Finger shot him down with a sharp glance.

Gabriel frowned. "Artistic control."

"What about it?"

"I want artistic control," Gabriel said. He was returning to the real world. "This show has got to have one strong conceptual vision, a consistent point of view . . . we can't have directors and assistant producers and script girls screwing things around from one week to the next."

Finger was too experienced to give in immediately, but after fifteen minutes of discussion, he had his arm around Gabriel's shoulders as they walked together toward the door.

"You've convinced me," Finger was saying expansively. "When you're right, you're right. Artistic control will be in your hands. One guy has got to keep the central vision of the show consistent from week to week. That's important."

"And it'll be written into my contract," Gabriel said warily.

"Of course! Everything down in black and white so there's no misunderstanding."

They shook hands at the door. Gabriel still looked uneasy, almost suspicious. Finger had his friendliest smile on.

"My agent will get in touch with you tomorrow," Gabriel said.

"Who you got . . . still Jerry Morgan?"

"Yeah."

"Good man, We'll work out the clauses with no trouble."

Gabriel left and Finger closed the door firmly. Fad was standing in the middle of the living room, shaking his head. He looked like Gary Cooper with an ulcer.

"What's the matter?"

"You let him have artistic control of the series! He'll want to do everything *his* way! The expense. . . ."

Finger raised a calming hand. "Listen. Right now he's cn the other side of that door, going through his pockets to see what I stole from him. And he won't find a thing missing. Tonight he'll have wet dreams about Rita and tomorrow morning he'll phone Jerry Morgan and tell him to be sure to get a clause about artistic control into his contract."

"But we can't. . . ."

"Who gives a damn about artistic control?" Finger laughed at the perplexed producer. "There's a million ways to get around such a clause. We'll have clauses in there about financial limits and decisions, clauses that tie him up six ways from Sunday. And even in his artistic control clause we'll throw in the line about no holding up production with unreasonable demands. Ever see anybody win a lawsuit by proving his demands were not unreasonable? We got him by the balls and he won't know it until we go into production."

"In Canada?"

"In Canada."

Sheldon's worried-hound face relaxed a little.

Someone tapped timidly at the door. Finger yanked it

open. A waiter stood there, bearing a tray with three snifters of brandy and three cigars on it.

"S . . . sorry to take so long, Mr. Finger. Your special cigars were in the vault and. . . ."

"Nah, don't worry about it." Finger ushered him in with a sweeping gesture of his arm. "It's good timing. I'd hate to waste a good cigar on that little punk."

It was dawn.

Finger sat on the edge of his bed and gazed down at Rita Yearling. Even under the bedclothes she looked incredibly beautiful.

Best money I ever spent, he told himself.

Her lovely eyelids fluttered and she awoke languorously. She smiled at Finger, stretched like a cat, then turned and looked out the porthole at the gray-white sky.

"Ain't it kinda early?"

"I want to go up to the bridge and see the sunrise over the mountains. We're almost back in port."

"Oh."

"How're you feeling?"

She stretched again. "Fine. Not an ache or pain anywhere."

He stroked her bare shoulder. "They did a beautiful job on you. When I had my Vitaform operations I was in agony for months."

"You didn't take good care of your original body," she chided, almost like Shirley Temple bawling out Wallace Beery. "I may have been older than you, but I took care of myself. The girls always said I had the best-kept body since Ann Corio."

"What about Mae West?" he joked.

"That hag!" Rita's luscious lips pulled back in a snarl, revealing slightly pointed teeth. "Her and her deepfreeze. As if anybody'd revive her in a hundred years."

Patting her in a fatherly way, Finger said, "I'm going to get dressed. I'll call you in an hour or so. We can have breakfast up on the bridge."

"Okay." She turned over and pulled up the covers.

"I want to talk to you about Ron Gabriel. He's going to be the head writer on the show, up in Canada."

"He's the Cagney that was in here last night?"

"Right. He can be troublesome. . . ."

She smiled at him; there was no innocent little girl in her face. "I can handle him and a dozen more like him, any time." Her tongue flicked across her sharp little teeth "Any time," she repeated.

It was bracing up on the bridge. The sea breeze stirred Finger, invigorated him. Up ahead he could see the smog bank that marked the beginning of Los Angeles' territorial waters and the oil rigs that kept the city supplied with fuel.

He paced the open deck of the flying bridge, glancing inside now and then to see how the ship was being handled. A solitary officer slouched lazily in a soft chair, toking happily, while the automated radar, sonar, robot pilot and computer steered the *Adventurer* toward its smog-shrouded pier.

It always unnerved Finger just the slightest bit to realize that the ship's crew was more machine than human. And with the exception of the captain, who was a boozer, most of the crewmen were heads.

Finger turned his back on the lazing officer and stepped to the rail. Leaning over it slightly, he could see the white foam of the ship's wake cutting through the oily waters. He looked up at his last glimpse of blue sky. Gripping the rail with both hands, he was suddenly on the deck of a whaling vessel out of New Bedford, an iron captain running a wooden ship.

Thar she blows! he heard in his mind's inner ear. And with the eye of imagination he saw a wild and stormy ocean, with the spout of a gigantic whale off near the white-capped horizon.

After him, me hearties! Finger shouted silently. *A five-dollar gold piece to the boat that harpoons him!*

He grunted to himself. Maybe a whaling show would

make a good series. The econuts would object to it, but they object to everything anyway. Special effects would be expensive: have to make a dummy whale. Nobody's seen a whale since the last Japanese expedition came back empty. Even the dolphins are getting scarce.

A frown of concentration settled on his face. The government would probably help with a series like that. They're always looking for outdoor stuff, so people will stay home and watch their three-dees instead of messing up the National Parks. And it could be a spectacular show—storms, shipwrecks, all that stuff. Got to be careful of the violence, though; get those parents and teachers on your neck and the sponsors disappear. Maybe a comedy show, with a crew that never catches a whale. A bunch of schmucks.

No. Finger shook his head. *A serious show. Iron men in wooden ships. Give the viewers some heroes to admire.* He squared his shoulders and faced straight into the wind. *Maybe I could do a sneak part in it, like Hitchcock used to do.*

He drew himself up to his full height. *Hell,* he told himself, *I could be the whaling ship's captain. Why not? I've got the look for it now.*

Why not do a whaling show instead of this science fiction thing with Gabriel?

Because, his business sense told him, it would be too realistic. Historicals are dead. Nobody watched them. The Hallmark Hall of Fame killed them years ago and nobody's had the guts to try them again. Too dull. And too realistic.

Still, he thought, it'll be good to have something like this in reserve. Doesn't have to be realistic or even historical. Maybe a science fiction whaler, on another planet. *Yeah!* With a different monster every week! He smiled; felt almost giddy. *Bernie,* he told himself, *you're a genius.* He made a mental note to look into the possibility of taking acting lessons. In secret. Like that football player for the Jets had done.

And then the *real* idea hit him. It came in a flash, the

whole of it, so completely detailed that he saw the columns of figures adding up to a fortune, nine digits worth. It was blinding. Terrifying. He sagged against the rail.

"That's it," he whispered to himself. "That'll do it! But it's got to be done in secret." He squeezed his eyes shut and locked the secret deep within his convoluted brain.

"You looking for me?"

Finger whirled, startled, and saw Brenda Impanema standing at the hatch that led inside to the bridge. She was out of costume now, wearing a comfortable kaftan that billowed in the breeze against her lean figure.

"I got a phone message from the computer that said you wanted to see me," Brenda said.

Gathering himself together, Finger grumbled, "That was last night."

"Gabriel's two goons wouldn't let me out of the bar until you two had finished your business talk," she said. "By the time I got to my stateroom and saw the message, I figured you were asleep . . . or at least in bed."

From someone else, Finger would have taken that for insolence. But from Brenda—he smiled.

"You were right. Smart girl." Then he looked sharply at her. She seemed weary, red eyed. "You didn't sleep good?"

"Not very."

"Who were you with?"

"Nobody," she said.

Finger considered the pros and cons for a moment. His ultimate, secret new idea glowed within him like a warming beacon. "Gabriel and I came to an agreement last night. We're going to do the show up in Canada. Les will check on the available studios up there. The talent office will start looking for a suitable male lead this morning."

"What about the female lead?"

"Rita Yearling."

Brenda's mouth went tight.

Nobody's going to find out about her previous life. That's why I've got a publicity department, to keep things quiet."

"Sure," Brenda said.

"So you don't like her," Finger said. "That's too bad."

Brenda looked away from him and let the salt wind blow at her hair. "No problem for me. I'm not going to have to work with her."

Taking a step closer to her, Finger said, "I still want you to go to Canada and keep an eye on things for me."

"You mean service Ron Gabriel."

"No. He's seen Rita and he's gone crazy over her. She'll keep him busy enough."

"You don't know Ron." Still looking away from Finger, she said, "I don't want to go."

"You're going!"

"I don't want to!"

"You'll do what I tell you. That's all there is to it."

"Thanks."

"I wouldn't send you up there if Gabriel was going to make things tough for you. You know that."

"Like hell."

She still wouldn't look at him. Feeling hurt, Finger said. "It's for the good of the show. There'll be a promotion in it for you."

"Wonderful," Brenda said. "But I'd rather jump over the rail."

He could feel his face getting red with anger. "So jump already!" he snapped and stamped off to the hatch.

It was spring in Southern California. The rains had finally stopped and for a few weeks everything was green and flowering. As long as it was domed over or otherwise protected from the smog.

Bill Oxnard's Holovision Laboratory was perched high enough on a Malibu hillside to be out of the usual smog banks, although when there was inversion the tinted clouds crept up and engulfed even the highest of the hills. But at the moment it was a beautiful spring day. Oxnard could lean back in his desk chair and see the surfers 'way down on the beach, in their colorful anticorrosion suits and motorized surfboards. In a few weeks—or perhaps days— he'd see the gardeners painting the lawns green and starting to worry about brush fires again. But for the moment, everything was beautiful.

His phone buzzed. He clicked it on and his secretary's grandmotherly face appeared on the screen.

"Ms. Impanema's here," she said.

Oxnard couldn't keep himself from grinning. "Send her right in."

Maybe she's the reason why I feel . . . he tried to identify exactly what it was that he did feel, and could only come up with a lame . . . *happy*.

Brenda strode into his office: tall, leggy, brightly dressed in a flowered slit-skirt sari that was becoming the hit of the new Oriental decorative style. Oxnard himself still wore his regular business clothes: an engineer's zipsuit of plain orange.

"Hope I'm not late," she said, smiling at him.

Oxnard came around the desk and took her hand. "No. Right on the tick. Here, have a seat. How's everything in Toronto? Have you eaten? Want some coffee or something?"

She took the chair and let the heavy-looking handbag she was carrying clunk to the floor. "A Bloody Mary, if you can produce one. I haven't had any breakfast. The damned airline didn't serve anything *again*. It's getting to be a regular scrooging with them."

Leaning over his desk to get at the phone, Oxnard called, "May . . . can you dig up two Bloody Marys and some breakfast?"

His secretary's face showed that she clearly disapproved of drinking on company time. But after all, it *was* his company. She nodded and switched off.

"So what's happening in Toronto?" Oxnard asked as he went back around the desk and sat down. For some reason he felt that he needed the desk between them.

"Everything's in a whirl," Brenda replied. "Let's see . . . when's the last time we talked?"

"A week after you first went up there. Ron hadn't gone yet; he was still here."

She nodded. "Right . . . that was the flight where they didn't serve any dinner. 'Sorry to inconvenience you,' she whined nasally, 'but the food service on this flight has been rendered inoperative due to a malfunctioning of the ground-based portion of our logistical system.' Fancy way of saying they didn't stash any food aboard the plane."

They chatted easily for a while. May brought in a pair

of drinks in plastic cups and a tray of real eggs and imitation bacon from the cafeteria. Brenda wolfed down everything hungrily. Oxnard answered a couple of routine phone calls while she ate, then told his secretary to hold all calls and visits.

"So what's happening in Toronto?" he asked again as she finished the last crumbs of her English muffin.

"Everything," Brenda said between dabs at her lips with a paper napkin. "It's wild."

"Ron's there? The scripts are being written?"

"Well. . . ." she cocked her head slightly to one side, as if waiting for the right words to come out of the air. "He's there . . . and there's a lot of writing being done. The production team is starting to put the sets together. . . ."

"But?"

Brenda's smile turned a little desperate. "Wasn't it you who told me about Murphy's Law?"

He grinned. "If anything can go wrong with an experiment, it will."

"Right. Well, that's what's happening in Toronto."

"That's too bad."

"It's worse than that. The show might never get on the air. All sorts of troubles have hit us."

Oxnard shook his head sympathetically. "Everything's going smoothly on this end. The new transmitters and cameras have tested out fine. We'll be ready to ship them up to Toronto right on schedule. And I've got some new ideas, too, about . . . well. . . ." Oxnard let his voice trail off. *She's got enough problems without listening to my untested brainstorms.*

"Will you be coming up to Toronto with the equipment?" Brenda asked.

"No need to," said Oxnard.

"But I thought. . . ."

"Oh, we'll send a couple of technicians along. I wouldn't dump the equipment on you without somebody to show your crew how to work it. . . ."

"I know," she said. "But I thought you would come up yourself."

For some reason, Oxnard's insides went fluttery.

"I'd like to," he said quickly. "But I can't leave the lab here . . . I'm not just an executive, you know. I *work* here; the rest of the staff depends on me."

Brenda nodded and looked distressed. "Bill . . . I wouldn't want you to hurt your own company, of course. But we *need* you in Toronto. Ron needs you. He's being driven crazy up there, trying to whip the scripts into shape and handle the technical details of building the sets and working out the special effects and a million other things. I've tried to help him all I can, but you're the one he needs. You've got the scientific know-how. Nobody else up there knows *anything. . . .*"

He refused, of course. He explained to her, very carefully, how his laboratory operated and how much he was needed for day-by-day, hour-by-hour decisions. He took her down to the labs and shop, showed her what a small, tightly integrated group he had. He explained to her over and over that these men and women didn't work *for* him, they worked *with* him. And he worked with them. Every day; ten, twelve hours per day.

He explained it all morning. He explained it over lunch. He took the afternoon off and drove her down the coast so that they could be alone and away from phones and business conferences while he explained it thoroughly. He explained it over dinner at a candlelit table looking out at the surf, not far from La Jolla.

He wanted to explain it to her in bed, in one of those plush La Jolla hotels, but at the last minute he lost his nerve. Brenda nodded and smiled and accepted everything he said without argument. But she kept repeating that Ron Gabriel, and the whole show, was in dire trouble and needed *him.* Now. In Toronto. And he kept getting the unspoken message from her that she needed him. Not that she promised anything or even hinted at it. But Oxnard realized that if he helped the show, helped Gabriel and Finger and Montpelier, he would be helping her.

And Bill Oxnard found that more than anything else in the world, he wanted to help her.

So he drove her back to the airport and agreed that he would join her in Toronto.

"Only for the weekend," he said. "I really can't stay away from the lab during regular working days."

"I know," she answered, as they hurried down the terminal corridor toward her flight's loading gate.

They made it to the gate with half a minute to spare. Brenda turned to him, breathless from running, while the gate computer examined her ticket and the overhead sensors scanned them both for everything from contraband lemons to plastic explosives.

"I really appreciate it, Bill. I'll set you up with a hotel room and try to make your weekend comfortable. Thanks for a fun day!"

He stood there tonguetied, trying to think of an appropriate answer: something witty, maybe poetic.

The computer's scratchy voice upstaged him: "Final boarding for Flight 68. Final boarding."

She reached up on tiptoes and kissed him lightly on the cheek. Oxnard stood there grinning like a schoolboy as she scampered through the doorway of the access tunnel that led to the plane.

Two lights later, on Friday, he followed her.

The studio was impressive.

It was huge, about the size of a modern jetliner hangar, Oxnard realized. But it looked even bigger because it was almost completely empty. The bare skeleton of its wall bracings and rows of rafter-mounted old-fashioned spotlights looked down on a bare wooden floor.

"You won't need all those lights," Oxnard said to his guide. "With laser holography, you can. . . ."

"We know all about it," said Gregory Earnest. He was small and wiry, with thickly curled dark hair and beard that hid most of his face, so that Oxnard couldn't see that he looked like one of Canada's most numerous residents— a weasel. "We're just as modern and up-to-date as you Yanks, you know."

Oxnard completely missed the edge to Earnest's voice. They continued their tour of Badger Studios, with Earnest proudly showing off his company's shops, equipment and personnel—most of them idle.

They ended in the model shop, where a half dozen intense young men and women were putting together a four-meter-long plastic model. It lay along a table that was too short for it, overlapping both ends. To Oxnard it looked something like a beached whale in an advanced stage of decomposition.

"The latest and most modern modeling techniques," Earnest told Oxnard. "Straight from Korea. No second-rate stuff around here."

"I see," Oxnard said.

"Americans always think that we Canadians are behind the times," Earnest said. "But we've learned to survive in spite of Yankee chauvinism. Like the flea and the elephant." His voice had an irritating nasal twang to it.

Oxnard replied with something like "Uh-huh."

His main interest was focused on the modeling team. They were buzzing around the long cylindrical model that rested on the chest-high worktable. They had a regular bucket brigade system going: two girls were taking tiny plastic pieces from their packing boxes and using whirring electrical buffers to erase the Korean symbols painted on them. Another woman and one of the men took the clean pieces and dabbed banana-smelling plastic glue on them. Then the remaining two men took the pieces, walked around the model slowly and stuck pieces onto the main body.

At random, apparently, thought Oxnard.

"Hand craftsmanship," exuded Earnest. "The mark of true art."

Still watching the team at work, Oxnard asked, "What's it supposed to be?"

"The model? It's one of the starships! For the series, of course."

"Why does it have fins on it?"

"Huh? What do you mean?"

Ignoring the business-suited executive, Oxnard stepped between the two gluers and asked one of the stickers:

"What're you using for a blueprint?"

The youth blinked at him several times. "Blueprint? We don't have no blueprint."

One of the young women said with a slightly French sneer, "This is artistry, not engineering."

Oxnard scratched at his nose. The banana smell made him want to sneeze. "Yes," he said mildly. "But this model is supposed to be a starship, right? It never flies in a planet's atmosphere . . . it stays out in space all the time. It doesn't need aerodynamic fins."

"But it looks smash-o with the fins!" said one of the other young men.

"It looks like something out of the Nineteen Fifties," Oxnard replied, surprised at the sudden loudness of his own voice. "And out of Detroit, at that!"

"Now wait a moment," Earnest said, from well outside the ring of workers. "You can't tell these people how to do their jobs. . . ."

Oxnard asked, "Why? Union rules?"

"Union?"

"We don't have trade unions."

"Lord, that's *archaic!*"

Earnest smiled patiently. "Trade unions were disbanded in Canada years ago. That's one of the many areas where our society is far ahead of the States."

Shaking his head, Oxnard said, "All right. But a starship can't have wings and fins on it. What it does need is radiative surfaces. You can change those fins from an aerodynamic shape. . . ."

They listened to him with hostile, sullen countenances.

Earnest folded his arms across his chest and smiled, like an indulgent uncle who would rather let his oddball nephew make an ass of himself than argue with him. Oxnard tried to explain some of the rationale of an interstellar vehicle and when he saw that it wasn't penetrating, he asked the crew if they'd ever seen photos of spacecraft or satellites.

"They don't look like airplanes, do they?"

They agreed to that, reluctantly, and Oxnard had to settle for a moral victory.

For the time being, he thought.

When Earnest showed him the set they were constructing for the bridge of the starship, it was the same battle all over again. But this time it was with Earnest himself, since the carpenters and other contractors were nowhere in sight.

"But this looks like the bridge of a ship . . . an ocean liner!" Oxnard protested.

Earnest nodded. "It's been built to Mr. Finger's exact specifications. It's a replica of the bridge on his ship, the *Adventurer.*"

Oxnard puffed out an exasperated breath. "But a starship doesn't sail in the ocean! It wouldn't have a steering wheel and a compass for godsake!"

"It's what Mr. Finger wants."

"But it's *wrong!*"

Earnest smiled his patient, infuriating smile. "We're accustomed to you Yanks coming here and finding fault with everything we Canadians do."

And no matter what Oxnard said, the Badger Studios executive dismissed it as Yankee imperialism.

Brenda met him for lunch and drove out to one of the hotel restaurants, away from the studio cafeteria.

"I'm beginning to see what you're up against," Oxnard told her. "They're all going every which way with no direction, no idea of what the show needs."

"That's right," Brenda agreed.

"But where's Ron? Why isn't he straightening this out? He knows better. . . ."

"After lunch," Brenda said, "I'll take you to Ron's place . . . if the guards let us through, that is."

She wasn't kidding.

Two uniformed security police flanked the door of Gabriel's hotel suite. One of them recognized Brenda, asked her about Oxnard, then reluctantly let them both through.

The foyer of the suite looked normal enough, although there was an obviously broken typewriter on the floor next to the door. Its lid was open and it looked as if someone had stomped on its innards in a rage of frustration.

The sitting room was a mess. Wadded up sheets of paper were strewn everywhere, ankle deep. The sofas and chairs were covered with paper. The chandelier was piled high with it. The paper crackled and scrunched underfoot as they walked into the room. Invisible beneath the wads lay a luxurious carpet. Two more typewriters sat on two separate desks, near the windows. A huge pile of papers loomed over one of the typewriters.

"Ron?" called Brenda.

No answer.

She looked into the bedroom on the right, as Oxnard stood in the middle of the paper sea feeling rather stunned.

"Ron?" Brenda called again.

With a worried expression on her face, she waded through the litter and went into the other bedroom.

"Ron?" Her voice sounded panicky now.

Oxnard went into the bedroom after her. The double bed was rumpled. Drawers were hanging out of the dresser. The TV—a flat, two-dimensional set—was on and babbling some midday women's show.

The window was open.

"My god, he escaped!" Brenda shouted. "Or jumped!"

She ran to the window and peered down.

Oxnard pushed open the door to the bathroom. The floor was wet. Towels were hanging neatly beside the tub. The shower screen was closed.

Almost as if he were a detective in a mystery show,

Oxnard gingerly slipped the shower screen back a few centimeters, wondering if he ought to be careful about fingerprints.

"Brenda," he said. "Here he is."

She hurried into the bathroom. "Is he. . . ."

Gabriel lay in the tub, up to his armpits in water. His eyes were closed, his mouth hung open. There was several days' stubble on his chin. His face looked awful.

Brenda gulped once and repeated, "Is he. . . ."

Without opening his eyes, Gabriel said, "He *was* asleep, until you two klutzes came barging in here."

Brenda sagged against Oxnard and let out a breath of relief.

Within a few minutes they were all sitting in the sitting room, Gabriel with the inevitable towel draped around his middle.

"They've had me going over these abortions they call story treatments for six days straight! They won't let me out of here. They even took out the goddamned phone! I'm a prisoner."

Brenda said, "They need the scripts, Ron. We're working against a deadline now. If we're not in production by. . . ."

"In production?" Gabriel's voice rose. "With what? Have you looked at these treatments? Have you tried to *read* any of them? The ones that are spelled halfway right, at least?"

"Are they that bad?" Oxnard asked.

"Bad?" Gabriel jumped to his feet. "Bad? They're abysmal! They're insufferable! They're rotten! Junk, nothing but junk. . . ."

He kicked at the paper on the floor and stomped over to the desk. "Listen to these treatments . . . these are the ideas they want to write about. . . ." Riffling through the pile of papers on the desk, he pulled out a single sheet.

Oxnard started to say, "Maybe we ought to. . . ."

"No, no . . . you listen. And you!" he jabbed a finger toward Brenda—"You better get back to Big Daddy in

L.A. and tell him what the hell's going on here. If we were in the States, I'd call the Civil Liberties Union. If I had a phone."

"What about the story ideas, Ron?" she asked.

"Hah! Story ideas. Okay, listen . . . here's one about two families working together to build a dam on a new planet that's described as, get this now . . . 'very much like upper Alberta Province, such as around Ft. Vermillion.' "

Oxnard looked at Brenda. She said, "Okay, so you don't care for the setting. What's the story idea?"

"That *is* the story idea! That's the whole treatment . . . about how to build a dam! Out of logs, yet!"

Brenda made a disapproving face. "You picked the worst one."

"Oh yeah? Lemme go down the list for you. . . ."

Gabriel spent an hour reading story treatments to them:

• A monster from space invades one of the starships, but it turns out to be a dream that the hero is having.

• The heroine (Rita Yearling) gets lost on an unexplored planet and the natives find her and think she's a goddess. She gets away by explaining astronomy to them.

• The heads of the two competing families of star traders engage in an Indian wrestling match in a frontier saloon "very much like those in upper Alberta Province, such as around Ft. Vermillion."

• The hero and heroine are stranded on an unpopulated planet and decide to call themselves Adam and Eve. Before they can bite the apple, they are rescued.

• A war between the two families is averted when the women of both families decide to stop cooking for their men if they fight.

By the end of the hour, Oxnard felt as if his head was stuffed with cotton wool. Brenda was stretched out on one of the sofas, looking equally dazed.

"And those are the best of them," Gabriel finished grimly.

"That's the best they can do?" Oxnard asked.

"Who's doing the writing?" Brenda wanted to know.

Gabriel glowered from his desk chair. "How the hell should I know? This Earnest Yazoo from Beaver Studios. . . ."

"Badger," Oxnard corrected.

"Same damned thing," Gabriel grumbled. "Earnest won't let me meet any of the writers. I have to write memos, suggestions, rewrites . . . which means I have to start from scratch and write everything! All thirteen goddamned scripts. I'm gonna have to do it all myself."

Brenda sat up and ran a hand through her hair. "But you can't! Our agreement with Badger and the Canadian government says that at least fifty percent of the scripts have to be written by Canadian citizens."

Gabriel threw a fiistful of papers into the air.

"This is terrible," Oxnard said.

"I would've walked out a week ago," Gabriel told him, "if it wasn't for the goddamned guards. They've got me locked up in here!"

Brenda looked at him. "That's because you yelled so much about walking out on them when they first gave you the story treatments."

Oxnard was shaking his head. "And I thought the modeling and sets were bad. . . ."

"What?" Gabriel was beside him instantaneously. "What about the models and the sets? What're they doing to *them?*"

Oxnard told him of his morning's tour of the studio shops.

"That did it!" Gabriel screeched. "Get that sonofabitch in here! I'll kill him!"

Wearily, Brenda asked, "Which sonofabitch do you mean?"

"Any of them! All of them! I'll take them all on at once!"

Oxnard got up and stood beside the betoweled writer. "We'll both take 'em on," he said grimly. "I don't like what they're doing either."

Brenda grinned at the two of them. "Laurel and Hardy,

ready to take on the whole Canadian army. Okay . . .
I'll get you some action."

She returned twenty minutes later with an already
flustered-looking Gregory Earnest.

In the interval, a maid had cleared up most of the mess,
Oxnard had ordered a bottle of beer for himself and
Gabriel had started packing. The two men were in the
bedroom when they heard the front door of the suite open
and Brenda call, "Ron? Bill?"

"In here," Gabriel yelled, as he tossed handsful of socks
into his open suitcase.

Oxnard saw that Earnest's face was red and he was a
trifle sweaty. *Brenda must have filled his ears but good,*
he thought.

"What're you doing?" Earnest asked as soon as he saw
the half-filled suitcase on the bed.

"Leaving," replied Gabriel.

"You can't go."

"The hell I can't!"

Brenda walked over to the edge of the bed and sat
down. "Ron," she said, her voice firm, "I brought him
here to listen to your problems. The least you can do is
talk to him."

"I'm talking," Gabriel said as he rummaged through a
dresser drawer and pulled out a heap of underwear.

Oxnard sat back in the room's only chair and tried to
keep himself from grinning.

"I, uh . . . understand," Earnest said to Gabriel's back,
"that you're not, uh, happy with the story material so far."

Gabriel turned and draped a bathrobe over the bed,
alongside the suitcase. He started folding it.

"You understand correctly," he said, concentrating on
the folding. The robe was red and gold, with a barely
discernible image of Bruce Lee on its back.

"Well," said Earnest, "you knew when you came here
that fifty percent of the scripts would have to be written
by Canadians."

"Canadian *writers*," Gabriel said, as he tenderly placed the folded robe in the suitcase. "What you've given me was produced by a team of Mongoloid idiots. It's hopeless. I'm leaving."

"You can't leave."

"Watch me."

"The guards won't let you out of here."

Oxnard raised his beer bottle. "Have you ever had your nose broken, Mr. Earnest?"

The Canadian backed away a short step. "Now listen," he said to Gabriel, "you know that Titanic hasn't given us the budget to take on big-name writers. . . ."

"These guys couldn't even *spell* a big name."

". . . and we're on a very tight production schedule. You can't walk out on us. It would ruin everything.

Gabriel looked up at him for the first time. "I can't make a script out of a turd. Nobody can. I can't write thirteen scripts, or even six and a half, in the next couple of weeks. We need writers!"

"We've got writers. . . ."

"We've got shit!" Gabriel yelled. "Excrement. Poop. Ka-ka. I've seen better-looking used toilet paper than the crap you've given me to work with!"

"It's the best available talent for the budget."

"Where'd you get these people?" Gabriel demanded. "The funny farm or the Baffin Island Old Folk's Home?"

He snapped the suitcase lid shut, but it bounced right up again.

"Too much in there," Oxnard said.

Gabriel gave him a look. "It'll close. I got it here and I'll get it out." He pushed the lid down firmly and leaned on it.

"Ron, those are the only writers we can *afford*," Earnest said, his voice taking on a faint hint of pleading. "We don't have the *money* for other writers."

Gabriel let go of the suitcase and the lid bounced up again. "As if that explains it all, huh? We go on the air with a public announcement: "Folks, please excuse the cruddy quality of the scripts. We couldn't afford better writers.' That's what you want to do?"

"Maybe if you worked with the writers. . . ."

"You won't even let me meet them!"

Earnest shifted back and forth on his feet uneasily. "Well, maybe I was wrong there. . . ."

But Gabriel was peering at the suitcase again. "It won't work."

"I told you it wouldn't" Oxnard said.

Brenda added, "Try putting it on the floor and then leaning on it."

Earnest gaped at her, shocked.

Gabriel picked up the open suitcase and carefully placed it on the floor. "Where'd you get these so-called writers from?" he asked, squatting down to lean on the lid again.

Earnest had to step around the bed to keep him in sight. "Uh . . . from here in the city, mostly."

"What experience do they have? What credits?"

"Well," Earnest squirmed, "not much, truthfully."

Holding down the lid, Gabriel said to Earnest, "Hey, you look like the heaviest one here. Stand on it."

Obediently, Earnest stepped up on the jiggling, slanting lid. Gabriel began to click the suitcase shut.

"Where'd you get these writers?" he asked again.

Earnest stood on the now-closed suitcase, looking foolish and miserable. "Uh, we had a contest. . . ."

"A contest?"

"In the local high schools. . . ."

Brenda gasped.

Oxnard began to laugh.

Gabriel got to his feet. His nose was about at the height of Earnest's solar plexus.

"You didn't say what I just heard," he said.

"What?"

Looking murderously up into Earnest's flustered face, Gabriel said, "You didn't tell me just now that the story treatments I've been beating out my brains over for the past two weeks were written by high school kids who sent them in as part of a writing contest."

"Uh . . . well. . . ."

"You didn't *imply*," Gabriel went on, his voice low, "that you haven't spent penny number one on any writers at all."

"We can use the money on. . . ."

Oxnard didn't think that Gabriel, with his short arms, could reach Earnest's head. But he did, with a punch so blurringly swift that Oxnard barely saw it. He heard the solid *crunch* of fist on bone, though, and Earnest toppled over backwards onto the bed, his face spurting blood.

"Sonofagun," Oxnard said, "you broke his nose after all."

Earnest bounced up from the bed and fled from the room, wailing and holding his bloody nose with both hands.

Brenda looked displeased. "You shouldn't have done that. It just complicates things."

Gabriel was rubbing his knuckles. "Yeah. I should've belted him in the gut a few times first. Would've been more satisfying."

"He's probably going straight to the lawyers. Or the police," she said.

Starting for the door, Oxnard said, "I'm going to the American consulate. They can't hold an American citizen prisoner like this."

"No. Wait," Brenda said. "Let me handle this."

"I don't care how you do it," Gabriel said, "but I want out."

Brenda faced him squarely. "Ron, that would be the end of everything. The show, the series, the whole Titanic company. . . ."

"What do I care? Those bastards have been screwing me. . . ."

"Ron, please!" Now it was Brenda who was pleading, and Oxnard wished he were in Gabriel's place.

"I'm walking," Gabriel insisted. "High school kids in a

writing contest . . . making models and sets like tinker-toys. . . ."

"I'll straighten things out," Brenda said, as strongly as Gabriel. "That's why I'm here. That's why you wanted me here, wasn't it?"

"Well. . . ." He kicked lightly at the suitcase, still on the floor.

Brenda turned to Oxnard. *Her eyes are incredibly green,* he noticed for the first time. "Bill, if I get B.F. to straighten out Earnest and give you authority to act as science consultant, will you stay?"

"I've really got to get back. . . ."

She bit her lower lip, then said, "But you can come up here on weekends, can't you? To make sure that the crew's building things the right way?"

With a shrug, he agreed, "Sure, I suppose I could do that."

Turning to Gabriel again, Brenda went on, "And Ron, if I get you complete authority over the scripts and make Earnest bring in some real writers and a story editor, will you stay?"

"No."

"Why not?"

Gabriel scuffed at the suitcase again, like a kid punishing the floor for tripping him. "Because these flatworm-brained idiots are just going to screw things over, one way or the other. They're a bunch of pinheads. Working with them is hopeless."

"But we'll form a team, the three of us," Brenda said. "You head up the writing and creative side, Ron. Bill will handle the scientific side. And I'll make sure that Titanic does right by you."

Gabriel shook his head.

"Listen," Brenda said, with growing enthusiasm. "They haven't made a decision on the male lead for the series. Suppose I tell B.F. that if we don't get a major star the show will fold. He'll understand that kind of talk. We can go out and get a big name. That'll force everybody else to live up to the star's level."

Gabriel's eyebrows inched upward. "A big name star?"

"Right." Brenda smiled encouragingly.

Oxnard could see wheels within wheels at work inside Gabriel's head.

"Okay," the writer said at last. "You go talk to B.F. But first . . . get Rita Yearling over here. I want to talk with her. About who she thinks would make a good co-star."

Oxnard looked at Brenda. She understood perfectly what was going on in Gabriel's mind. And she didn't like it.

But she said, "All right, Ron. If that's what you want." Flat. Emotionless.

She started for the door. Gabriel stooped down and pushed the suitcase under the bed. Oxnard called out:

"Wait up, Brenda. I'm going with you."

The studio was alive at last. It rang with the sounds of busy workmen: carpenters hammering; electricians yelling to each other from atop giddy-tall ladders; painters and lighting men and gofers carrying the tools of their trades across the vast floor of the hanger-sized room.

Four different sets were being erected in the four corners of the studio, fleshing over its bare metal walls and reaching upward to the girders that supported row after row of lights which seemed to stare down at the beehive below in silent disbelief.

Ron Gabriel was standing in the middle of the big, clangorous whirl. He wore what had come to be known over the past few months as his "official working costume:" a pair of cutoff levis and a tee shirt with *Starcrossed* lettered on front and back. Somewhere in the offices and workshops adjoining the studio, the art director was dreaming up a special symbol for the show. Gabriel would get Badger or Titanic to make tee shirts for the entire cast and crew with the symbol on them, no matter who protested about the cost.

Standing beside him, in a conservative one-piece business suit, was Sam Lipid. He was only slightly taller than Gabriel, roundish, with a prematurely balding pate. His face was soft and young looking. Lipid was Production Manager for the show and Gabriel's major point of contact with Badger Films. Gregory Earnest had given Gabriel a wide berth ever since bouncing off the bed in his hotel room, months earlier. There had been some talk of a lawsuit, but Brenda got Titanic to pay for a nose job and Earnest wound up looking better than he ever had before Gabriel socked him.

". . . and here on the turntable," Lipid was saying, "will be the 'planet' set. We'll redress it every week to make it look like a different world."

Gabriel nodded. "Why the turntable?"

Lipid's babyface actually pinked sightly with enthusiasm, "Oh, we used to use this studio for filming a musical show, the Lawrence Welk Simulacrum, you know? It was very popular. They had audience seats along all four walls of the studio and the orchestra rotated at a different speed for each song, in time with the music."

"You're kidding," Gabriel said.

"No, they really did it." His face went pinker. "That is, until the speed mechanism broke down and flung all those animated dummies into the audience. It was a terrible scene. That's when they cancelled the show."

Gabriel chuckled to himself as he and Lipid slowly walked across the noisy studio to inspect the "bridge" set. This would be used as the bridge of both starships, with slight redressings to change it from one ship to the other.

"What do you think of it?" Lipid asked, over the shouting and hammering.

Gabriel took it in. The two walls of the corner were now lined by desk-type consoles studded with elaborate keyboard buttons and viewing screens. About them were big observation screens, taller than a man and many times wider. They were blank, of course, nothing but sheets of painted plastic covering the studio's bare walls. But with electronic picture matting, they would appear to look out on the vast universe and reveal stars, strange new worlds, other spaceships of the series. The floor had been turned into a metalized deck, thanks to judicious spray painting, and there were very modernistic chairs and crew stations arranged in a semicircle facing the corner.

Nodding, Gabriel admitted, "It looks good. Real substantial. Needs some personalized touches, though."

Lipid quickly agreed. "Oh sure. Right. We've been talking with one of our Ontario vineyards . . . they might come in as a sponsor for part of the show. One of the captains can have a flask of wine set up at his command console."

Gabriel said, "Just make sure it's a futuristic flask. We're seven hundred years in the future, remember."

"Oh, sure."

Gabriel stood there and tried to visualize how the actors would look on the set. *Not bad,* he thought. *It's finally starting to shape up.*

"You like it?" Lipid asked. His voice went a little squeaky, like a kid who's desperately anxious for a word of approval.

"It'll do, I guess. At least we got rid of that damned steering wheel."

Lipid blushed. "Oh. That. I didn't understand what you needed. Dr. Oxnard straightened me out on that."

"He's been a help," Gabriel said.

Lipid stared down at his sneakers. "You don't like it, do you? What'd we do wrong?"

"I like it," Gabriel said. "It's okay. Nothing's wrong."

Looking up at him, the Production Manager said, "But you're . . . well, you're not excited by it. It doesn't really raise your metabolism."

With a weary smile, Gabriel said, "Listen kid. I've been going flat out for more than three months now. I've been trying to get the scripts in shape, working with high school kids and every amateur playwright north of Saskatoon. I haven't seen a single script or story treatment that I didn't have to rewrite from start to finish. I'm hoarse from talking to these bean-brains and going blind from reading and typing twenty-eight hours a day. My ass hurts from sitting and my feet hurt from running and my gut hurts from fighting. So don't expect me to flip handstands and start swinging from the rafters. Okay?"

Lipid's face glowed with awe. "Oh sure, Mr. Gabriel. I understand. There's been a lot of talk around the studio about how hard you've been working on the scripts."

"Okay," Gabriel said. Then, looking at Lipid's trembling lower lip, he added, "And call me Ron. I don't like this Mr. Gabriel shit."

"Oh . . . okay, Mr. Ga . . . uh, Ron."

Gabriel forced a smile and they started for the next set, in the next corner of the studio.

Lipid asked as they walked, "Uh, Ron . . . can I ask you a question?"

"Sure." They had to detour around a burly guy carrying a long plank on his shoulder. *Laurel and Hardy would have a field day in here,* Gabriel thought.

"Why do you do it?" the Production Manager asked, his voice filled with admiration and wonder.

"Do what?"

"Why do you put up with us? I mean, you could be working with the bigtime outfits down in Hollywood. Or writing books. I've been reading your sci-fi books since I was a kid. . . ."

Gabriel winced. Twice.

But Lipid didn't notice it. "You're a famous writer. You've won a lot of awards. Why are you putting up with this cheap outfit? I mean, this is the best job *I* can get right now. But you . . . you can do a lot better."

Gabriel looked at him. *The kid means it. He's not putting me on.*

Without breaking stride, he said gruffly, "This is *my* show. Comprend? Mine. I *created* this idea; it came out of my brain. I may have to deal with shitheads at Titanic and beaver-brains at Badger, but that doesn't matter. I want this show to be *good,* man. Not pretty good. Not good enough to get some sponsors. Not good enough to get renewed after the first thirteen weeks."

His voice was rising and the heat was building up inside him. Months of anger and frustration were bubbling close to the surface.

"I want it to be *good!* Good enough to satisfy me. Good enough for any one of us to point at with pride. I want you and me and every carpenter and electrician in this crazy cave to be proud to have worked on 'The Star-crossed.' I want even assholes like Earnest—and Finger back in his padded room in California—to feel proud of this show. They won't, because they haven't got the capacity. But we do, you and me. That's what I want. Pride of accomplishment."

"Wow," gasped Lipid. "What commitment."

And the money helps, Gabriel added silently. *And the fact that nobody else in town would touch my work because Mongoloid idiots like Finger convinced everybody I'm too tough to get along with. And I'm broke. And this is the only decent idea I've had in the past year. And if I don't make some money out of this I'll have to give up my house.*

As they stopped and looked over the next set, Gabriel realized that even those eminently practical reasons that didn't sound so good when you voiced them, even they didn't go deep enough.

I'm staying because she's here, he admitted to himself. *Rita's close enough to touch and so beautiful that she's driving me crazy. She smiles and says all the right words to me, but she never gets within arm's reach.*

He laughed silently, sardonically, at himself. *They do articles in magazines about me, one of the ten most available bachelors in Hollywood. I have all the women I want. I spend half my Blue Cross getting cleaned up from them. And this one goddamned girl just smiles at me and I'm all putty inside.*

His mind completely detached from his physical surroundings, Gabriel wondered where Rita Yearling was at that precise moment. *Getting her costumes fitted? Taking color tests with the new camera system? Talking on the three-dee phone Finger gave her? Talking to him? Planning to go back to L.A. for the weekend to be with him?*

Gabriel grimaced inwardly. *I haven't been writing fiction,* he realized. *I know exactly how Romeo felt.*

Rita Yearling did not go to Los Angeles that weekend. Bernard Finger came to Toronto.

Gabriel was standing on the balcony of his hotel room, looking out disconsolately at the park-like front grounds of the hotel and beyond to the towers of the city that blocked what had once been a decent view of Lake Ontario. There wasn't much smog in Toronto, since the Canadians used nuclear energy to a large extent. But the lake was still a fetid cesspool of industrial wastes.

Rita had smilingly accepted Gabriel's dinner invitation the night before; he had treated her to a quick jet flight to New York for authentic delicatessen fare. All through the evening she was warm, friendly, outgoing, obviously happy to be with Gabriel. And that's as far as it went. She eluded his grasp. Even in the plush passenger compartment of the rented jet (five thousand bucks, Canadian, for the night) she somehow managed to stay at arm's length.

Gabriel couldn't figure it out. Women didn't act that way. Or at least, he'd never had any patience with those who did. "You either do or you don't," he had told hundreds of girls. *But Rita's different.* Shy yet friendly. Innocent yet knowing. Desirable but distant. *She's driving me nuts,* Gabriel told himself for the thousandth time.

He burped pastrami. The morning air wasn't helping to settle his stomach. Just as he decided to go back inside and take some antacid, a long stream of cars came purring off the superhighway and onto the hotel's approach road.

Finger! Gabriel knew instantly. No one else would demand such commotion. The carefully landscaped grounds of the old hotel had never seen such a flurry of sychophants. Bellmen and doormen seemed to spring out of the front entrance. Yesmen by the dozens poured out of the cars and yeswomen, too. Finger was no sexist.

As Gabriel leaned over his balcony railing to watch, it seemed as if the hotel was disgorging whole phalanxes of flunkies. It was easy to tell the Californians from the Canadians. The L.A. contingent wore the latest *mode*: fur-trimmed robes and boots and hats that made them look like extras from an old Ivan the Terrible flick. *Or the minions of Ming the Merciless.* The locals wore conservatively zippered business suits, while the hotel staff was decked out in bluish uniforms faintly reminiscent of the old RAF.

The whole conglomeration swirled and eddied around the car for nearly fifteen minutes. Then everyone seemed to fall into a prearranged pattern, and the rear door of the longest, blackest, shiniest limousine was opened by one of the RAF uniforms. Despite himself, Gabriel grinned. *He ought to have a line of trumpeters announcing his arrival.*

Bernard Finger's expensively booted foot appeared in the limousine's doorway, followed by the rest of his Cary Grant body. He looked gorgeous, resplendent in royal purple and ermine. And he bumped his head on the car's low doorway.

Gabriel hooted. "You're still a klutz, you klutz!" he hollered. But his balcony was too far above street level for anyone to hear him. Briefly he wondered if he'd have time enough to make a water bomb and drop it on Finger's ermine-trimmed hat. But he couldn't tear himself away from the barbaric splendor of the scene below, even for an instant.

Finger straightened his hat and sneaked a small rub on the bump he'd just received, then stood tall and beaming at the sea of servility surrounding him.

Rita's not there to greet him Gabriel noticed, and felt good about it.

Then with an expansive gesture, Finger said something to the people nearest him. Several of them were holding recorders and minicameras, Gabriel noticed. *Media flaks.*

Finger turned back toward his limousine and ducked slightly, beckoning to someone inside. *New girlfriend?* Gabriel wondered.

It was a man who got out. A guy who wasn't terribly tall, but looked wide across the shoulders and narrow at the hips. Muscleman. He wasn't wearing Hollywood finery, either. He wore a simple turtleneck sweater and a very tight pair of pants. Athlete's striped sneakers. Dirty blond hair, cropped short and curly. Rugged looking face; nose must've been broken more than once. Good smile, dazzling teeth. Must be caps.

The newcomer grinned almost boyishly at the cameras, then turned and, grabbing Finger by the shoulders so strongly that he lifted the mogul off his feet, he kissed B.F. soundly on both cheeks.

As he let Finger's boots smack down on the pavement again, Gabriel howled to himself, *He's got a new girl-friend, all right! Wait'll Rita sees this!*

But Gabriel was completely wrong.

Les Montpelier phoned almost as soon as Gabriel stepped back inside his room, inviting him to a "command performance" dinner.

"The whole team's going to be here tonight," Les said gravely, "to meet the show's male lead."

Gabriel blinked at Montpelier's image on the tiny phone screen. "You mean that guy is going to be our big star?"

"That's right." Montpelier cut the connection before Gabriel could ask who the man was.

Briefly, Gabriel considered throwing himself off the balcony. But he decided to attend B.F.'s dinner instead.

Finger bought out the hotel's main restaurant for the evening and filled it with media people and the top-level crew of "The Starcrossed." *No working types allowed,* Gabriel grumbled to himself. No painters or electricians or carpenters. Just us white-collar folks. Not even Bill Oxnard had been invited, although Gabriel knew he was in Toronto for the weekend.

Finger sat at the head table, flanked by Rita Yearling on one side and the rugged-looking, erstwhile star of the show on the other. Gabriel had been placed halfway across the big dining room, as far removed from Gregory Earnest as possible, and seated at a table of what passed for writers. They were a grubby lot. The high schoolers weren't allowed to stay up late or drink alcoholic beverages (and marijuana was still illegal in Canada), so they hadn't been invited. Gabriel sat amid a motley crew of semi-retired engineers who had always wanted to write sci-fi, copyboys and reporters from the area news media who saw their futures in dramaturgy, and one transplanted Yank who had exiled himself to Canada millenia ago and could outwrite the entire staff, when he wasn't outdrinking them.

Something about Finger's male "discovery" was bothering Gabriel. His face looked vaguely familiar. Gabriel spent the entire dinner—of rubber chicken and plastic peas—trying to figure out where he had seen the man before. A bit player in some TV series? An announcer? One of the gay blades who're always hanging around the studios and offices? Maybe a dancer?

None of them seemed to click.

Then, as coffee and joints were passed around by the well-beyond-retirement-age waiters, Finger got to his feet.

"I suppose you're wondering why I asked you here this evening."

Everyone roared with laughter. Except Gabriel, who clutched his stomach and tried to keep from shrieking.

"Even though I've been staying in sunny Southern California. . . ." More canned laughter from the throats of Finger's lackeys. ". . . I've been keeping a close eye on your work up here. 'The Starcrossed' is an important property for Titanic and even though we're working with an extremely tight budget. . . ." *Who's paying for this bash tonight?* Gabriel wondered. ". . . I can assure you that Titanic is doing everything possible to make this show a success."

Loud applause. Even the media people clapped. *Local flaks,* Gabriel knew. *They want the show to succeed, too.*

Finger cocked his head in Gabriel's direction, like Cary

Grant sizing up Katherine Hepburn. "I know we've had some troubles in the script department, but I think that's all been ironed out satisfactorily." *Maybe,* Gabriel answered silently.

"And thanks to our foresight in hiring one of the world's foremost scientists as our technical consultant—Dr. William Oxnard, that is, who unfortunately couldn't be with us here tonight because he's literally spending night and day at the studio . . . let's hear it for Dr. Oxnard. . . ."

They all dutifully applauded while Finger tried to figure out where he was in his speech. "Um, well, as I was saying, we've got terrific scientific advice. And we're going to have the best show, from the technical standpoint, of anything in the industry."

More applause.

"But when you get right down to it. . . ." Finger went on, reaching for a napkin to dab at his brow. The lights were hot, especially under those fur-trimmed robes. "When you get right down to it, what the audience sees is mainly the performers. Sure, the scripts and the sets are important, but those millions of viewers out there, they react to *people* . . . the performers who perform for them, right there in their living rooms—or bedrooms, whichever the case may be."

I'll never make it all the way through this speech without throwing up, Gabriel told himself.

"It's crucially important to have a pair of brilliant costars," Finger said, gesturing with the white napkin, "especially for a show like 'The Starcrossed,' which is, after all, a show about two young people, lovers, who will captivate the millions of viewers out there."

Someone broke into enthusiastic applause, found that he was alone, quickly stopped, looked around and slid down in his chair halfway under the table.

Finger glanced in his direction, then resumed. "We are extremely fortunate in having one of the most exciting young new talents in the world to play our feminine lead, our Juliet: Rita Yearling."

Rita stood up amid a pleasant round of applause and took a cautious bow. Considering the gown she'd been poured into and her cleavage, caution was of utmost importance. She remained standing as Finger went on:

"Isn't she beautiful? And she can *act!*" Some laughter; Rita herself smiled tolerantly, while Gabriel squirmed in his chair with indignation for her.

"But although Rita Yearling will be a superstar by the end of the coming season, she's still relatively unknown to the TV audience. So what we needed, I knew, was a male costar who would be instantly recognizable to the whole world. . . ."

Gabriel found his puzzlement deepening. The guy sitting at Finger's right side looked vaguely familiar, but Gabriel *knew* he wasn't a well-known actor.

"So I went out and got a guy who *is* known the whole world over," Finger was at his self-congratulatory best, "and signed him up to play our Romeo, our male lead. And here he is! A superstar in his own right! Francois Dulaq!"

Everyone in the big dining room rose to their feet and roared approval. "Du-*laq!* Du-*laq!*" they began chanting. Even the crystal chandeliers started swaying in rhythm with their shouts.

And then it hit Gabriel. Francois Dulaq. The hockey star. The guy who broke Orr's old scoring record and made the Canadian Maple Stars world champions. They even beat the Russo-Chinese All-Stars, Gabriel remembered from last season's sportscasts.

A hockey player as the male lead? *It's Buster Crabbe all over again,* Gabriel moaned to himself.

He had to climb up on his chair to see what was going on. The crowd was still on its feet, roaring. Dulaq had gone around Finger to where Rita was standing. They put their arms around each other and bared the most expensive sets of teeth in television history for the media cameramen. Finger beamed approvingly.

The expatriate American tugged at Gabriel's sleeve and yelled over the crowd's hubbub, "Whaddaya think?"

Gabriel shrugged. "He might be okay. Looks good enough. Probably can't act worth shit, but he wouldn't be the first big star who couldn't act."

Frowning and shaking his head, the expatriate said, "Yeah, but he can't even speak English."

Gabriel almost fell off his chair. "What? What's he speak, French?"

"Nope. Neanderthal."

Not knowing whether it was a joke or not, Gabriel climbed off his perch and sat down. The crowd settled down, too, as Finger nudged Dulaq to the microphone.

"I wancha t'know," Dulaq said, "dat I'll t'row evert'ing I got into dis job . . . jus' like I t'rew dem body checks inta dem Chinks last May!"

They all roared again. Gabriel sank his head down onto his arms and tried to keep from crying.

At precisely two a.m. Gabriel's phone buzzed.

He wasn't sleeping. His trusty suitcase was open on the bed, half filled with his clothes. Since the end of the dinner, Gabriel had spent the night phoning Finger, Montpelier, Brenda, Sam Lipid and anyone else who would listen, telling them that if Dulaq was the male star of the show, they could get themselves another chief writer.

They all argued with him. They cited contracts and clauses. They spoke glowingly of Dulaq's magnetic personality and star quality and sex appeal. They promised voice coaching and speech therapy and soundtrack dubbing. Still, Gabriel packed his suitcase as he fought with them.

Then his phone buzzed.

Gabriel leaned across the bed and flipped the switch that turned it on. Rita Yearling's incredibly lovely face appeared on the phone's screen.

"Hi," she breathed.

Gabriel hung suspended, stretched across the bed with one foot in his suitcase, tangled in his dirty underwear.

"Hello yourself," he managed.

Her eyes seemed to widen as she noticed the open suitcase. "You're not leaving?"

Gabriel nodded. He couldn't talk.

"Don't you care about the show?" she asked.

He shook his head.

"Don't you care about me?"

With an effort, Gabriel said, "I care a lot. Too much to watch you ruin your career before it really starts. That hockey puck of a leading man is going to *destroy* this show."

She dimpled at him. "You're jealous!"

"No," he said. "Just fed up."

"Oh Ron. . . ." Her face pulled together slightly in a small frown.

"I can't take it anymore," Gabriel said. "It's just one battle after another . . . like fighting with a Hydra. Every time I chop off one head, seven more pop up."

But she wasn't listening. "Ron . . . you poor sweet boy. Come out onto your balcony. I've got a surprise for you."

"On the balcony?"

"Go out and see," Rita cooed.

Untangling himself from the suitcase, Gabriel padded barefoot to the balcony. He was wearing nothing but his knee-length dashiki and the chill night air cut into him the instant he opened the sliding glass door.

"Surprise!" he heard from over his head.

Looking up, he saw Rita smiling lusciously down at him. She was on the balcony one floor up and one room over from his own. She stood there smiling down at him, clothed in a luminous whisp of gown that billowed softly in the breeze.

"I took this room for the weekend. I wanted to get away from the suite where B.F. is," she said.

Ron's knees went weak. "It is the east," he murmured, "and Juliet is the sun."

"This is a lot more fun than talking over the phone, isn't it?" Rita gave a girlish wriggle. "Like, it's more romantic, huh?"

Without even thinking about it, Gabriel leaped up on the railing of his own balcony. He stretched and his fingertips barely grazed the bottom of Rita's balcony.

"Hey! Be careful!"

Gabriel glanced below. Ten floors down, the street lamps glowed softly in the cold night air. Wind whipped at his dashiki and his butt suddenly felt terribly exposed.

"What are you *doing?*" Rita called, delighted.

He jumped for her balcony. His fingers clutched at the cold cement, then he reached, straining, and grabbed a fistful of one of the metal posts supporting the railing.

His feet dangled in empty air and his dashiki billowed in the wind. Somewhere far back in his mind, Gabriel realized what a ridiculous picture this would present to anyone passing below. But that didn't matter.

Beads of cold sweat popped out all over his body as he strained, muscles agonized by the unaccustomed effort, hand over hand to the edge of the balcony's railing. His bare toes found a hold on the balcony's cement floor at last and he heaved himself, puffing and trembling wtih exertion, over the railing to collapse at Rita's feet.

She dropped to her knees beside him. "Ron, darling, are you all right?"

He smiled weakly up at her. "Hiya kid." It wasn't Shakespeare, he knew, but it was the best he could manage under the conditions.

They went arm in arm into her hotel room. Rita's gown was a see-through and Gabriel was busily looking into it.

She sat him down on the edge of the bed. "Ron," she said, very seriously, "you can't leave the show."

"There's no reason for me to stay," he said.

"Yes there is."

"What?"

She lowered her eyelids demurely. "There's me."

10: THE DIRECTOR

Mitch Westerly sat scowling to himself behind his archaic dark glasses. The other passengers on the jet airliner shuffled past him, down the narrow aisle, overcoats flopping in their arms and hand baggage banging against the seats and each other.

Westerly ignored them all, just as he had ignored the stewardesses who had recognized him and asked for his autograph. They were up forward now, smiling their mechanical "Have a good day" at the outgoing passengers and sneaking glances at him.

I should never have come back, he thought. *This is going to be a bad scene. I can feel it in my karma.*

He was neither tall nor particularly handsome, but since puberty he had somehow attracted women without even trying. His face was rugged, weatherbeaten, the face of an oldtime cowboy or mountaineer, even though he had spent most of his life in movie sound stages—and even in Nepal, where he had been for the past two years, he had seen the Himalayas only through very well-insulated windows. His body was broad shouldered, solid, stocky, the kind that goes to fat when you reach forty. But Westerly had always eaten very sparingly and hardly ever drank at all; there was no fat on him.

He wore his standard outfit, a trademark that never

changed no matter what the current fashion might be: a pullover sweater, faded denims, boots, the dark shades and a pair of soft leather race driver's gloves. He had started wearing the gloves many years earlier, when he had been second-unit director on a racing car TV series. The gloves kept him from biting his fingernails, and he rarely took them off. It ruined his image to be seen biting his fingernails.

Finally, all the passengers had left. The plane was empty except for the three stewardesses. The tallest one, who also seemed to be the boss stew, strode briskly toward him, her microskirt flouncing prettily and revealing her flowered underpants.

"End of the line, I'm sorry to say," she told him.

"Hate to leave," Westerly said. His voice was as soft as the leather of his gloves.

"I hope you enjoyed the flight."

"Yeah. Sure did." *And the offers of free booze, the names and numbers your two assistants scribbled on my lunch tray and the note you slipped under the washroom door.*

He slowly pulled himself out of the plush seat, while the stewardess reached up into the overhead rack and pulled out his sheepskin jacket.

"Will you be in Toronto for long?" she asked, as they started up the aisle together, with him in the lead.

"Directing a TV series here," Westerly said, over his shoulder.

"Oh really?" Her voice said *How exciting!* without using the words. "Will you be staying at the Disney Hilton? That's where we stay for our layovers."

That dump. Not even the fleas go there anymore. "Nope. They've got us at one of the older places—Inn on the Park."

"Ohhh. That's beautiful. A . . . friend, he took me to dinner there once."

They were at the hatch now. The other two stews were smiling glitteringly at him. With his Himalayan-honed senses he could almost hear them saying, *Put me in your*

*TV series. Make me famous. I'll do anything for that.
Glamour, glamour, romance and glamour.*

He hesitated at the hatch and made a smile for them.
They shuddered visibly. "Y'all come out to the studio when
you get a chance. Meet the TV people. Just ask for me at
the gate. Anytime."

"Ohh. We will!"

His smile self-destructed as soon as he turned his back
on them and trudged down the connecting tunnel that led
into the airport terminal building.

They were at the gate area waiting for him. The
photographers, the media newshounds, the newspaper reporters, the lank-haired droopy-mouthed emaciated young
women who covered Special Events for the local TV
stations and show business magazines, the public relations
flaks for Titanic and Badger and Shiva knows who else.
They all looked alike, from Bhutan to Brooklyn.

*They might be the same people who were at the airport
in Delhi* . . . *and in Rome* . . . *and in London,* Westerly
realized with a thrill of horror. *My own personal set of
devils hounding me wherever I go. Eternally. Hell is an
airport terminal!*

He kept his head down and refused even to listen to
their shouting, pleading questions until the PR flaks—
Why are they always balding and desperate faced?—
steered him to one of those private rooms with unmarked
doors that line the long impersonal corridors of every
airport terminal in the world.

The room inside had been set up for a press conference. A table near the door was groaning with bottles
of liquor and trays of hors d'oeuvres. A battery of
microphones studded a small podium at the front of the
room. Folding chairs were neatly arranged in rows.

Inside of three minutes, Westerly was standing at the
podium (which bore the stylized trademark of Titanic
Productions, a rakishly angled "T" in which the cross
piece was a pair of wings), the hors d'oeuvres were totally
demolished, half the booze was gone, the chairs were

scattered as if by a *tsunami* and the PR men were smiling with self-satisfaction.

One of the lank-haired young women was asking, "When you left Hollywood two years ago, you vowed you'd never return. What changed your mind?"

Westerly fiddled with his glasses for a moment. "Haven't changed my mind," he said slowly, with just a trace of fashionable West Virginia accent. "Didn't go back to Hollywood. This is Toronto, isn't it?"

The news people laughed. But the scrawny girl refused to be embarrassed.

"You said you were finished with commercial films and you were going to seek inner peace; now you're back. Why?"

Because inner peace comes at eleven-fifty a week at the Katmandu-Sheraton, baby. "I spent two years absorbing the wisdom of the East in the Himalayas," Westerly replied aloud. "One of the most important things the lamas taught me is that a man should use his inborn talents and use them wisely. My talent is making movies and television shows. It's my karma . . . my destiny."

"Didn't you make a movie in Tibet last year?" asked an overweight, mustachioed reporter.

"Surely did," said Westerly. "But that was purely for self-expression . . . to help release my soul from its bondage. That film will never be released for commercial viewing." *Not that bomb. Never make that mistake again —hash and high altitudes just don't mix.*

One of the media interviewers, his videotape camera strapped securely to the side of his head, asked, "You left the States right after the Academy Awards dinner, with no explanations at all except that you had to—quote, find yourself, end quote. Why did you turn down the Oscar?"

"Didn't think I deserved it. A director shouldn't get an Oscar for his first feature film. There were many other directors who had amassed a substantial body of work who deserved to get an Oscar before Mitch Westerly did." *And the IRS and the Narcs were getting too close; it was no time to show up at a prearranged affair.*

"Do you still consider yourself the Boy Genius of Hollywood?"

"Never been a boy." *Pushing forty and running scared.*

"Why have you come here to Toronto, instead of going back to Hollywood?"

Taxes, pushers, alimony . . . take your pick. "Gregory Earnest convinced me that 'The Starcrossed' was a vehicle worthy of my Krishna-given talents."

"Have you met the people who'll be working for you on 'The Starcrossed'?"

"Not yet."

"Have you read any of the scripts?"

I gagged over the first six pages. "Looked over some of the scripts and read the general concept of the show. Looks great."

"Do you think Shakespeare and science fiction can be mixed?"

"Why not? If Will were alive today, he'd be writing science fiction."

"What do you think is the best film you've ever directed?"

Without an instant's hesitation, Westerly replied, "The one I'm working on now. In this case, the entire series, 'The Starcrossed.' "

But in his mind, his life flashed before his consciousness like a videotape spun at dizzying, blurring speed. He knew the best film he had done; everyone in the room knew it; the one original piece of work he had been able to do, the first major job he had tackled, as a senior back at UCLA: *The Reawakening*. The hours, the weeks, the months he had spent. First as a volunteer worker at the mental hospital, then convincing them to let him bring his tiny pocket camera in. Following Virginia, sallow, pathetic, schizophrenic Virginia through the drug therapy, the primal sessions, the EEGs, the engram reversals. Doctors, skinny fidgety nurses who didn't trust him at first, Virginia's parents tight and suspicious, angry at her for the dream world they had thrust her into, the psychotechs and their weird machines that mapped the brain and put the *mind* on a viewscreen. Virginia's gradual awakening to the real world, her understanding that the parents who said they loved her actually wanted nothing to do with her, her acceptance of adulthood, of maturity, of her own individuality and the fact that she was a lovely, desirable woman. Mitch's wild hopeless love for her and that heart-stopping instant when she smiled and told him in a voice so low that he could barely hear it that she loved him too. That was his best film; his life and hers recorded in magnetic swirls on long reels of tape. Truth frozen into place so that people could see it and understand and cry and laugh over it.

He had never done anything so fine again. He became successful. He directed "True to Life" TV shows and made money and fame. He married Virginia while they were both still growing and changing. Unlike the magnetic patterns on video tape, they did not stay frozen in place forever. They split, slowly and sadly at first, then with the wild burning anger of betrayal and hate. By the time he directed his first major production and was nominated for an Oscar, his world had already crashed around him.

"Do you really think 'The Starcrossed' is award-winning material?"

The question snapped him back to this small stuffy overcrowded room, with the news people playing their part in the eternal charade. So he went back to playing his.

" 'The Starcrossed' has the potential of an award-winning series. I won't be eligible for an Oscar because it's not a one-time production. But it should be in contention for an Emmy as Best Dramatic Series."

Satisfied that they had put his neck in the noose, the news people murmured their thanks and headed on to their next assignments.

Westerly went straight to the studio, while two of the PR flaks took his luggage to the hotel. He almost asked why it took a pair of them to escort his one flight bag to the hotel, but thought better of it. If he raised a question about it, Westerly knew, they'd wind up assigning a third PR man to supervise the first two.

Gregory Earnest met him at the studio, looking somber in a dark gray jumpsuit. His face was as deeply hidden by bushy beard and tangled mane as ever, but since Westerly had seen him last—many months earlier, in Nepal—Earnest's face had subtly changed, improved. His nose seemed slightly different, somehow.

"I'm glad you're finally here," Earnest said, with great seriousness. "Now maybe we can start to bring some order out of this chaos."

He showed Westerly around the sets that had been built in the huge studio. The place was empty and quiet, except for a small group of people off to one side who were working on some kind of aerial rigging. Westerly ignored them and studied the sets.

"This is impossible," he said at last.

"What?" Earnest's eyebrows disappeared into his bushy forelocks. "What do you mean?"

"These sets." Westerly stood in the middle of the starship bridge, surrounded by complicated-looking cardboard consoles. "They're too deep. How're we going to move cameras in and out around all this junk? It'll take hours to make a single shot!"

Earnest sighed with relief. "Oh *that*. You've never directed a three-dee show before, have you?"

"No, but. . . ."

"Well, one of the things audiences like is a lot of depth in each scene. We don't put all the props against the walls anymore . . . we scatter them around the floor. Makes a better three-dimensional effect."

"But the cameras. . . ."

"They're small enough to move through the standing props. We measured all the tolerances. . . ."

"But I thought three-dee cameras were big awkward mothers."

Earnest cast a rare smile at him. It was not a pleasant thing to see. "That was two years ago. Time marches on. A lot of transistors have flown under the bridge. You're not in the Mystic East anymore."

Westerly pushed his glasses up against the bridge of his nose. "I see," he said.

"Hey! There you are!" A shout came echoing across the big, nearly empty room.

Earnest and Westerly turned to see a stubby little guy dashing toward them. He wore a *Starcrossed* tee shirt and a pair of old-fashioned sailor's bell-bottoms, complete with a thirteen-button trapdoor in front.

"Oh *God*," Earnest whined nasally. "It's Ron Gabriel."

Gabriel skidded to a halt in front of the director. They were almost equal in height, much to Earnest's surprise.

"You're Mitch Westerly," Gabriel panted.

"And you're Ron Gabriel." He grinned and took Gabriel's offered hand.

"I've been a fan of yours," Gabriel said, "ever since 'The Reawakening.' Best damned piece of tape I ever saw."

Westerly immediately liked the writer. "Well, thanks."

"Everything else you've made since then has been crap."

Westerly liked him even more. "You're damn right," he admitted.

"How the hell they ever gave you an Oscar for that abortion two years ago is beyond me."

Westerly shrugged, suddenly carefree because there were no pretenses to maintain. "Money and politics, man. You know the game. Same thing goes for writers' awards."

Gabriel made a face that was halfway between rue and embarrassment. Then he grinned. "Yeah. Guess so."

Earnest said, "I'm taking Mr. Westerly on a tour of the studio facilities. . . ."

"Go pound sand up your ass," Gabriel said. "I've gotta talk about the scripts." He grabbed at Westerly's arm. "Come on, I'll buy you a beer or something."

"I don't drink."

"Great Neither do I." They started off together, leaving Earnest standing there. Behind his beard, his face was redder than a Mounties jacket at sunset.

The studio cafeteria was murky with pot smoke, since

smoking of all sorts was forbidden on the sets because of the fire hazard.

"Now let me get this straight," Westerly was saying. "The original scripts were written by high school kids as part of a contest?"

They were sitting at a corner table, near the air conditioning blowers, sipping gingerales.

Gabriel nodded slowly. "I've been working since summer with Brenda and Bill Oxnard to make some sense out of them. I've also written two original scripts of my own."

"And that's all we've got to shoot with?"

"That's right."

"Krishna's left eyebrow!"

"Huh?"

Westerly waved at the encroaching smoke. "Nothing. But it's a helluva situation."

"They didn't tell you about the scripts?"

"Earnest said there were some problems with you . . . you're supposed to be tough to get along with."

"I am," Gabriel admitted, "when I'm being shat on."

"I don't blame you."

Gabriel hunched forward in his chair. "So what do we do?"

With a small shrug, Westerly said, "I'll have to talk to Fad about it . . . it's the Executive Producer's job. . . ."

Gabriel shook his head. "Sheldon split. Went back to L.A. as soon as his girl moved out of his apartment, and turned over the E.P. title to Earnest."

"Earnest?" Westerly felt his lip curling.

"The boll weevil of the north," said Gabriel.

"Well," with a deep sigh, "I guess I'll have to mention it to Finger. I'm supposed to have a conference with him tonight. . . ."

"I thought he was back in L.A."

"He is. We're talking by phone. Private link . . . satellite relay, they tell me."

"Oh."

"I'll just tell Finger we have to get better script material."

"You can read the scripts, if you want to."

"I already saw a couple. I thought they were rejects. I'd like to see yours. At least we'll have a couple to start with."

Gabriel looked pleased, but still uncertain.

"Is there anything else?" Westerly asked.

With a grimace, Gabriel said, "Well, I hate to bring it up."

"Go on."

For an instant, the writer hesitated. Then, like a man who's decided to step off the high board no matter what, "You've got a reputation for being an acid freak. Did they bring you in here just for the name or are you gonna stay straight and do the kind of work you're capable of doing?"

So there it is, right out in the open. Westerly almost felt relieved. "Both," he said.

"Huh?"

"Finger and Earnest called me back from the Roof of the World because I have a big name with the public and I need money so bad that I'm willing to work cheap. They know I've blown my head off; I doubt that they care."

Gabriel gritted his teeth but said nothing.

"But *I* care," Westerly went on. "I finally got off the stuff in Nepal and I want to stay off it. I want to do a good job on this series. I want to get back to work again."

"No shit?"

"No shit, buddy."

"You're not kidding me? Or yourself?"

"No kidding."

Gabriel broke into a grin. "Okay, *buhbie*. We'll show the whole world."

By the time Westerly got back to the studio, the quiet little knot of technicians who had been working on the aerial rigging had turned into a studio full of shouting, milling people. One of the men was hanging suspended in the rig, wires disappearing up into the shadows of the high ceiling, his feet dangilng a good ten meters off the floor.

Gregory Earnest seemed to rise up out of the floor-boards as Westerly stood near the studio's main door, watching.

"That's Francois Dulaq, our star," Earnest explained, pointing to the dangling man. "We're geting him accustomed to the zero-gravity simulator."

"Shouldn't we use a stuntman? It looks kind of dangerous. . . ."

Earnest shook his head. "We don't have any stuntmen on the budget. Besides, Dulaq's a trained athlete . . . strong as an ox."

Dulaq hung in midair, shouting at the men below him. To Westerly, there was a faint tinge of terror in the man's voice. Someone yelled from off in the distance, "Okay, try it!" Dulaq's body jerked into motion. The rig started moving him across the vast emptiness of the studio's open central area.

'Hold it!" the voice yelled; the rig halted so abruptly that Dulaq was almost thrown out of his skin. Westerly could feel his own eyeballs slam against his lids, in psychic communion with the man in the rig.

"Shouldn't we test the rig with a dummy first?" he asked Earnest.

For the second time that day the executive smiled. "What do you think we've got up there now?"

It was agonizing to watch. The technicians spent hours setting up the lights and whisking Dulaq backward and forward through the spacious studio on the aerial rig. They slammed him against walls, amidst frantic yells of "Slow it down!" or "Watch it!" Once the rig seemed to slip and Dulaq went hurtling to the floor, only to be snatched up again and yanked almost out of sight, into the shadows up near the ceiling. From the far corner where the technicians manipulated the controls came the sounds of multilingual swearing. And from the rigging itself came shrieks and groans.

Finally, the star of the show went gracefully swooping past Westerly, smiling manfully, as a trio of tiny unattended cameras automatically tracked him from the floor, like radar-directed antiaircraft guns getting a bead on an intruding attack plane. The technicians were clustered around the controls and watched their monitor screens.

"Beautiful!" somebody shouted.

Meanwhile, Dulaq had traversed the length of the studio, still smiling, sailing like Superman through thin air and rode headfirst into the upper backwall of the starship bridge set.

Westerly heard a concussive *thunk!* The backwall tottered for a moment as Dulaq hung there, suddenly as stiff and wooden as a battering ram. Then the wall tumbled, taking most of the set apart with a series of splintering crashes. Amidst the flying dust and crashing two-by-threes, and all the rending, shrieking noises, Westerly clearly heard the same master technician shout out, "Hold it!"

They got Dulaq down from the rig, nearly dropping him from ten meters up in the process. He was still smiling and apparently conscious, although to Westerly his eyes definitely looked glassy. The technicians bundled him off to the infirmary, which fortunately was in the same building as the studio. By the time Westerly got there, a smiling medic was telling the assembled technicians:

"He's all right . . . didn't even get a splinter. I took an x-ray of his head and it showed nothing."

The technicians smiled and joked and went back to their work. As they dispersed, Westerly introduced himself to the medic and asked permission to see the star of the show.

The medic graciously ushered him into the infirmary's tiny emergency room. Dulaq was sitting up on the only cot, still smiling, with an icepack perched on his head.

"Hi," Westerly said. "How're you feeling?"

"Okay."

"That was one terrific shot you took out there."

"I got worst," Dulaq mumbled. "Onst, against de Redwings, I went right t'rough da glass."

They talked together for about a half hour, as Westerly's heart sank lower and lower. *This is the star of the show?* he kept asking himself.

"Do you think you'll be all right to start working on

Monday?" he asked, feeling his head give a body-language *no*, despite his conscious efforts to keep it from shaking.

"Sure. I could go back now, if ya wanna."

"No! No . . . that's all right. You rest."

Westerly got up to leave, but Dulaq grasped his wrist in a grip of steel.

"Hey, one t'ing you do for me, huh?"

"Uh, sure. What?"

"Don' gimma no long speeches t'remember, huh? I don' want no long speeches. Too tough."

Krishna, Shiva and Vishnu, Westerly prayed. *Why have they done this to me?*

"Sure, he told Dulaq. "Don't worry about it."

"Okay. No long speeches."

"Right."

Dulaq let go of him and Westerly ducked through the accordian-fold door of the little sickroom, rubbing his wrist.

The doctor was at his cubbyhole desk.

"You examined him thoroughly?" Westerly asked.

"Yep," said the doctor.

"Did he talk that way before he hit his head?"

The doctor glowered at him.

Westerly had dinner with Rita Yearling, who seemed incredibly beautiful, utterly sure of herself and dismally cold toward him.

His hotel suite was sumptuously furnished, including a strange electronic console of shining metal and multicolored buttons that squatted bulkily in the far corner of the sitting room. Gregory Earnest had explained that the device was a three-dee phone station, which would link him instantaneously via satellite with Finger's private office in Los Angeles.

Somehow the phone loomed in his mind like an alien presence as he and Rita ate their dinner at the other end of the sitting room, near the windows.

Rita was polite, respectful and distant. The vibes coming from her were strictly professional, totally impersonal.

"Do you know Bernie Finger very well?"

"Of course."

"He discovered you?"

"Yes."

"Through an agent?"

"Oh, on his own."

"Where was that?"

"It doesn't really matter, does it?"

"No, I guess not. Um . . . what do you think of Ron Gabriel?"

"His brain's in his crotch."

"And your costar, Dulaq?"

"No brains at all."

And so it went, right through dinner, all the way through to the ice cream dessert that neither of them would do more than taste.

A part of Westerly's mind was almost amused. Here he was having dinner with the loveliest woman he had seen in years and he was bored silly by her. While she referred to other people as brainless, she came across as heartless, which in many ways was infinitely worse.

Finally he pushed aside his coffee cup and glanced at his wrist. "Finger will be calling in a few minutes, if he's on time."

"He's always on time," Rita said. She got up from her chair, a vision of Venus, Helen of Troy, Cleopatra, Harlow, Hayworth, Monroe—and equally cold, unalive.

"I'll let you two talk business together," Rita said.

Westerly got up and went to the door with her. She stopped just as he reached for the doorknob.

Without so much as a smile, Rita said, "B.F. won't mind if we ball, but we'll hafta keep it quiet from Gabriel. Ron thinks he's got me falling for him."

"Oh," was just about all that Westerly could manage.

"Just let me know where and when," she said.

He opened the door and she left the room.

For several minutes Westerly leaned against the closed door, his mind spinning. *It's not me,* he kept telling himself. *She really said it and that's the way it is with her. It*

*means as much to her as filling out an application blank
at the unemployment office.*

Still his hands trembled. He wished for the pleasant
euphoria that a pinch of coke would bring. Or even the
blankness of cat, the synthetic hypnotic drug that he started taking when Virginia was still in chemotherapy.

The phone chimed.

For an instant, Westerly didn't understand what the
sound was. He had started the day in Rome, stopped in
London and now—he remembered Earnest's instructions
on operating the three-dee phone. He went to the desk
near the rolling dinner table and picked up the handset.
The red button, he mused. Turning toward the strange,
squat apparatus across the room, he thumbed the red
button.

The far half of the room seemed to disappear, dissolving
into a section of Bernard Finger's Los Angeles office. The
bright blue sky of early twilight was visible in the window
behind Finger's imposing high-backed chair.

"H . . . hello," Westerly said shakily.

"Surprises you, eh?" Finger said back at him. "Just like
being in the same room. That's how good Oxnard's new
three-dee system is. It's the system we're using on 'The
Starcrossed' and *that's* what's gonna make it a great show."

"I'm glad we've got something going for us," said
Westerly.

"Huh?" Whaddaya mean by that?" Finger said.

Westerly pulled up his chair. This wasn't going to be a
pleasant chat, he realized. "Well," he said, "I've only been
here a few hours, but this is the way it looks to me. . . ."

He outlined what he had heard and seen, from his opening discussions with Earnest through his talk with Gabriel
and the accident with Dulaq and its aftermath. He stopped
short of telling about his dinner with Rita. Finger looked
slightly upset at first, angry when he heard Gabriel's name,
then ultimately bored of the whole litany of problems.

"You finished?" he asked when Westerly stopped.

"That seems like enough for the first day."

"H'mmp." Finger got up from his desk and the camera

tracked him. To Westerly, it looked as if half his sitting room was shifting around, the walls and furnishings moving, as Finger paced slowly toward a sofa that appeared in one corner and then centered itself in his view.

Finger sat on the sofa and touched a button that was set into its arm. On the wall behind him, a professional football game suddenly appeared on a flat, two-dimensional wall-sized TV screen.

"You see that?"

"Pro football. That's our competition?"

Finger shook his head. "That's our salvation, if everything works out right."

"What do you mean?" asked Westerly.

Glancing furtively on either side of himself, Finger said, "This is a private, scrambled connection. If you try to tell anybody about this, I'll deny it and sue you. I'll make sure that you never work again *anywhere!*"

"What in hell. . . ."

"Shut up and listen. Part of the money that the bankers put up for 'The Starcrossed' is now invested in the Honolulu Pineapples."

"The what?"

"The football team! The Honolulu Pineapples! If they win the Superbowl, Titanic Productions is out of the red."

Westerly's mind was reeling again. For a moment he couldn't remember if he had brought the pills with him or not. *I was going to dump them in the Ganges, but I think I left them. . . .*

"I'll give you the whole story," Finger was saying, "because you're the guy who's got to come through for me."

. . . in the zipper compartment of the flightbag.

"The bankers gave me enough money for one series. If it hits, Titanic gets more money to pull us out of debt. Got that? But we're up to our assholes in bills right now, baby! Now! Not the end of next season, but now!"

None of this is real, Westerly told himself.

"So I'm using some of the bankers' money to keep our heads above water, pay a few bills here and there. And the rest of it I'm betting on the Pineapples. As long as they keep winning, we can keep treading water. If they take the Superbowl, we're home free."

"What's this got to do with 'The Starcrossed'?" Westerly heard himself ask.

"Don't you understand? The money for the show is already spent!" Finger's voice was almost pleading. *For what? Understanding? Mercy? Appreciation?* "There isn't any more money for 'The Starcrossed.' It's spent. Bet on the Pineapples. The budget you've got is *all* you're going to get. There's not another nickel in the drawer."

"There's no money for writers?"

"No."

"No money for better actors?"

"No."

"No money for staff or technicians or art directors or. . . ."

"No money for nothing!" Finger bellowed. "Not another penny. Just what's on the budget now. Nothing more. You've got enough to do thirteen shows. That's it. If the series isn't a hit after the first couple weeks, it's over."

"I can't work like that," Westerly said. "I've got to have decent material, competent staff. . . ."

"You work with what you've got. That's *it*, baby!"

"No sir. Not me."

"That's all there is," Finger insisted.

"I can't work that way."

"Yes you can."

"I won't!"

"You've got to!"

Westerly got to his feet. For an instant he was tempted to walk over and grab Finger by the throat and *make* him understand. Then he realized that the man was a safe five thousand kilometers away.

"I won't do it," he said quietly. "I quit."

"You can't quit."

"Says who?"

"Says me." Finger's voice went low and ugly. "You try

quitting and I'll send you some visitors. Guys you owe money to."

"Who? The IRS? My ex-wife's lawyers? They can't touch me in Canada."

"Not them. The guys you bought your goodies from, just before you took off for the far hills. *They* can touch you . . . oh, brother, can they touch you."

Westerly felt a river of flame run through his guts. "You told me you had squared that!" he shouted.

"I told *them* that I'd square it . . . after you'd done the first thirteen shows. They're waiting. Patiently."

"You lying sonofabitch. . . ."

"And you're a cathead, an acid freak. So what? You do your job and you'll be okay. You just make do with what you've got there. And no complaints."

With his eyes closed, Westerly echoed, "No complaints."

"Good," Finger said. "Maybe we can all get out of this in one piece. Even if the show flops, the Pineapples are winning pretty good."

"Wonderful."

"Damned right it's wonderful. Now you take good care of yourself and have fun. I'm already contacting the right people about the Emmies. They'll be watching you. Them . . . and others."

"Thanks."

"You're entirely welcome. Good night."

Finger and his office abruptly disappeared, replaced by the rest of the sitting room and the ugly three-dee console.

Westerly stood without moving for several minutes. Then he stirred himself and headed for the bedroom. The flightbag was on the bed. And inside the zipper compartment, he knew, were enough pills to make him forget about this phone conversation.

At least, for a little while.

▦ 11: THE FIRST DAY'S SHOOTING

Gregory Earnest sat in the control booth, high above the rebuilt starship bridge set.

Directly in front of him were the engineers and technicians who ran the complex three-dee holographic equipment. They sat along a row of desk consoles, earphones clamped to their heads, eyes fixed on the green, glowing dials and viewscreens that were the only illumination in the darkened control booth.

Beyond the soundproof window in front of them, the set was alive with crewmen and actors. Electricians were trailing cables across the floor; cameramen were jockeying their self-propelled units and nodding their laser snouts up and down, right and left, like trainers taking high-spirited horses for a morning trot. Mitch Westerly was deep in conversation with Dulaq, one arm around the burly hockey star's shoulders. Rita Yearling lounged languidly on her special liquafoam couch, glowing with the metallic sheen of her skintight costume. Ron Gabriel paced nervously around the set, orbiting closer and closer to Rita.

Earnest's nose throbbed whenever he saw Gabriel. And a special vein in his forehead, reserved exclusively for passions of hatred and revenge, pulsed visibly.

"The first take of the first scene," a voice whispered from behind Earnest.

He turned to scowl, but saw that the speaker was Les Montpelier, from Titanic. He let his scowl vanish. Montpelier was B.F.'s special representative, here to lend an air of official enthusiasm to the first day's shooting. He was higher in the pecking order than the Executive Producer, entitled to scowl but not to be scowled at.

For a moment neither man said anything. They simply sat there looking at each other, Montpelier's trim little red beard nearly touching the Canadian's shaggier black one.

Then, over the loudspeaker, they heard Westerly's voice crackle: "Okay, let's get started."

A technician held out the clapboard and shouted, "Starcrossed. Episode One. Scene One. Take One."

"We're on our way!" Montpelier said with almost genuine enthusiasm, as the clapboard cracked and fell apart. The embarrassed technician picked up the pieces and scuttled out of camera range, shaking his head at the broken clapboard in his hands.

An omen? Earnest wondered.

Brenda Impanema stayed well back in the shadows, away from the bustling men and women on the blazingly lighted set.

"Would you like a chair?"

Startled, she looked around to see Bill Oxnard smiling at her. He was carrying a pair of folding chairs, one in each hand.

"I won't be able to see if I sit down," she whispered.

"Then stand on it," he said as he flicked the chairs open and set them down on the cement floor.

With a grin of thanks, Brenda clambered up on a chair. Oxnard climbed up beside her.

"I thought you were back at Malibu," she said, without taking her eyes from the two minor actors who were going through their lines under the lights.

"Couldn't stay there," he replied. "Kept fidgeting. Guess

I wanted to see how the equipment works the first day. And I've got some new ideas to discuss with you, when you have some free time."

"Business ideas?"

He looked at her and Brenda saw a mixture of surprise, hurt and anticipation in his face.

With a slow nod, he replied, "Uh, yes . . . business ideas."

"Fine," said Brenda.

The actors were clomping across the bridge set, pronouncing their lines and fiddling with the props that were supposed to be the starship's controls. Out of the corner of her eye, Brenda could see Oxnard shaking his head and muttering to himself.

"What's the matter?" she whispered.

"The lights. I told them we don't need so much wattage with this holographic system. They're going to wash out everything . . . the tape will be overexposed."

"Can't they take care of that electronically, up in the control booth?"

"Up to a point. I just wish they'd listen to what I tell them. Once, at least."

His teeth were clenched and he looked very unhappy.

"It'll be all right," she said soothingly.

Oxnard grimaced and jabbed a finger toward the actors. "You don't use an astrolabe for navigating a starship! I *told* Earnest and the rest of them . . . why don't they *listen?*"

Mitch Westerly wasn't worried about the astrolabe or any other technical details. His head was still buzzing from last night's high. Faced with the first day's shooting, he hadn't been able to get to sleep without help. Which came in the form of pills that floated him up among the stars and then dumped him on the cement floor of the studio with a bad case of shakes.

Liven it up, you guys! he ordered the actors, mentally.

We don't have time or money for retakes. Put some life into it.

"We haven't seen any signs of the Capulet starship since we left Rigel Six," said the first bit player, pronouncing "Wriggle" instead of "Rye-gel."

"Maybe they never got away from the planet," spoke the second, as if he were being forced to repeat the words at gunpoint. "They were having trouble with their engines, weren't they?"

With some feeling! Westerly pleaded silently.

"I'll check the radars," said Actor One.

"Cut!" Westerly yelled.

Both actors looked blankly toward him. "What's the matter?"

Westerly strode out onto the set. He felt the glare of the lights on his shoulders like a palpable force.

"The word in the script is 'scanners,' not 'radar,'" Westerly said, squinting in the light despite his shades.

The actor shrugged. "What's the difference?"

Ron Gabriel came trotting up. "What's the difference? You're supposed to be seven hundred years in the future, dim-dum! They don't use radar anymore!"

The actor was tall and lanky. When he shrugged, it looked like a construction crane stirring into motion. "Aww, who's gonna know the difference?"

Gabriel started hopping up and down. "*I'll* know the difference! And so will anybody with enough brains in his head to find the men's room without a seeing-eye dog!"

Westerly placed a calming hand on the writer's shoulder. "Don't get worked up, Ron."

"Don't get worked up?"

Turning back to the actor, Westerly said, "The word is *scanners.*"

"Scanners." Sullenly.

"Scanners," Westerly repeated. "And you two guys are supposed to be joking around, throwing quips at each other. Try to get some life into your lines."

"Scanners," the actor repeated.

Westerly went back to his position next to the Number One camera unit. The script girl—a nondescript niece of somebody's who spoke nothing but French—pointed to the place in the scene where they had stopped.

"Okay," Westerly said, with a deep breath. "Let's take it from . . . 'Maybe they never got away from that planet.' With life." *Cat,* he said to himself. *I've got to find some cat or I'll never sleep again.*

Ron Gabriel was trying not to listen. He prowled around the edges of the clustered crew, peeking between electricians and idle actors as they stood watching the scene being taped. *They're mangling my words,* he knew. *They're taking the words I wrote and grinding them up in a cement mixer. Whatever's left, they're putting into a blender and then beating it with a stick when it comes crawling out.*

He felt as if he himself was being treated the same way. He paced doggedly, his back to the lighted set.

Farther back, away from the action, Brenda and Oxnard were standing on their chairs, watching. Off to one side, Rita Yearling reclined on her couch, the one Finger had flown up from Hollywood for her.

Gabriel stopped pacing and stared at her. *If it wasn't for her,* he thought, *I'd have walked out on this troop of baboons long ago. Maybe I ought to split anyway. She's a terrific lay, but. . . .*

Rita must have felt him watching her. She looked up and smiled beckoningly. Gabriel went over to her side and hunkered down on his heels.

"Nervous?" he asked her.

Her eyes were extraordinarily blue today and they widened with girlish surprise. "Nervous? Why should I be nervous? I know all my lines. I could say them backwards."

Gabriel frowned. "We've already got one clown who's going to be doing that."

"What do you mean?" Her voice was an innocent child's.

"Dulaq. He's going to get it all ass-backwards. I just know it."

"Oh, he'll be all right," Rita said soothingly. "Don't get yourself flustered."

"He's an idiot. He'll never get through one scene."

Rita smiled and patted Gabriel's cheek. "Francois will be all right. He can be very much in control. He's a take-charge kind of guy."

"How do you know?" Gabriel demanded.

She made her surprised little girl face again, and Gabriel somehow found it irritating this time. "Why, by watching him play hockey, of course. How else?"

Before Gabriel could answer, the assistant director's voice bellowed (assistant directors are hired for their lungpower): "Okay, set up for Scene Two, Dulaq and Yearling, front and center."

"I've got to go to work," Rita said, swinging her exquisite legs off the couch.

"Yeah," said Gabriel.

"Wish me luck."

"Break a fibia."

She blew him a kiss and slinked off toward the set. Gabriel watched her disappear among the technicians and actors, and suddenly realized that her walk, which used to be enough to engorge all his erectile tissue, didn't affect him that way anymore. The thrill was gone. With a rueful shake of his head, he walked toward the set like Jimmy Cagney heading bravely down the Last Mile toward the little green door.

> *Scene Two:* Int., starship bridge. BEN is sitting at the control console, watching the viewscreens as the ship flies through the interstellar void at many times the speed of light. On the viewscreens we see nothing but scattered stars against the blackness of space.

BEN

(To himself.) Guess we've shaken
off those Capulets. Haven't seen
another ship within a hundred
parsecs of us.

ROM enters. He is upset, despondent. (Tell
Dulaq that the Redwings will win the Stanley
Cup next year; that should work him up enough
for this scene.) He glances at the viewscreens,
then goes to BEN and stands beside him.

BEN

(Looking up at Rom.) Greetings,
cousin. How are you this day?

ROM

Not as good. (Shakes his head)

BEN

What's the trouble, cousin?

ROM

I dunno. Must'a been somet'in I
picked up back on Rigel Six.
Maybe a bug. . . .

"*Cut!*"

"Francois . . . the script says 'virus,' not 'bug.' "

"Ahh. 'bug' sounds better. I don't like all dose fancy
words."

"Try to say 'virus,' will you? And watch your diction."

"My what?"

"Your pronunciation!"

"Hey, you want me to say all dose funny words and
pernounce everyt'ing your way? At de same time? Come
on!"

"Take it from, 'What's the trouble, cousin.' "

BEN
What's the trouble, cousin?

ROM
I dunno. Must'a been somet'in I picked up back on Rigel Six. Maybe a b...a virus or somet'ing.

BEN
(With a grin.) Or that Capulet girl you were eyeing, Julie.

ROM grabs BEN's lapels and lifts him out of his chair.

ROM
(With some heat.) Hey, I don't mess around with Capulets. Dey're our enemies!

BEN
(Frightened.) Okay ... okay! I was only joking.

ROM
(Lets him go. He drops back into his seat.) Some t'ings you shouldn't kid about. ... Go on back and grab somet'ing to eat. I'll take over.

BEN
(Glad to get away.) Sure. It's all yours, cousin.

BEN hurries off-camera. ROM sits at the command console, stares out at the stars.

> ROM
> (Pensively.) All dose stars . . . all
> dat emptiness. I wish she was right
> here, instead of back on Rigel Six.

JULIE steps out from behind the electronic computer, where she's been hiding since she stowed
away on the Montague starship.

> JULIE
> (Shyly.) I *am* here, ROM. I stowed
> away aboard your ship.

> ROM
> (Dumbfounded.) You . . . you . . .
> Hey, Mitch, what th'hell's my next
> line?

"Cut!!!"

From up in the control booth, Les Montpelier kept
telling himself, *It's not as bad as it looks. They'll fix up all
the goofs in the editing process. Maybe we can even get
somebody to dub a voice over Dulaq's lines. He looks
pretty good, at least.*

At that moment, Dulaq was pointing to the blank side
wall of the set, where the Capulets' starship would be
matted in on the final tape.

"How'd your ship catch up wit' us so soon?" he was
asking Rita Yearling. But he was looking neither at her
nor the to-be-inserted view of the other starship. He was
peering, squint-eyed, toward Mitch Westerly. The director
had his face sunk in his hands, as if he were crying.

"Rita looks stunning," said Gregory Earnest, with a
hyena's leer on his face.

"She sure does," Montpelier agreed. "But there's something wrong about her . . . something. . . ."

Rita's face was all dewy-cheeked youth, her eyes wide and blue as a new spring sky. But her body was adult seductress and she slinked around the set with the practiced undulations of a bellydancer.

". . . something about her that doesn't seem quite right for the character she's supposed to be playing," Montpelier finished.

"The audience will love her," Earnest said. "We've got to give them a little pizzazz."

Montpelier started to answer, but hesitated. *Maybe he's right.*

"And Dulaq looks magnificent," the Canadian went on. "Look at that costume. Shows plenty of muscles, doesn't it?" Earnest's voice was almost throbbing with delight.

"Too bad it doesn't cover his mouth," Montpelier said.

Earnest shot him an angry glance.

On the set, Dulaq was staring off into space. He thought he was looking at the red light of an active camera unit, as Westerly had instructed him to do. Actually, he was fixing his gaze on a red EXIT sign glowing in the darkness on the other end of the huge studio. Dulaq's eyes weren't all that good.

"I know it's wrong," he was saying, "But I love you, Julie. I'm mad about you."

Rita was entwining herself about his muscular frame, like a snake climbing a tree.

"And I love you, Rom darling," she breathed. The boom microphone, over her head, seemed to wilt in the heat of her torridly low-pitched voice.

"That's a shy, innocent young girl?" Montpelier asked rhetorically.

Dulaq finally focused his ruggedly handsome gaze on her, as their noses touched. Suddenly he gave a strangled growl and clutched at her. Rita shrieked and they both went tumbling to the floor.

"Cut!" Mitch Westerly yelled. "Cut!"

The cameramen were grinning and training their equipment on the squirming couple. Then, out of the crowd, came a blur of fury.

Ron Gabriel leaped on Dulaq's back and started pounding the hockey star's head. "Leggo of her, you goddamn ape!" he screamed.

It took Dulaq several moments to notice what was happening to him. Then, with a roar, he swung around and flipped Gabriel off his back. The writer staggered to his knees, got up quickly and launched himself at Dulaq.

With a surprised look on his face, Dulaq took Gabriel's charge. The writer's head rammed into his stomach, but produced nothing except a slight "Oof" which might have come from either one of them. Gabriel rebounded, looking a bit glassy eyed. He charged at Dulaq again and kicked him in the shins, hard.

It finally seemed to penetrate Dulaq's head that he was being attacked by someone who had no hockey stick in his hands. The athlete's face relaxed into a pleasant grin as he picked Gabriel up off his feet with one hand and socked him between the eyes so hard that the writer sailed completely off the set while his shirt remained in Dulaq's left fist.

Pandemonium raged. The only recognizable sound to come out of the roiling crowd on the set was Westerly, pathetically screaming "Cut! Cut!"

Montpelier and the technicians in the control booth bolted out the door and down the steps to the floor of the studio. Gregory Earnest sat in the darkened booth alone, watching the riot develop, and smiled to himself.

He knew at last how to get rid of Ron Gabriel. And how to cash in on what little money would be made by "The Starcrossed."

12: THE SQUEEZE PLAY

Gregory Earnest's home was a modest ranch house in one of the new developments between Badger Studio and the busy Toronto International Jetport. Although nearly half the expense of the house had gone into insulation—thermal and acoustic—the entire place still rumbled and shivered with the infrasonic, barely audible vibrations of the big jets screaming by just over the roof.

The living quarters were actually underground, in what was originally the basement level. Earnest had spent many weekends digging, cementing, enlarging the underground portion of the house, until now—after five years' occupancy—he had a network of bunkers that would have made Adolf Hitler feel homesick. His wife made all her neighbors envious with tales of Gregory's single-minded handiness and devotion to home improvement. While she turned the neighborhood women green and they nagged their husbands, Earnest dug with the dedication of a Prisoner of War, happily alone and free of his wife and their two milk-spilling, runny-nosed, grammar-school children.

Les Montpelier was a little puzzled when he first rang Earnest's doorbell. It was Sunday, the studio was still closed for repairs. Ron Gabriel had left the hospital with two black eyes and several painfully cracked ribs, but no broken bones. Francois Dulaq had a bruised hand and some interesting bite marks on his upper torso. Rita Yearling was doing television talk shows all weekend, back in the States. Mitch Westerly had disappeared under a cloud of marijuana smoke.

Montpelier was not in the jauntiest of moods. "The

Starcrossed" was a dead duck, he knew, even before the second day of shooting in the studio. It was hopeless.

Yet Gregory Earnest obviously had something optimistic in mind when he had called Montpelier at the hotel.

So, puzzled and depressed, with a microfilm copy of the *LA Free Press-News-Times* Sunday help wanted ad section in the pocket of his severely styled mod Edgar Allen Poe business suit, he leaned on the bell button of Earnest's front door. A jumbo jet came screaming up from what seemed like a few meters away, making the very ground shake with the roar of its mighty engines, and spewing fumes and excess kerosene in its wake. Montpelier suddenly realized why the lawns looked so greasy. He was glad that his suit was dead black.

The door opened and he was greeted by a smiling Eskimo. At least, she looked like an Eskimo. Her round face was framed by a furry hood. Her coat was trimmed with antlered designs from the far north. She smiled and moved her mouth, but Montpelier couldn't hear a word over the rumbling whine of the dwindling jet.

"Can't hear you," he said and found that he couldn't even hear himself.

They stood in the doorway smiling awkwardly at each other for a few minutes as the jet flew off into the distance.

"You must be Mr. Montpelier," said the round-faced woman. Her accent was more Oxford than igloo and Montpelier realized that her face really had none of the oriental flatness of an Eskimo's.

"I'm Gwendoline Earnest, Gregory's wife. I was just taking Gulliver and Gertrude to the skating rink. . . ."

Two more Eskimos appeared. Little ones, round and furry in their plastiskin parkas. It wasn't that cold outside, Montpelier realized. *Maybe Eskimo is the next big style trend.*

Gwendoline Earnest shooed her two little ones out and down the driveway. "Greg's down in the study, waiting for you," she said, squeezing past Montpelier at the doorway. She started down the driveway toward the minibus parked at the curb. "And thank you," she called over her shoulder, "for taking him away from his eternal digging for one Sunday! It's such a pleasure not to hear the pounding and the swearing!"

She waved a cheery "Ta-ta!" and pushed the kids into the yawning side door of the minibus.

With a bewildered shake of his head, Montpelier stepped inside what he thought would be the house's living room. It looked more like an attic. There were bicycles, toys, crates, suitcases, piles of books and spools of videotape. Another jetliner roared overhead; even with the front door closed, the ear-splitting sound made Montpelier's teeth ache.

He threaded his way through the maze of junk, looking for a living area. The entire house seemed to be cluttered with storage materials.

It took ten minutes of shouting back and forth before Montpelier tumbled to the fact that Earnest—and the real living quarters—were downstairs in the erstwhile basement. Another few minutes to find the right door and the stairs leading down, then the usual meaningless words of greeting, and Montpelier found himself sitting in a comfortable panelled den, in a large overstuffed chair, with a beer in his hand.

Gregory Earnest sat across the corner from him, equally at ease with a beer mug in one hand. It had an old corporation logo on it: GE. *Gregory, Gwendoline, Gulliver and Gertrude Earnest,* Montpelier reflected. *He must've bought a case of those mugs when the antitrust boys broke up old GE.*

In the opposite corner of the den, the three-dee set was tuned to the National Football League's game of the week. Montpelier couldn't tell who was playing: all he saw was a miniature set of armored players tumbling and grunting across the other side of Earnest's den, like Lilliputian buffoons who'd been hired to entertain a sadistic king. Only the scintillations and shimmerings of the imperfect three-dee projection betrayed the fact that they were watching holographic images, rather than real, solid, miniature figures.

Earnest touched a button in the keyboard that was set into the arm of his recliner chair and the sound of pain and cheering disappeared. But the game went on.

"Imagine how terrific the games will look," Earnest said in his nasal, oily way of speaking, "when Oxnard's new system is used. Then you can buy giant-sized three-dee tubes. It'll look like you're right there on the field with them."

Montpelier nodded. There was something about Earnest that always disturbed him. The man was too sly, too roundabout. He'd fit in well at Titanic.

Earnest was wearing a pullover sweater and an ancient pair of patched jeans. He seemed utterly a ease, smiling. Montpelier was reminded of the cobra and the mongoose, but he didn't know who was supposed to be which.

"You look relaxed and happy," Montpelier said.

Earnest's smile showed more teeth. "Why shouldn't I be?"

After a sip of beer, Montpelier said, "If I were the producer of a show that started off as disastrously as 'The Starcrossed' did last week. . . ."

"Oh that." Earnest made a nonchalant gesture. "I wouldn't worry about that."

"No?"

"Why worry? Is B.F. worried?"

"He sure is," Montpelier said. "He almost went into shock when I told him what happened in the studio."

"Really?"

Earnest's voice got so arch that Montpelier found himself getting angry, something he never did with a potential ally. Or enemy. It was a luxury you couldn't afford in this business. Not if you wanted to survive.

"What are you driving at?" Montpelier asked, trying to keep his voice level.

Earnest nodded toward the three-dee game that still rolled and thudded across the far side of the den.

"The Pineapples," he said. "They're winning."

"So?"

"So long as they keep winning, B.F.'s money is safe. Right?"

Montpelier fought down a gnawing panic. Either Earnest had completely flipped, which was not too unlikely, and was now certifiably insane—or he knew something that he himself didn't know, which was a very dangerous position for Montpelier to be in.

"Are, ah . . . you betting on the Pineapples?" he fished.

"Sure I am. Especially since I found out that B.F. is sinking almost all his cash into them. When they win the title, we can forget about 'The Starcrossed.' Won't matter if the show never goes beyond the first seven weeks."

Slowly, without revealing how little he actually knew, Montpelier coaxed the story out of Earnest. It wasn't difficult. The Canadian was very proud of himself. He had some friends in the local phone company tap all the special three-dee phones that Finger had installed in the various hotel suites. Montpelier was suddenly grateful that he didn't rank high enough for such luxury. Only Westerly, Gabriel and Yearling had them. And Gabriel got one only because he screamed and threw tantrums until Brenda put through a call to Finger's office.

"You should hear the conversations between Rita and B.F.," Earnest said, licking his chops. "And *see* the display she puts on for him. In three-dee yet! I've got some of them taped, you know."

Montpelier guided him back to the main subject. "So as long as the Pineapples keep winning their football games, Titanic's cash is safe."

"Right," Earnest answered. "And 'The Starcrossed' is just a front operation to keep those New York bankers convinced that B.F. has invested their money in a show."

"So the show gets as little money as possible. . . ."

"Sure. Just enough to keep it going. Oh, I think B.F. really wants to make Rita into a star . . . but that doesn't mean he's going to spend more than he has to. Just enough to get her on The Tube for a few weeks and see how the public reacts to her."

"Yeah, that sound like B.F.'s way of doing business," Montpelier agreed.

But Earnest had turned his attention to the football game. One of the miniature players was scampering like mad and other players were chasing after him while the background whizzed past. Yet none of them actually moved very far across Earnest's floor. It was like watching midgets struggling on a treadmill.

"The Pineapples just intercepted another pass!" Earnest was chortling. "I *knew* those Mexicans couldn't play our style of football!"

Montpelier leaned over and nudged his shoulder. "I didn't come here to watch a football game. You said you had something important to tell me."

Earnest's smile went nasty. "That's right. What do you think would happen if those New York bankers found out what B.F.'s doing with their money? Those banks are *Mafioso,* you know. The mob owns the banks and the WASPS are just frontmen."

Montpelier didn't answer. But he had figured out which of them was the cobra.

"Now, I happen to be smart enough," Earnest went on, "To understand what's going on in B.F.'s mind. 'The Starcrossed' is *supposed* to flop. When it does, B.F. will tell his bankers that the show went broke and their investment is down the drain. Maybe they'll get Rita or some other goods as a booby prize." He grinned at his feeble pun.

"That's crazy. . . ."

"Is it?" Earnest shrugged, then scratched at his beard. "Maybe so. But it would make a fun story in New York, don't you think?"

"If anybody believed you. . . ."

"They would. But why should I cut off the hand that feeds me? Especially when it's going to feed me so well."

"You mean blackmail."

Earnest shook he head. "No, That's not nice. And it could be risky. No, you just tell B.F. that I understand what he wants and I'm willing to help him. It won't cost him an extra cent."

"What do you want?"

"Nothing very much. I'll bet on the Pineapples, too. Maybe he can put me in touch with his own brokers, so that I can get the same rates he does."

From the inflection in Earnest's voice, Montpelier knew that there was more.

"And what else?" he asked.

"Oh nothing much, really." Earnest spread his arms out, expansively. "Just control of the show. I *am* the Executive Producer, after all. All I want is complete authority. I want to do the hiring and firing. All of it. From here on. With no interference from you or Brenda or anybody at Titantic."

"Complete authority," Montpelier echoed.

"Right. I can handle Westerly. He's through as a director, but he still has a good name. I can keep him supplied with enough cat to make him docile. . . ."

"Cat?" Montpelier's insides winced, as if they'd been electroshocked.

"Oh, it's all completely legal," Earnest assured him. "I have a few friends at the hospital here who'll make out prescriptions for him. I get a cut of their fees and the pharmacy price, of course; cat's *very* expensive stuff, you know. But that'll keep Westerly happy and under control."

Montpelier found that his hands were shaking.

"And then there's Gabriel," Earnest said with relish. "He goes. I'm going to fire his ass right out of here so fast he won't know what hit him."

"Now wait . . . we need him for the scripts. Those high school kids can't turn out shootable scripts and you know it."

"I can find a dozen writers who'll work for *free*," Earnest crowed, "just for the glory of getting their names on The Tube. The local science fiction writers' chapter has plenty of people who'll gladly fill in."

"But Gabriel has talent! His scripts are the only decent thing we've got going for us!"

"Who cares?" The show's not supposed to be a hit. Get that through your skull. Think of it as a tax writeoff."

Montpelier felt his jaw muscles clenching. "But Ron is. . . ."

"Ron Gabriel is out!" Earnest shouted, a vein on his forehead throbbing visibly. "His scripts are out, too. Wait until the network censors see them! There won't be enough left to wipe your backside with."

"But the censors have already. . . ."

"No they haven't," Earnest said, with the most malicious grin Montpelier had ever seen. "Gabriel was so late turning them in. . . ."

"That's because he had to work on all the other scripts."

". . . that I let the crew start up production *before* sending the scripts to the censors. I'll be meeting with them tomorrow. And with the sponsor's representatives, too. *That* will finish Mr. Gabriel and his high-and-mighty scripts!"

"But. . . ."

"And what do you think B.F. is going to say about Gabriel when I tell him how he's been sacking with Rita all these weeks, behind his back?"

"It hasn't been exactly behind his back."

Earnest smiled another chilling smile. "I know that, and you know that, and B.F. knows that. But what will the gossip programs say about it? Eh? Can B.F. afford to have his image belittled in public?"

Calling this character a snake is insulting the snakes, Montpelier told himself. But he said nothing.

"Come on," Earnest said, suddenly very hearty and full of beery good cheer. "Don't look so glum. We're all going to make a good pile of money out of this. So what if the series folds early? We'll cry all the way to the bank."

For the first time in many years, Montpelier found himself contradicting one of his primary survival rules. Out of the depth of his guts, he spoke his feelings:

"I'd always heard that the rats were the first to leave a sinking ship. But I never realized that some of the rats are the sonsofbitches that scuttled the ship in the first place."

13: THE THREE MONKIES

The restaurant was poised atop Toronto's tallest office tower, balanced delicately on a well-oiled mechanism that smoothly turned the entire floor around in a full circle once every half hour. It was too slow to be called a merry-go-round, so the restaurant management (it was part of an American-owned chain) called it the Roundeley Room.

The building was very solidly constructed, since there were no earthquakes fears so close to the Laurentian Shield. Since the world wide impact of a theater movie a generation earlier, dealing with a fire in a glass tower, there were sprinklers everywhere—in the ceilings, under the tables of the restaurant, in the elevators and restrooms and even along the walls, cleverly camouflaged as wrought iron decorations.

The restaurant was up high enough so that on a clear day, diners could see the gray-brown smudge across Lake Ontario that marked the slums of Buffalo. To the north, they could watch the city of Toronto peter out into muskeg and dreary housing developments.

The weather had turn cold, with an icy wind howling down from the tundra. But it was a clear, dry cold, the kind of air meteorologists call an Arctic High. Air crisp enough to shatter like crystal.

From his seat in a soundproofed booth, Les Montpelier watched the last rays of the sinking sun turn the city into a vermillion fantasyland. Lights were winking on; automobile traffic made a continuous ribbon of white light on one side of the highways, red on the other. Safely behind the insulated windows, Montpelier could hear the polar wind whispering past. But he felt warm and comfortable. Physically.

"It's a beautiful view," said the man across the booth from him.

"That it is," Montpelier agreed.

The man was Elton Good, who had flown up from New York. He was a tall, spare, almost cadaverous man in that indistinct age category between Saturday afternoon softball games and Saturday afternoon checkers games. His eyes were alive, deep brown, sparkling. He wore an almost perpetual smile, but it looked more like an apology than anything joyful. His clothes were straight Madison Avenue chic—neo-Jesuit, minus the religious icons, of course.

Elton Good worked for the Federal Inter-Network Combine (FINC), the quasipublic, quasigovernmental, quasicorporate overview group that interconnected the rulings of the Federal Communications Commission, the pressures of the Consumer Relations Board, the demands of the national networks, and the letters from various PTA and religious groups. Since network executives usually filled the posts of the FCC and CRB, the job wasn't as taxing as it might sound to an outsider.

Elton Good was a censor. His job was to make certain that nothing disturbing to the public, contrary to FCC regulations or harmful to network profits got onto The Tube.

"Is Mr. Gabriel always this late?" Good asked, with a slight edge to his reedy voice.

Montpelier couldn't reconcile the voice with the sweetly smiling face. "He had to stop at the hospital. They're taking the bandages off his face."

"Oh, yes . . . that . . . brawl he got himself into." Good

edged back away from the table slightly, as if he might become contaminated by it all. "Very ugly business. Very ugly."

This is going to be some dinner, Montpelier knew.

In another soundproofed booth, across the restaurant, Brenda Impanema was smiling at Keith Connors, third assistant vice president for marketing of Texas New Technology, Inc.

Connors wore a Confederate-gray business suit, hand-tooled Mexican boots, and had an RAF mustache that curled up almost to the corners of his eyes.

"I knew I'd spot y'all in the middle of a crowded restaurant even though I'd never see y'all befoah," he was saying. "I jes' tole myself, Keith, ol' buddy, y'all jes' go lookin' for the purtiest gal in the place. These Canadian chicks don't have the class of California gals."

Brenda smiled demurely. "Actually, I was born in New Mexico."

"Hey! That's practically in Texas! No wonder yo're so purty."

Connors was beaming at her, the glow of his toothy smile outshining the candle on their table by several orders of magnitude. He had already shown Brenda holograms of his Mexican wife and their six children—all under seven years of age. "Guess I'm jes' a powerful ol' lover," he had smirked when she commented on the size of his family.

Brenda hadn't quite known what to expect of the executive from TNT. Bernard Finger had called her that afternoon and ordered her to have dinner with the man and show him some of Toronto's night life.

"TNT could take over sponsorship of the whole show, all by themselves," Finger had said. "They're big and they're not afraid to spend money."

Brenda glowered at Titanic's chief. "How nice do you want me to be to him?"

Finger glowered back at her. "You get paid for using your brains, not your pelvis. There's plenty action for a

Texas cowboy in town. You just show him where the waterholes are."

So she had dressed in a demure, translucent knee-length gown and decorated it with plenty of the electronic jewelry that TNT manufactured. As she sat in the booth, silhouetted against the gathering twilight, she glittered like an airport runway.

"Yessir, you shore are purty," Connors said, with a puppydog wag in his voice.

"Do you think," Brenda asked coolly, "that your company will want to advertise your electronic jewelry on 'The Starcrossed?' Seems like a natural, to me."

The booths at the Roundeley Room were soundproofed so that private conversations could not be overheard, and also to protect the restaurant's patrons from the noisy entrances made by some customers.

Gloria Glory swept into the restaurant's foyer, flanked by Francois Dulaq, Rita Yearling and Gregory Earnest. The effect was stunning.

Once a regally tall, statuesque woman, Gloria Glory had allowed many years of success as a gossip columnist to freeze her self-image. While she still thought of herself as regal and statuesque, to the outside world she closely resembled an asthmatic dirigible swathed in neon-bright floor-length robes.

No one ever told her this, of course, because her power to make or destroy something as fragile as a "show-business personality" was enormous. In the delicate world of the entertainment arts, where talent and experience counted for about a tenth of what publicity and perseverance could get for you, Gloria Glory possessed a megatonnage unapproached by any other columnist. Her viewers were fanatically devoted to her: what Gloria said was "in" was *in;* who she said was "out" went hungry.

So words such as *fat, overweight* and *diet* had long since disappeared from Gloria's world. They were as unspoken near her as descriptions of nasal protuberances went unsaid near Cyrano de Bergerac.

The maitre d', the hatcheck girl, two headwaiters who usually did nothing but stand near the entrance and look imperious, and a dozen other customers all clustered around Gloria and her entourage.

The hatcheck girl and most of the customers were asking Dulaq for his autograph. They recognized the hockey star's handsome face, his rugged physique, and his name spelled on the back of the All-Canadian All-Stars team jacket that he was wearing.

The headwaiters and most of the men in the growing crowd were panting around Rita Yearling, who wore a see-through clingtight dress with nothing under it except her own impressive physique. The traffic jam was beginning to cause a commotion and block the newcomers who were piling up at the head of the escalator.

The maitre d', with the unerring instinct of the breed, gravitated toward Gloria Glory. He had never seen her before and never watched televison. But he knew money when he sniffed it. Calmly ignoring the rising tide of shrieks and curses from the top of the escalator as body tumbled upon body, he gave Gloria the utmost compliment: he didn't ask if she had a reservation.

"Madam would prefer a private room, perhaps?"

Gregory Earnest, roundly ignored by all present, started to say, "I made a reserva. . . ."

But Gloria's foghorn voice drowned him out. "Naah . . . I like to be right in the middle of all the hustle and bustle. How about something right in the center of everything?"

"Of course," said the maitre d'.

Gloria swept regally across the crowded restaurant, like a Montgolfier Brothers hot-air balloon trailing pretty little pennants and fluttering ribbons of silk. Earnest and the two stars followed in her wake, while the maitre d' preceded her with the haughty air of Grand Vizier. The jumbled, tumbled, grumbling crowd at the top of the escalator was left to sort itself out. After all, that's what insurance lawyers were for, was it not?

Montpelier couldn't hear the shouts and shrieks from the foyer, of course. But he watched Gloria and her entourage march to the table nearest the computer-directed jukebox. He breathed a silent thanksgiving that Gabriel hadn't arrived at the same time as Earnest.

"Um, would you like a drink, Mr. Good?" he asked.

Good held up a long-fingered hand. "Never touch alcohol, Mr. Montpelier. . . ."

"Les."

"Alcohol and business don't mix. Never have."

"Well, that's one thing you and Ron Gabriel have in common," Montpelier said.

"Oh? What's that?"

"He doesn't drink, either."

"Really?" Good's perpetual smile got wider and somehow tenser. "That's a surprise."

"What do you mean?"

"From all the depravity in his scripts, I assumed he was either an alcoholic or a drug fiend. Or both."

"Depravity?" Montpelier heard his voice squeak.

"Yer not married or nuthin', are yew?" asked Connors.

Brenda shook her head slowly. "No, I'm a rising young corporate executive."

He was working on his second bourbon and water. Their dinners remained on a corner of the table, untouched.

"Must be tough to get ahead. Lotsa competition."

"Quite a bit." Brenda sipped at her vodka sour.

"If TNT sponsored yer new show, it'd be a real feather in yore cap, huh?"

"Yes it would. But I won't go to bed with you for it."

Connor's face fell. "Wh . . . who said anything about *that?* I'm a married man!"

Now Brenda permitted herself to smile again. "I'm sorry," she said with great sincerity. "I didn't mean to shock you. But, well . . . there are lots of men who try to take advantage of a woman in a situation like this. I'm glad you're not that kind of man."

"Hell no," said Connors, looking puzzled, disappointed and slightly nettled.

Brenda sweetened her smile. *Have to introduce him to some of the professional ladies working at the hotel*, she knew, *before he decides to get angry.*

Earnest sat across the table from Dulaq. Between the two men sat Gloria Glory and Rita Yearling. Four appetizers had been served; two were still sitting untouched, but Dulaq's and Gloria's were already demolished.

"And you, you great big hunk of muscle," Gloria turned to Dulaq, "how do you like acting?"

The hockey star shrugged. "It's okay. Ain't had a chance t'really do much . . . wit' the riot and all. . . ."

Earnest felt his blood pressure explode in his ears.

"Riot?" Gloria looked instantly alert. "What riot?"

"It wasn't a *riot*," Earnest said quickly. "It was just a bit of a misunderstanding. . . ."

"I'm afraid it was all my fault," Rita offered.

"Dis Gabriel guy gimme a hard time, so I punched him out."

"You *hit* Ron Gabriel?"

For an instant there was absolute silence at the table. Even Dulaq seemed to realize, in his dim way, that Gloria's reaction would have enormous implications for his future in show business.

"Uh . . . yeah. Once. Between de eyes."

Gloria's bloated face seemed to puff out even more and she suddenly let loose a loud guffaw. "Oh no! You punched that little creep between the eyes! Oh, it's *too* marvelous!" She roared with laughter.

Dulaq and Rita joined in. Earnest laughed too, but his mind was racing. Fearfully, he touched Gloria's bouffant sleeve. She wiped tears from her eyes as she turned to him.

"Um, Gloria," he begged. "You're not going to, uh . . . broadcast this, are you?"

"Broadcast it? Ron Gabriel getting what he's always asking for? It's too delicious!"

"Yes, but it could, well . . . it could reflect poorly on the show."

Gloria put her napkin to her lips and for a wild instant Earnest thought she was going to devour it. But instead she wiped her mouth and then flapped the napkin in Earnest's direction, saying:

"Greg . . . you don't mind me calling you Greg, do you?"

Earnest hated being called Greg, but he said, "No, of course not."

"All right, Greg, now listen. It has always been my policy to speak no evil of the people I like. I like Bernie Finger and I *love* this heavyweight champion you've got here. . . ." She nodded in Dulaq's direction. "And you've got a lovely new starlet. She's going to be a winner, I know. So, no matter how much I loathe Gabriel, I won't breathe a word about the fight over the air."

Earnest sighed. "Oh, thank you, Gloria."

"Nothing to it. You *are* getting rid of the little creep, though, aren't you?"

"Oh we certainly are," Earnest assured her. "He's on his way out. Never fear."

Ron Gabriel, meanwhile, had arrived and let himself be led quietly to Les Montpelier's booth. He didn't see Gloria, Earnest, *et. al.*, mainly because he was wearing dark glasses and the restaurant's twilight lighting level was quite dim. As it was, Gabriel had a little difficulty following the head waiter who showed him to the booth. He tripped over a step and bumped into a waitress on the way. He cursed at the step and made a date with the girl.

As he slid into the booth, he said, "I'm not eating anything. They just pumped me so full of antibiotics at the hospital that all I want to do is go home and sleep. Let's just talk business and skip the socializing."

Before Montpelier could respond, Elton Good pulled a thick wad of notes from his jacket pocket.

"Very well, Mr. Gabriel. I like a man who speaks his

mind. There are eighty-seven changes that need to be made in your script before it's acceptable to FINC."

"Eighty-seven?"

Good nodded smilingly. "Yes. And as you know, heh-heh, without FINC's mark of approval, your script cannot be shown on American television."

"Eighty-motherloving-seven," Gabriel moaned.

"Here's the first of them," said Good, peering at his notes in the dim lighting. His smile widened. "Ah, yes . . . when you have the character Rom standing behind the character Ben, who's sitting at the command console, I believe. . . ."

"That's in the second scene," Montpelier murmured.

"Yes. Rom puts his hand on Ben's shoulder . . . that's got to come out."

"Huh? Why?"

Good's smile turned sickening. "Can't you see? It's too suggestive. One man standing behind another man and then touching him on the shoulder! Children will be watching this show, after all!"

Gabriel looked across the table at Montpelier. Even though half the writer's face was covered by dark glasses, Montpelier could read anguish and despair in his expression.

"I shorely do love my wife," Connors was telling Brenda, between bites of steak. "But, well, hell honey . . . I travel an awful lot. And I'm not exactly repulsive. When I see somethin' I like, I don't turn my back to it."

"That's understandable," Brenda said. She toyed with her salad for a moment, then asked, "And what does your wife do while you're away on all these business trips?"

He dropped his fork into his lap. "Whattaya mean?"

Brenda widened her eyes. "I mean, does she fill in the time with volunteer work or social clubs or at the golf course? She doesn't stay home with the children *all* the time, does she?"

Connors scowled at her. "No, I reckon she doesn't. We

belong to the country club. And she's a voluntary librarian, over t'the school."

"I see."

He retrieved his fork and studied it for a moment, then changed the subject as he went back to the attack on his steak. "I wanted t'get yore opinion about how many TNT products we can use on the show? As props, I mean."

"Well," Brenda said, "the action's supposed to be taking place seven hundred years in the future. I don't think too many existing products will be in keeping with the scenario. . . ."

Connors' face brightened. "They'll still be usin' wrist-watches, won't they? We make wristwatches. And pocket radios, calculators, all sorts of stuff."

"Yes, but if they're the same products that are being advertised during the commercial breaks, then the viewers will. . . ."

"Well, spit, why not? The viewers'll think that TNT's stuff's so good people'll still be usin' 'em seven hunnert years from now. That's terrific!"

"I don't know if that will work. . . ."

"Shore it will. And I'll tell yew somethin' else, honey. I don't want any shows about computers breakin' down or goin' crazy or any of that kinda stuff. We make computers that *don't* break down or go crazy and we ain't gonna sponsor any show that says otherwise."

Brenda nodded. "I can understand that."

"And where do you get your hair done?" Gloria Glory was asking Rita.

Earnest watched with growing concern as the two women chatted about clothes, hairdos, cosmetics, vitamins. *Is Gloria probing Rita to find out about her real age? Does she know about Rita's earlier life and her Vitaform Processing?*

Across the table from him, Dulaq was demolishing a haunch of venison, using both hands to get at the meat.

If he had thumbs on his feet he'd use those, too, Earnest told himself with an inward wince of distaste.

Then he felt something odd. Something soft and tickly was rubbing against his left ankle. *A cat? Not in a place like this. Don't be absurd.* There it was again, touching his ankle, just above his low-cut boots and below the cuff of his Fabulous Forties trousers.

He pulled his left foot back abruptly. It bumped into something. Glancing surreptitiously down to the floor, Earnest saw the heel of a woman's shoe peeking out from under the tablecloth. A pink shoe. Gloria's shoe. And the tickling, rubbing sensation started on his right ankle.

She's playing toesies with me!

Earnest didn't know what to do. One doesn't rebuff the most powerful columnist in the business. Not if one wanted to remain in the business. Yet. . . .

He frankly stared at Gloria's face. She was still chatting with Rita, eyes focused—glowing, actually—on the beautiful starlet. But her toes were on Earnest's ankle.

Suddenly his stomach heaved. He fought it down, manfully, but the thought of getting any closer to that mountain of female flesh distressed him terribly. *She's fat and ugly and . . . old!* But what really churned his guts was the realization that whatever Gloria wanted, Gloria got. There were no exceptions to the rule; in her own powerful way, she was quite irresistible.

Maybe it's Dulaq she's after. How to let her know she had the wrong ankle? Earnest pondered the problem and decided that the best course of action was a cautious retreat.

Slowly he edged his right foot back toward the safety of his own chair, where his left foot cowered. He tried not to look directly at Gloria as he did so, but out of the corner of his eye he noticed a brief expression of disappointment cross her bloated face.

His feet tucked firmly under his chair, Earnest watched as Gloria squirmed slightly and seemed to sink a little lower in her seat. Dulaq chomped away on his venison, oblivious to everything else around him. *If she's made contact with him,* Earnest raged to himself, *he hasn't even noticed it. He'll ruin us all!*

Rita was saying, "And I take all the megavitamins. Have you tried the new multiple complexes? They're great for your complexion and they give you scads of energy. . . ."

Earnest squeezed his eyes shut with the fierceness of concentrated thought. *If she's after Dulaq and he doesn't pay attention to her, we're all sunk. I'll have to get into the act and* (his stomach lurched) *volunteer for duty with her. At least, she'll be flattered enough to forget about Dulaq.*

Trying not to think of what he'd have to do if Gloria liked him or was after him in the first place, Earnest quietly slipped off one boot and stuck his toes out cautiously toward Dulaq's side of the table.

His stockinged toes bumped into a leg. He quickly pulled back. Trying not to frown, he wished he could see what was going on under the table. Gloria's leg shouldn't be extended so far; she was missing Dulaq entirely, no doubt.

Very carefully, he sent his toes on a scouting mission *around* Gloria's extended foot, trying to find where Dulaq's massive hooves might be. And he bumped into another leg. Rita gave a stifled little yelp as he touched the second leg. It was hers.

Earnest froze. Only his eyes moved and they ping-ponged back and forth between Gloria and Rita. *They're playing toesies with each other!* he realized, horrified.

But from the smiles on both their faces, he saw that he was the only one startled by the idea.

Dulaq kept on eating.

". . . and here in Act Two, shot twenty-seven," Elton Good was saying, "you can't have the girl and the man holding each other and kissing that way. This is a family show."

Montpelier hadn't bothered to order dinner. He kept

a steady flow of beer coming to the table. It was a helluva way to get drunk, but Good didn't seem to consider beer as sinful as hard liquor. Or wine, for some reason. So Montpelier sipped beer and watched the world get fuzzier and fuzzier.

As Ron Gabriel bled to death.

"They can't hug and kiss?" Gabriel was a very lively corpse. He was bouncing up and down as he sat in the booth. The seat cushions complained squawkingly under him. "They're *lovers,* for god's sake. . . ."

"Please!" Good closed his eyes as tightly as his mind. "Do not take the Deity's name in vain."

"What?" It was a noise like a goosed duck.

"You don't seem to understand," Good said with nearly infinite patience, "that children will be watching this show. Impressionable young children."

"So they can't see two adults kissing each other? They can't see an expression of love?"

"It could affect their psyches. It would be an inconsistency in their young lives, watching adults act lovingly toward each other."

Gabriel shot a glance at Montpelier. The executive merely leaned his head on his hand and propped his elbow on the table next to the beer. It was an age-old symbol of noninvolved surrender.

"But . . . but. . . ." Gabriel sputtered and flapped back through several pages of Good's notes, startling the gentleman. ". . . back here in shot seventeen, where the two Capulets beat up the Montague . . . you didn't say anything about that. I was worried about the violence. . . ."

"That's not 'violence,' Mr. Gabriel," Good said, with a knowing condescension in his voice. "That's what is called 'a fight scene.' It's perfectly permissible. Children fight all the time. It won't put unhealthy new ideas into their heads."

"Besides," Montpelier mumbled, "maybe we can get Band-Aids or somebody to sponsor that segment of the show."

Good smiled at him.

"What about the night life in this hyar town?" Connors was asking. "I hear they got bellydancers not far from here."

Brenda nodded. "Yes, that's right. They do."

"Y'all wanna come along with me?"

"I'd love to, but I really can't. We start shooting again tomorrow and I have to get up awfully early."

Connors' normally cheerful face turned sour. "Shee-it, I shore don't like the idea of prowlin' around a strange city all by meself."

Thinking about the Mexican wife and six children back home in Texas, Brenda found herself in a battle with her conscience. She won.

"I'll tell you what, Mr. Connors . . . there are a couple of girls here at the hotel—they're going to be used as extras in some of our later tapings. But they're not working tomorrow." *Not the day shift!* "Would you like me to call one of them for you?"

Connors' face lit up. "Starlets?" he gasped.

Hating herself, Brenda said, "Yes, they have been called that."

Earnest was still in a state of shock. Dulaq had polished off two desserts and was sitting back in his chair, mouth slack and eyes drooping, obviously falling asleep. Gloria and Rita had joined hands over the table now, as well as feet underneath. They spoke to each other as if no one else was in the restaurant.

But Earnest reconciled himself with the thought, *at least we ought to get some good publicity out of the old gasbag.*

Gabriel was acutally pulling at his hair.

"But why?" His voice was rising dangerously, like the steam pressure in a volcano vent just before the eruption.

"Why can't they fight with laser guns? That's what people will *use* seven hundred years in the future!"

His beneficent smile absorbing all arguments, Good explained, "Two reasons: first, if children tried to use lasers they could hurt themselves. . . ."

"But they can't buy lasers! People don't buy lasers for their kids. There aren't any laser toys."

Good waited for Gabriel to subside, then resumed: "Second, most states have very strict safety laws about using lasers. You wouldn't be able to employ them on the sound stage."

"But we weren't going to use real lasers! We were going to fake it with flashlights!"

Real lasers are too expensive, Montpelier added silently, from the slippery edge of sobriety.

"No, I'm sorry." Good's smile looked anything but that. "Lasers are on FINC's list of forbidden weapons and there's nothing anyone can do about it. Lasers are out. Have them use swords, instead."

"Swords!" Gabriel screamed. "Seven hundred years in the future, aboard an interstellar spaceship, you want them to use *swords!* Aaarrgghhhh. . . ."

Gabriel jumped up on the booth's bench and suddenly there was a butterknife in his hand. Good, sitting beside him, gave a startled yell and dived under the table. Gabriel clambered up on top of the table and started kicking Good's notes into shreds that were wafted into the air and sucked up into the ceiling vents.

"I'll give you swords!" he screamed, jumping up and down on the table like a spastic flamenco dancer. Montpelier's beer toppled into his lap.

Good scrambled out past Montpelier's legs, scuttled out of the booth on all fours, straightened up and started running for his life. Gabriel gave a war screech that couldn't be heard outside the booth, even though it temporarily deafened Montpelier, leaped off the table and took off in pursuit of the little censor, still brandishing his butterknife.

They raced past Connors and Brenda, who had just

gotten up from their booth and were heading for the foyer.

"What in hell was *that?*" Connors shouted.

Brenda stared after Gabriel's disappearing, howling, butterknife-brandishing form. The waiters and incoming customers gave him a wide berth as he pursued Good out beyond the entryway.

"Apache dancers, I guess," Brenda said. "Part of the floorshow. Very impromptu."

Connors shook his head. "Never saw nuthin' like them back in Texas and we got plenty Apaches."

"No, I suppose not."

"Hey," he said, remembering. "You were gonna make a phone call fer me."

Since their table was not soundproofed, Earnest heard Gabriel's cries for blood and vengeance before he saw what was happening. He turned to watch the censor fleeing in panic and the enraged writer chasing after him.

No one else at the table took notice: Dulaq was snoring peacefully; Gloria and Rita were making love with their eyes, fingertips and toes.

Earnest smiled. *The little bastard's finished now, for sure. I won't even have to phone Finger about him. The show is mine.*

It was snowing.

Toronto International Jetport looked like a scene from *Doctor Zhivago*. Snowbound travelers slumped on every bench, chair and flat surface where they could sit or lie down. Bundled in their overcoats because the terminal building was kept at a minimum temperature ever since Canada had decided to Go Independent on Energy, the travelers slept or grumbled or moped, waiting for the storm to clear and the planes to fly again.

Ron Gabriel stood at the floor-to-ceiling window of Gate 26, staring out at the wind-whipped snow that was falling thickly on the other side of the double-paned glass. He could feel the cold seeping through the supposedly vacuum-insulated window. The cold, gray bitterness of defeat was seeping into his bones. The Unimerican jet-liner outside was crusted over with snow; it was beginning to remind Gabriel of the ancient wooly mammoths uncovered in the ice fields of Siberia.

He turned and surveyed the waiting area of Gate 26. Two hundred eleven people sitting there, going slowly insane with boredom and uncertainty. Gabriel had already made dates with seventeen of the likeliest-looking girls, including the chunky security guard who ran the magnetic weapons detector.

He watched her for a moment. She was sitting next to the walkthrough gate of her apparatus, reading a comic book. Gabriel wondered how bright she could be, accepting a date from a guy she had just checked out for the flight to Los Angeles. *Maybe she's planning to come to L.A.,* he thought. Then he wondered briefly why he had tried to make the date with her, when he was leaving Toronto forever. He shrugged. *Something to do. If we have to stay here much longer, maybe I can get her off into. . . .*

"Ron!"

He swung around at the sound of his name.

"Ron! Over here!"

A woman's voice. He looked beyond the moribund waiting travelers, following the sound of her voice to the corridor outside the gate area.

It was Brenda. And Bill Oxnard. Grinning and waving at him.

Gabriel left his trusty suitcase and portable typewriter where they sat and hurried through the bundled bodies, crumpled newspapers, choked ashtrays and tumbled suitcases of the crowd, out past the security girl—who didn't even look up from her *Kookoo Komix*—and out into the corridor.

"Hey, what're you two doing here? You're not trying to get out of town, are you?"

"No," Brenda said. "We wanted to say goodbye to you at the hotel, but you'd already left."

"I always leave early," Gabriel said.

"And when we heard that the storm was expected to last several hours and the airport was closed down, we figured you might like some company," Oxnard explained.

"Hey, that's nice of you. Both of you."

"We're sorry to see you leave, Ron," Brenda said; her throaty voice sounded sincere.

Gabriel shrugged elaborately. "Welll . . . what the hell

is left for me to stay here? They've shot the guts out of my scripts and they won't let me do diddely-poo with the other writers and the whole *idea* of the show's been torn to shreds."

"It's a lousy situation," Oxnard agreed.

Brenda bit her lip for a moment, then—with a *damn the torpedoes* expression on her face—she said, "I'm glad you're going, Ron."

He looked at her. "Thanks a lot."

"You know I don't mean it badly. I'm glad you found the strength to break free of this mess."

"I had a lot of help," Gabriel said, "from Finger and Earnest and the rest of those bloodsuckers."

Brenda shook her head. "That's not what I'm talking about. I thought Rita really had you twisted around her little finger."

"She did," Gabriel admitted. "But I got untwisted."

"Good for you," Brenda said. "She's trouble."

Oxnard said, "I just hate to see you getting screwed out of the money you ought to be getting."

"Oh, I'm getting all the money," Gabriel said. "They can't renege on that . . . the Screen Writers Guild would start napalming Titanic if they tried anything like that. I'll get paid for both the scripts I wrote. . . ."

"But neither one's going to be produced," Oxnard said. "Earnest has scrapped them both."

"So what? I'll get paid for 'em. And I've been getting my regular weekly check as Story Editor. And they still have to pay me my royalties for each show, as the Creator."

With a smile, Brenda asked, "You're going to let them keep your name on the credits?"

"Hell no!" Gabriel grinned back, but it was a Pyrrhic triumph. "They'll have to use my Guild-registered pen name: Victor Lawrence Talbot Frankenstein."

"Oh no!" Brenda howled.

Oxnard frowned. "I don't get it."

"Frankenstein and the Wolfman," Gabriel explained. "I

save that name for shows that've been screwed up. It's my way of telling friends that the show's a clinker, a grade B horror movie."

"His friends," Brenda added, giggling, "and everybody in the industry."

"Oh." But Oxnard still looked as if he didn't really understand.

Laughing at the thought of his modest revenge, Gabriel said, "Lemma grab my bags and take you both to dinner."

"The restaurants are closed," Oxnard said. "We checked. They ran out of food about an hour ago."

Gabriel held up one hand, looking knowledgeable: "Have no fear. I know where the aircrews have their private cafeteria. One of the stewardesses gave me the secret password to get in there."

Oxnard watched the little guy scamper back through the now-dozing security girl's magnetic detector portal and head for his bags, by the window. It was still snowing heavily.

"Victor Lawrence Talbot Frankenstein?" he muttered.

Brenda said to him, "It's the only satisfaction he's going to get out of this series."

"He's getting all that money. . . ."

She rested a hand on his shoulder and said, "It's not really all that much money, compared to the time and effort he's put in. And . . . well, Bill . . . suppose your new holographic system won the Nobel Prize. . . ."

"They don't give Nobels for inventions."

"But just suppose," Brenda insisted. "And then one of the people who decide on the Prize comes to you and says they're going to name Gregory Earnest as the inventor. You'll get the money that goes with the Prize, but he'll get the recognition."

"Ohh. Now I see."

Gabriel came back, lugging his suitcase and typewriter. As they started down the corridor, Oxnard took the typewriter from him.

"Thanks."

"Nothing to it."

Brenda said, "Looks like we'll be here a long time."

"Good," said Oxnard. "It'll give me a chance to ask you some questions about a new idea of mine."

"What's that?" Gabriel asked.

Oxnard scratched briefly at his nose. "Oh, it's just a few wild thoughts I put together . . . but it might be possible to produce a three-dee show without using any actors. You. . . ."

"What?" Gabriel looked startled. Brenda pursed her lips.

Oxnard nodded as they walked. "After watching how pitiful Dulaq is as an actor, I got to thinking that there's no *fundamental* reason why you couldn't take one holographic picture of him—a still shot—and then use a computer to electronically move his image any way you want to . . . you know, make him walk, run, stand up, sit down. Some of the work they've been doing at the VA with hemiplegics. . . ."

Gabriel stopped and dropped his suitcase to the floor. Brenda and Oxnard took a step or two more, then turned back toward him.

"Don't say anything more about it," Gabriel warned.

"Why not?" Oxnard looked totally surprised at his reaction. "You could do away with. . . ."

"He's right," Brenda agreed. "Forget about it. You'll produce nothing but trouble."

Oxnard stared at them both. "But you could lower the costs of producing shows enormously. You wouldn't have to hire any act. . . ."

Gabriel put a hand over his mouth. "For Chrissake, you wanna start a revolution in L.A.? Every actor in the world will come after you, with guns!"

Oxnard shrugged as Gabriel took his hand away. "It's just an idea . . . might be too expensive to work out in real-time." He sounded hurt.

"It would cause more trouble than it's worth," Brenda said, as they resumed walking. "Believe me, a producer would have to be utterly desperate to try a scheme like that."

:::::::

HONOLULU PINEAPPLES WIN EIGHTH STRAIGHT, 38-6
QB Gene Toho Passes
For Three Scores

:::::::

Gregory Earnest stood beside the reclining plush barber chair, watching the skinny little old man daub Francois Dulaq's rugged features with makeup.

"What is it this time, Francois?" he asked, barely suppressing his growing impatience.

Dulaq's eyes were closed while the makeup man carefully filled in the crinkles at the corners and painted over the bags that had started to appear under them.

"I gotta leave early t'day. Th'team's catchin' the early plane to Seattle."

Earnest felt startled. "I thought you were taking the special charter flight, later tonight. You can still be in Seattle tomorrow morning, in plenty of time for the game."

"Naw . . . I wanna go wit' th'guys. They're startin' t'razz me about bein' a big TV star . . . and de coach ain't too happy, neither. Sez I oughtta get t'th'practices . . . my scorin's off and th'guys're gettin' a little sore at me."

"But we can't shoot your scenes in just a few hours," Earnest protested.

"Sure ya can."

Earnest grabbed the nearest thing at hand, a tissue box, and banged it viciously on the countertop. Dulaq opened one eye and squinted at him, in the mirror.

"Francois, you've got to *understand*," Earnest said. "We've stripped your scenes down as far as we can. We haven't given you anything more complicated to say than

'Let's go,' or 'Oh, no you don't.' We're dubbing all the longer speeches for you. But you've *got* to let us photograph you! You're the *star*, for goodness' sake! The people have to *see* you on the show!"

"I ain't gonna be a star of nuthin' if I don't start scorin' and th'team don't start winnin'."

Earnest's mind spun furiously. "Well, I suppose we *could* use Fernando to stand in for the long shots and the reverse angles, when you're back's to the camera."

"He still limpin'?"

"A little. That was some fight scene."

"Dat's th'only fun I've had since we started dis whole show."

The makeup man pursed his lips, inspected his handiwork and then said, "Okay, *mon ami*. That's the most I can do for you."

Dulaq bounded up from the chair.

"Come on," Earnest said, "you're already late for the first scene."

As they left the makeup room and headed down the darkened corridor toward the studio, Dulaq put his arm around Earnest's shoulders. "Sorry I gotta buzz off, but th'team's important, y'know."

"I know," Earnest said, feeling dejected. "It's just . . . well, I thought we were going to have dinner tonight."

Dulaq squeezed him. "Don' worry. I'll be back Wensay night. I'll take d'early plane. You meet me at th' airport, okay?"

Earnest brightened. "All right. I will." And he thrilled to the powerful grip he was in.

"But you can't walk out on us!" Brenda pleaded.

Mitch Westerly was slowly walking along the windswept parking lot behind Badger's square red-brick studio building. The night was Arctic cold and dark; even the brilliant stars seemed to radiate cold light.

"It's h . . . hopeless," Westerly said.

His head was bent low, chin sunk into the upraised collar of his mackinaw, hands stuffed into the pockets. The wind tousled his long hair. Brenda paced along beside him, wrapped in an ankle-length synthetic fur coat that was warmed electrically.

"You can't give up now," Brenda said. "You're the only shred of talent left in the crew! You're the one who's been holding this show together. If you go. . . ."

Westerly pulled one gloved hand out of his pocket. Under the bluish arclamps the leather looked strange, otherwordly. The hand was trembling, shaking like the strengthless hand of a palsied old man.

"See that?" Westerly said. "The only way I can get it to stop . . . make my whole body stop shaking . . . is to pop some cat. Nothing less will do the trick anymore."

"Cat? But I thought. . . ."

"I kicked it once . . . in the mountains, far away from here. But I'm right back on it again."

Brenda looked up at the director's face. It looked awful and not merely because of the lighting. "I didn't know, Mitch. How could. . . ."

It took an effort to keep his teeth from chattering. Westerly plunged his hand back into his pocket and resumed walking.

"How can anybody stay straight in this nuthouse?" he asked. "Dulaq is bouncing in and out of the studio whenever he feels like it. Half the time we have to shoot around him or use a double. Rita's spending most of her time with that snake from FINC . . . I think she's posing for pictures for him. He told me he's an amateur photographer. . . ."

Brenda huffed, "Oh for god's sake!"

"And when she's on the set all she wants to do is look glamorous. She can't act for beans."

"But you've gotten four shows in the can."

"In four weeks, yeah. And each week my cat bill goes up. Earnest is making a fortune off me."

"Earnest? He's supplying you with cat?"

"It's all legal . . . he tells me."

"Mitch . . . can you stay for just another three weeks? Until we get the first seven shows finished?"

He shook his head doggedly. "I'd do it for you, Brenda ... if I could. But I know what I went through the last time with cat. If I don't stop now, I'll be really hooked. Bad. It's me or the show ... another three weeks will kill me. Honest."

She said nothing.

"Earnest has a couple of local people who can direct the other three segments. Hell, the way things are going, anybody could walk off the street and do it."

Brenda asked, "Where will you go? What will you do?"

"To the mountains, I guess."

"Katmandu again?"

He shrugged. "Maybe. I'd like to try Aspen, if Finger will let me off the hook. I owe some debts. ..."

"I'll take care of that," Brenda said firmly. "B.F. will let you go, don't worry."

He looked at her from under raised eyebrows. "Can you really swing it for me?"

Brenda said, "Yes. I will ... but, what will you do in Aspen?"

He almost smiled. "Teach, maybe. There's a film colony there ... lots of eager young kids."

"That would be good," Brenda said.

He stopped walking. They were at his car. "I hate to leave you in this mess, Brenda. But I just can't cut it anymore."

"I know," she said. "Don't worry about it. You're right, the show's a disaster. There's no sense hanging on."

He reached out and grasped her by the shoulders. Lightly. Without pulling her toward him. "Why are you staying?" he asked. "Why do you put up with all this bullshit?"

"Somebody's got to. It's my job."

"Ever think of quitting?"

"Once every hour, at least."

"Want to come to Aspen with me?"

She stepped closer to him and let her head rest against

his chest. "It's a tempting thought. And you're very sweet to ask me. But I can't."

"Why not?"

"Reasons. My own reasons."

"And they're none of my business, right?"

She smiled up at him. "You've got enough problems. You don't need mine. Go on, go off to the mountains and breathe clean air and forget about this show. I'll square it with B.F."

Abruptly, he let go of her and reached for the car door. "Can I drop you off at the hotel?"

"I've got my own car." She pointed to it, sitting alone and cold looking a few empty rows down the line.

"Okay," he said. "Goodbye. And thanks."

"Good luck, Mitch."

She walked to her car and stood beside it as he gunned his engine and drove off.

::::::

PINEAPPLES CLINCH PLAYOFF SLOT AS TOHO LEADS 56-13 MASSACRE

::::::

It'll look like Orson Wells, Gregory Earnest told himself as he strode purposefully onto the set. *Script by Gregory Earnest. Produced by Gregory Earnest. Directed by Gregory Earnest.*

He stood there for a magnificent moment, clad in the traditional dungarees and tee shirt of a big-time director, surrounded by the crew and actors who stood poised waiting for his orders.

"Very well," he said to them. "Let's do this one *right*."

Four hours later he was drenched with perspiration and longing for the safety of his bed.

Dulaq had just delivered the longest speech in his script: "Oh yeah? We'll see about dat!"

He stood bathed in light, squinting at the cue cards that had his next line printed in huge red block letters, while the actor in the scene with him backed away and gave his line:

"Rom, we're going to crash! The ship's out of control!"

Dulaq didn't answer. He peered at the cue card, then turned toward Earnest and bellowed, "What th'hell's dat word?"

"Cut!" Earnest yelled. His throat was raw from saying it so often.

"Which one?" the script girl asked Dulaq.

"Dat one . . . wit' de 'S.' "

"*Stabilize,*" the girl read.

Dulaq shook his head and muttered to himself, "Stabilize. Stabilize. Stabilize."

This is getting to be a regular routine, Brenda told herself. *I feel like the Welcome Wagon Lady . . . in reverse.*

She was at the airport again, sitting at the half-empty bar with Les Montpelier. His travelbags were resting on the floor between their stools.

"I don't understand why you're staying," Montpelier said, toying with the plastic swizzle stick in his Tijuana Teaser.

"B.F. asked me to," she said.

"So you're going to stick it out until the bloody end?" he asked rhetorically. "The last soldier at Fort Zinderneuf."

She took a sip of her vodka gimlet. "Bill Oxnard still comes up every weekend. I'm not completely surrounded by idiots."

Montpelier shook his head, more in pity than in sorrow. "I could ask B.F. to send somebody else up here . . . hell, there's no real reason to have anybody here. The seventh show is finished shooting. All they have to do now is the editing. No sense starting the next six until we get the first look at the ratings."

"The editing can be tricky," Brenda said. "These people

that Earnest has hired don't have much experience with three-dee editing."

"They don't have much experience with anything."

"They work cheap, though."

Montpelier lifted his glass. "There is that. I'll bet this show cost less than any major network presentation since the Dollar Collapse of Eighty-Four."

"Do you think that there's any chance the show will last beyond the first seven weeks?" Brenda asked.

"Are you kidding?"

"Thank god," she said. "Then I can go home as soon as the editing's finished."

The P.A. system blared something unintelligible about a flight to Los Angeles, Honolulu and Tahiti.

"That's me," Montpelier said. "I'd better dash." He started fumbling in his pocket for cash.

"Go on, catch your plane," Brenda said. "I'll take care of the tab."

"Gee, thanks."

"Give B.F. my love."

"Will do." He grabbed his travelbags and hurried out of the bar.

Brenda turned from watching him hurry out the doorway to the three-dee set behind the bar. The football game was on. Honolulu was meeting Pittsburgh and the Pineapples' star quarterback, Gene Toho, was at that very minute throwing a long pass to a player who was racing down the sideline. He caught the ball and ran into the endzone. The referee raised both arms to signal a touchdown.

Brenda raised her glass. "Hail to thee, blithe spirit," she said, and realized she was slightly drunk.

The guy on the stool at her left nudged her with a gentle elbow. "Hey, you a Pineapples fan?"

He wasn't bad looking, if you ignored the teeth, Brenda decided. She smiled at him. "Perforce, friend. Perforce."

Even though he knew better than anyone else exactly what to expect, the sight still exhilarated Bill Oxnard.

He was sitting in the darkened editing room — more a closet than a real room. He knew that what he was watching was a holographic image of a group of actors performing a teleplay. (A poor teleplay, but that didn't matter much, really.)

Yet what he saw was Francois Dulaq, life-sized, three-dimensional, full, real, solid, standing before him. He was squinting a little and seemed to be staring off into space. Oxnard knew that he was actually trying to read his cue cards. He wore an Elizabethan costume of tights, tunic and cape. A sword dangled from his belt and got in his way whenever he tried to move. His boots clumped on the wooden deck of the set. But he was as solid as real flesh, to the eye.

"You!" Dulaq was saying, trying to sound surprised. "You're here!"

"You" was Rita Yearling, who in her own overly heated way, was every bit as bad an actor as Dulaq. But who cared? All she had to do was try to stand up and breathe a little. Her gown was metallic and slinky; it clung in all the right places, which was everywhere on her body. She was wearing a long flowing golden wig and her child-innocent face gave the final touch of maddening desirability to her aphrodisiacal anatomy.

"I have waited for you," she panted. "I have crossed time and space to be with you. I have renounced my family and my home because I love you."

"Caught up with you at last!" announced a third performer, stepping out of the shadows where the holo image ended. This one was dressed very much like Dulaq, complete with sword, although his costume was blood red whereas Dulaq's was (what else?) true blue.

"You're coming back with me," the actor recited to Rita Yearling. "Our father is lying ill and dying, and only the sight of you can cure him."

"Oh!" gasped Rita, as she tried to stuff both her fists in her mouth.

"Take yer han's off her!" Dulaq cried, even though the other actor had forgotten to grasp Rita's arm.

"We can dub over that," an engineer muttered in the darkness beside Oxnard.

"Don't try to interfere, Montague dog," said the actor. "Stand back or I'll blast you." But instead of pulling out the laser pistol that was in the original script, he drew his sword. It flexed deeply, showing that it was made of rubber.

"Oh yeah?" adlibbed Dulaq. And he drew his rubber sword.

They swung at each other mightily, to no avail. The engineers laughed and suddenly reversed the tape. The fight went backwards, and the two heroes slid their swords back into their scabbards. Halfway. Then the tape went forward again and they fought once more. Back and forth. It looked ludicrous. It *was* ludicrous and Oxnard joined in the raucous laughter of the editing crew.

"Lookit the expression on Dulaq's face!"

"He's trying to hit Randy's sword and he keeps missing it!"

"Hey, hey, hold it . . . right there . . . yeah. Take a look at that terrific profile."

"Cheez . . . is she *built!*"

Oxnard had to admit that structurally, Rita was as impressive as the Eiffel Tower—or perhaps the Grand Teton Mountains.

"A guy could bounce to death off those!"

"What a way to go!"

"C'mon, we got work to do. It's almost quittin' time."

The fight ran almost to its conclusion and then suddenly the figures got terribly pale. They seemed to blanch out, like figures in an overexposed snapshot. The scene froze with Dulaq pushing his sword in the general direction of his antagonist, the other actor holding his sword down almost on the floor so Dulaq could stab him and Rita in the midst of a stupifyingly deep breath.

"See what I mean?" came the chief engineer's voice, out of the darkness. "It does that every couple minutes."

Oxnard looked down at the green glowing gauges on the control board in front of him. "I told them not to light the set so brightly," he said. "You don't need all that candlepower with laser imaging."

"Listen," said the chief engineer, "if they had any smarts, would they be doin' this for a living?"

Oxnard studied the information on the gauges.

"Can we fix it?" one of the editors asked. Oxnard smelled pungent smoke and saw that two of the assistants were lighting up in the dimness of the room.

"We'll have to feed the tape through the quality control computer, override the intensity program and manually adjust the input voltage," Oxnard said.

The chief engineer swore under his breath. "That'll take all humpin' night."

"A few hours, at least."

"There goes dinner."

Oxnard heard himself say, "You guys don't have to hang around. I can do it myself."

He could barely make out the editor's sallow, thin face in the light from the control board. "By yourself? That ain't kosher."

"Union rules?"

"Naw . . . but it ain't fair for you to do our work. You ain't gettin' paid for it."

Oxnard grinned at him. "I've got nothing else to do. Go on home. I'll take care of it and you can get back to doing the real editing tomorrow."

One of the assistants walked out into the area where the holographic images stood. He wasn't walking too steadily. Taking the joint from his mouth, he blew smoke in Dulaq's "face."

"Okay, tough guy," he said to the stilled image. "If you're so tough, let's see you take a swing at me. G'wan

. . . I dare ya!" He stuck his chin out and tapped at it with an upraised forefinger. "Go on . . . right here on the button. I dare ya!"

Dulaq's image didn't move. "Hah! Chicken. I thought so."

The guy turned to face Rita's image. He walked all around her, almost disappearing from Oxnard's view when he stepped behind her. Oxnard could see him, ghost-like, through Rita's image. The other assistant drew in a deep breath and let it out audibly. "Boy," he said, with awe in his voice, "they really are three-dimensional, aren't they? You can walk right around them."

"Too bad you can't pinch 'em," said the chief engineer.

"Or do anything else with 'em," the assistant said.

Oxnard lost track of time. He simply sat alone at the control desk, working the buttons and keys that linked his fingers with the computer tape and instruments that controlled what stayed on the tape.

It was almost pleasant, working with the uncomplaining machinery. He shut off the image-projector portion of the system, so that he wouldn't have to see or hear the dreadful performances that were on the tape. He was interested in the technical problem of keeping the visual quality of the images constant; that he could do better by watching the gauges than by watching the acting.

All of physics boils down to reading a dial, he remembered from his undergraduate days. He chuckled to himself.

"And all physicists are basically loners," he said aloud. *Not because they want to be. But if you spend enough time reading dials, you never learn how to read people.*

Someone knocked at the door. Almost annoyed, Oxnard called, "Who is it?" without looking up from the control board.

Light spilled across his field of view as the door opened. "What are you doing here so late?"

He looked up. It was Brenda, her lean, leggy form silhouetted in the light from the hallway.

"Trying to make this tape consistent, on the optical quality side," he said. Then, almost as an afterthought, "What about you? What time is it?"

"Almost nine. I had a lot of paperwork to finish."

"Oh." He took his hands off the control knobs and gestured to her. "Come on in. I didn't realize I'd been here so long."

"Aren't you going back to L.A. tomorrow?" Brenda asked. She stepped into the tiny room, but left the door open behind her.

He nodded. "Yes. That's why I thought I'd stick with this until the job's done. The editors can't handle this kind of problem. They're good guys, but they'd probably ruin the tape."

"Which show are you working on?" Brenda asked, pulling up a stool beside him.

He shrugged. "I don't know. They all look alike to me."

Brenda agreed. "Will you be at it much longer?"

"Almost finished . . . another ten-fifteen minutes or so."

"Can I buy you dinner afterward?" she asked.

He started to say no, but held up. "I'll buy *you* some dinner."

"I can charge it off to Titanic. Let B.F. buy us both dinner."

With a sudden grin, he agreed.

He worked in silence for a few minutes, conscious of her looking over his shoulder, smelling the faint fragrance of her perfume, almost feeling the tickling of a stray wisp of her long red hair.

"Bill?"

"What?" Without looking up from the control board.

"Why do you keep coming up here every weekend?"

"To make sure the equipment works okay."

"Oh. That's awfully good of you."

He clicked the power off and looked up at her. "That's a damned lie," he admitted, to himself as much as to her. "I could stay down at Malibu and wait for you to have some trouble. Or send one of my technicians."

Brenda's face didn't look troubled or surprised. "Then why?"

"Because I like being with you," he said.

"Really?"

"You know I do."

She didn't look away, didn't laugh, didn't frown. "I hoped you did. But you never said a word. . . ."

Suddenly his hands were embarrassingly awkward appendages. They wouldn't stay still.

"Well," he said, scratching at his five o'clock shadow, "I guess I'm still a teenager in some ways . . . retarded . . . I was afraid . . . afraid you wouldn't be interested in me."

"You were wrong," she said simply.

She leaned toward him and his hands reached for her and he kissed her. She felt warm and safe and good.

They decided to have dinner in his hotel room. Oxnard felt giddy, as if he were hyperventilating or celebrating New Year's Eve a month early. As they drove through the dark frigid night toward the hotel, he asked:

"The one thing I was afraid of was that you'd walk out on the show, like everybody else has."

"Oh, I couldn't do that," Brenda said, very seriously.

"Why not?"

"B.F. wouldn't let me."

"You mean you allow him to run your whole life? He tells you to freeze your . . . your nose off here in Toronto all winter, on a dead duck of a show, and you do it?"

She nodded. "That's right."

He pulled the car into the hotel's driveway as he asked, "Why don't you just quit? There are lots of other studios and jobs. . . ."

"I can't quit Titanic."

"Why not? What's Finger got on you?"

"Nothing. Except that he's my father and I'm the only person in the world that he can really trust."

"He's your *father?*"

Brenda grinned broadly at him. "Yes. And you're the

only person in the whole business who knows it. So please don't tell anyone else."

Oxnard was stunned.

He was still groggy, but grinning happily, as they walked arm-in-arm through the hotel lobby, got into an elevator and headed for his room. Neither of them noticed the three-dee set in the lobby; it was tuned to the evening news. A somber-faced sports reporter was saying:

"There's no telling what effect Toho's injury will have on the playoff chances of the Honolulu Pineapples. As everyone knows, he's the league's leading passer."

The other half of the Folksy News Duo, a curly haired anchorperson in a gingham dress, asked conversationally, "Isn't it unusual for a player to break his leg in the shower?"

"That's right, Arlene," said the sports announcer. "Just one of those freak accidents. A bad *break*," he said archly, "for the Pineapples and their fans."

The woman made a disapproving clucking sound. "That's terrible."

"It certainly is. They're probably going crazy down in Las Vegas right now, refiguring the odds for the playoff games."

Room enough in town. You just show him where the
water is and—"
So we got dressed in a demure, translucent fine-leaf

"You don't understand!" Bernard Finger shouted.
"Every cent I had was tied up in that lousy football team!
I'm broke! Ruined!"

He was emptying the drawers of his desk into an impossibly thin attache case. Most of the papers and mementoes—including a miniature Emmy given him as a gag by a producer, whom Finger promptly fired—were missing the attache case and spilling across the polished surface of the desk or onto the plush carpet.

The usually impressive office reminded Les Montpelier of the scene in a war movie where the general staff has to beat a fast retreat and everybody's busy stripping the headquarters and burning what they can't carry.

"But you couldn't have taken everything out of Titanics' cash accounts," Montpelier said, trying to remain calm in the face of Finger's panic.

"Wanna bet?" Finger was bent over, pulling papers out of the bottommost drawer, discarding most of them and creating a miniature blizzard in the doing.

Montpelier found himself leaning forward tensely in his chair. "But we still get our paychecks. The accounting department is still paying its bills. Isn't it?"

Finger straightened up and eyed him with a look of scorn for such naiveté. "Sure, sure. You know Morrie Witz, down in accounting?"

"Morrie the Mole?"

"Who else? He worked out a system for me. We keep enough in the bank for two weeks of salaries and bills. Everything else we've been investing in the Pineapples. Every time they win, we bet on 'em again. The odds keep going down, but we keep making sure money. Better than the stock market."

"Then you must have a helluva cash reserve right now," Montpelier said.

"Its already bet!" Finger bawled. "And the Pineapples play the Montana Sasquatches this afternoon. . . ." He glanced at the clock on his littered desk. "They're already playing."

"Shall I turn on the game?" Montpelier asked, starting to get up from his chair.

"No! I can't bear to watch. Without Toho they're sunk." Montpelier eased back into the chair.

"Yes!" Finger burst. "Turn it on. I can't stand not knowing!"

He went back to rummaging through the desk drawers as Montpelier walked across the room to the control panel for the life-sized three-dee set in the corner.

"The Pineapples still have their defensive team intact," Montpelier reasoned. "And Montana's not that high-scoring a team. . . ."

He found the right channel and tuned in the game. The far corner of the office dissolved into a section of a football field. A burly man in a Sasquatch uniform was kneeling, arms outstretched, barking out numbers. The crowd rumbled in the background. It was raining and windy; it looked cold in Montana.

The camera angle changed to an overhead shot and Montpelier saw that the Sasquatches were trying to kick a field goal. The ball was snapped, the kicker barely got the kick past a pair of onrushing Pineapple defenders, who ruined their orange and yellow uniforms by sprawling in the mud.

Again the camera angle changed, to show the football sailing thrugh the uprights of the goal post. The announcer said, "It's gooood!" as the referee raised both arms over his head.

Finger groaned.

"It's only a field goal," Montpelier said.

"So as the teams prepare for the kickoff," the announcer said cheerily, "the score is Montana seventeen, Honolulu zero."

With a gargling sound, Finger pawed through the attache case. He grabbed a bottle of pills as he yelled, "Turn it off! Turn it off!" and poured half the bottle's contents down his throat.

Montpelier turned the game off, just catching a view of the scoreboard clock. Only eight minutes of the first quarter had elapsed.

He turned to Finger. "What are you going to do?"

His face white, Titanic's boss said softly, "Get out of town. Get out of the country. Get off the planet, if I can. Maybe the lunar colony would be a safe place for me . . . if I could qualify. I've got a bad heart, you know."

Like an ox, Montpelier thought. Aloud, he asked, "But you've been through bankruptcy proceedings before. Why are you getting so upset over this one?"

Raising his eyes to an unhelpful heaven, Finger said, "The other bankruptcy hearings were when we owed money to *banks.* Or to the government. What we owe now, we owe to the mob. When they foreclose, they take your head home and mount it on the goddamn wall!"

"The gamblers. . . ."

Finger wagged his head. "Not the gamblers. I'm square with them. The bankers who backed us on 'The Starcrossed.' It's their money I've been betting. When the show flops they're gonna want their money back. With interest."

"Ohhh."

"Yeah, ohhh." Finger knuckled his eyes. "Turn the game on again. Maybe they're doing something. . . ."

The three-dee image solidified, despite annoying flickers and shimmers, to show an orange-and-yellow Pineapple ball carrier break past two would-be tacklers, twist free of another Sasquatch defender and race down the sidelines. The crowd was roaring and Finger was suddenly on his feet, screaming.

"Go! Go! Go, you black sonofabitch!"

There was only one Sasquatch left in the scene, closing in on the Pineapple runner. They collided exactly at the Montana ten yard line. He twisted partially free, and as he began to fall, another Sasquatch pounced on him. The ball squirted loose.

"Aarrghh!"

What seemed like four hundred men in muddied uniforms piled on top of each other. There was a long moment of breathless suspense while the referees pulled bodies off the mountain of rain-soaked flesh.

Finger stood frozen, his fists pressed into his cheeks.

The bottom man in the pile was a Sasquatch. And under him was the ball.

"Turn it off! Turn it off!"

They spent the rest of the afternoon like that, alternately turning on the three-dee, watching the Sasquatches hurt the Pineapples, and turning off the three-dee. Finger moaned, he fainted, he swallowed pills. Montpelier went out for sandwiches; on Sunday the building's cafeterias were closed.

He idly wondered how far the bankers' revenge would go. *If they can't get B.F., will they come after me?* He tried to put the thought aside, but ugly scenes from Mafia movies kept crawling into his skull.

Finger wolfed down his sandwich as if it were his last meal. They turned the game on one final time, and the Sasquatches were ahead by 38-7 with less than two minutes to play. Finger started calling airlines.

He set up seven different flights for himself, for destinations as diverse as Rio de Janiero and Ulan Bator.

"I'll dazzle them with footwork," he joked weakly. His face looked far from jovial.

The phone chimed. With a trembling hand, Finger touched the ON button. The same corner that had showed the football game now presented a three-dee image of a gray-templed man sitting a a desk. He looked intelligent, wealthy, conservative and powerful. His suit was gray, with a vest. The padded chair on which he sat was real leather, Montpelier somehow sensed. The wall behind him was panelled in dark mahogany. A portrait of Nelson Rockefeller hung there.

"Mr. Finger," he said in a beautifully modulated baritone. "I'm pleased to find you in your office this afternoon. My computer doesn't seem to have your home number. Working hard, I see."

"Yes," Finger said, his voice quavering just the slightest bit. "Yes . . . you know how it is in this business, heh-heh."

The man smiled without warmth.

"I, uh . . . I don't think I know you," Finger said.

"We have never met. I am an attorney, representing a group of gentlemen who have invested rather substantial sums in Titanic Productions, Incorporated."

"Oh. Yes. I see."

"Indeed."

"The gentlemen who're backing 'The Starcrossed.' "

The man raised a manicured forefinger. "The gentlemen are backing Titanic Productions, not any particular show. In a very real sense, Mr. Finger, they have invested in *you*. In your business acumen, your administrative capabilities, your . . . integrity."

Finger swallowed hard. "Well, eh, 'The Starcrossed' is the show that we've sunk their . . . eh, invested their money into. It goes on the air in three weeks. That's the premier date, second week of January. Friday night. Full network coverage. It's a good spot, and. . . ."

"Mr. Finger."

Montpelier had never seen B.F. stopped by such a quiet short speech.

"Yessir?" Finger squeaked.

"Mr. Finger, did you happen to watch the Montana Sasquatch football game this afternoon?"

"Uh. . . ." Finger coughed, cleared his throat. "Why, um, I *did* take a look at part of it, yes."

The man from New York let a slight frown mar his handsome features. "Mr. Finger, the bankers whom I represent have some associates who—quite frankly—I find very distasteful. These, ah, associates are spreading an ugly rumor to the effect that you have been betting quite heavily on the Honolulu professional football team. Quite heavily. And since Honolulu lost this afternoon, my clients thought it might be wise to let you know that this rumor has them rather upset."

"Upset," Finger echoed.

"Yes. They fear that the money they have invested in Titanic Productions has been channeled into the hands of. . . ." he showed his distaste quite visibly ". . . bookies. They fear that you have lost all their money and will have nothing to show for their investment. That would make them very angry, I'm afraid. And justifiably so."

Finger's head bobbed up and down. "I can appreciate that."

"The proceedings that they would institute against you would be so severe that you might be tempted to leave the country or disappear altogether."

"Oh, I'd never. . . ."

"A few years ago, in a similar situation, a man who tried to cheat them became so remorseful that he committed suicide. He somehow managed to shoot himself in the back of the head. Three times."

What little color was left in Finger's face drained away completely. He sagged in his chair.

"Mr. Finger, are you all right? Does the thought of violence upset you?"

Finger nodded weakly.

"I'm terribly sorry. It's raining here in New York and I tend to get morbid on rainy Sunday afternoons. Please forgive me."

Finger raised a feeble hand. "Think nothing of it."

"Back to business, if you don't mind. Mr. Finger, there is a series called 'The Starcrossed'? And it will premier on the second Friday in January?"

"Eight p.m." Montpelier said as firmly as possible.

"Ah. Thank you, young man. This show does represent the investment that my clients have made?"

"That's right, it does," Finger said, his voice regaining some strength. But not much.

"That means," the New York lawyer went on, remorselessly, "that you have used my client's money to acquire the best writers, directors, actors and so forth . . . the best that money can buy?"

"Sure, sure."

"Which in turn means that the show will be a success. It will bring an excellent return on my clients' investment. Titanic Productions will make a profit and so will my clients. Is that correct?"

Sitting up a little straighter in his chair, Finger hedged, "Well now, television is a funny business. Nobody can *guarantee* success. I explained to. . . ."

"Mr. Finger." And again B.F. stopped cold. "My clients are simple men, at heart. If 'The Starcrossed' is a success and we all make money, all well and good. If it is not a success, then they will investigate just how their money was spent. If they find that Titanic did not employ the best possible talent or that the money was used in some other manner—as this regrettable betting rumor suggests, for instance—then they will hold you personally responsible."

"Me?"

"Do you understand? *Personally* responsible."

"I understand."

"Good." The lawyer almost smiled. "Now if you would do us one simple favor, Mr. Finger?"

"What?"

"Please stay close to your office for the next few weeks. I know you probably feel that you are entitled to a long vacation, now that your show is . . . how do they say it in your business? 'In the can?' At any rate, try to deny yourself that luxury for a few weeks. My clients will want to confer with you as soon as public reaction to 'The Starcrossed' is manifested. They wouldn't want to have to chase you down in some out-of-the-way place such as Rio de Janiero or Ulan Bator."

Finger fainted.

::: **16: THE REACTION**

On the second Friday in January, twenty-odd members of the New England Science Fiction Association returned to their clubroom after their usual ritual Chinese dinner in downtown Boston. The clubroom was inside the lead walls of what once had housed MIT's nuclear reactor—until the local Cambridge chapter of Ecology Now! had torn the reactor apart with their bare hands, a decade earlier, killing seventeen of their members within a week from the radiation poisoning and producing a fascinating string of reports for the obstetrics journals ever since.

The clubroom was perfectly safe now, of course. It had been carefully decontaminated and there was a trusty scintillation counter sitting on every bookshelf, right alongside musty crumbling copies of *Astounding Stories of Super Science.*

The NESFA members were mostly young men and women, in their twenties or teens, although on this evening they were joined by the President Emeritus, a retired lawyer who was regaling them with his Groucho Marx imitations.

"Okay, knock it off!" said the current president, a slim, long-haired brunette who ran the City of Cambridge's combined police, fire and garbage control computer system. "It's time for the new show."

They turned on the three-dee in the corner and arranged themselves in a semicircle on the floor to see the first episode of "The Starcrossed."

But first, of course, they saw three dozen commercials: for bathroom bowl cleaners, bras, headache remedies, perfumes, rectal thermometers, hair dyes, and a foolproof electronic way to cheat on your school exams. Plus new cars, used cars, foreign cars, an airline commercial that explained the new antihijacking system (every passenger gets his very own Smith & Wesson .38 revolver!), and an oil company ad dripping with sincerity about the absolute need to move the revered site of Disneyland so that "we can get more oil to serve *you* better."

The science fiction fans laughed and jeered at all the commercials, especially the last one. They bicycled, whenever and wherever the air was safe enough to breathe.

Then the corner of the room where the three-dee projector cast its images went absolutely black. The fans went silent with anticipation. Then a thread of music began, too faint to really pick out the tune. A speck of light appeared in the middle of the pool of blackness. Then another. Two stars, moving toward each other. The music swelled.

"Hey, that tune is 'When You Wish Upon a Star!' "

"Sssshhh." Nineteen hisses.

The two stars turned out to be starships and bold letters spelled out "The Starcrossed" over them. The fans cheered and applauded.

Two minutes later, after another dozen commercials, they were gaping.

"Look at how *solid* they are!"

"It's like they're really here in the room. No scintillations at all."

"It's a damned-near perfect projection."

"I wish we had a life-sized set."

"You can reach out and touch them!"

"I wouldn't mind touching *her!*"

"Or him. He's got muscles. Not like the guys around here."

"And she's got. . . ."

Twelve hisses, all from female throats, drowned him out.

Fifteen minutes later, they were still gaping, but now their comments were:

"This is pretty slow for an opening show."

"It's pretty slow, period."

"That hockey player acts better in the Garden when they call a foul on him."

"Shuddup. I want to watch Juliet breathe."

Halfway into the second act they were saying:

"Who wrote this crud?"

"It's *awful.*"

"They must be dubbing Romeo's speeches. His mouth doesn't sync with the words."

"Who cares? The words are *dumb.*"

They laughed. They groaned. They threw marshmallows at the solid-looking images and watched the little white missiles sail right through the performers. When the show finally ended:

"What a wagonload of crap!"

"Well, at least the girl was good-looking."

"Good-looking? She's sensational!"

"But the story. Ugh!"

"What story?"

"There was a story?"

"Maybe it's supposed to be a children's show."

"Or a spoof."

"It wasn't funny enough to be a spoof."

"Or intelligent enough to be a children's show. Giant amoebas in space!"

"It'll set science fiction back ten years, at least."

"Oh, I don't know," the President Emeritus said, clutching his walking stick. "I thought it was pretty funny in places."

"In the wrong places."

"One thing, though. That new projection system is terrific. I'm going to scrounge up enough money to buy a life-sized three-dee. They've finally worked all the bugs out of it."

"Yeah."

"Right. Let's get a life-sized set for the clubroom."

"Do we have enough money in the treasury?"

"We do," said the treasurer, "if we cancel the rocket launch in March."

"Cancel it," the president said. "Let's see if the show gets any better. We can always scratch up more money for a rocket launch."

In Pete's Tavern in downtown Manhattan, the three-dee set was life-sized. The regulars sat on their stools with their elbows on the bar and watched "The Starcrossed" actors gallumph across the corner where the jukebox used to be.

After the first few minutes, most of them turned back to the bar and resumed their drinking.

"*That's* Francois Dulaq, the hockey star?"

"Indeed it is, my boy."

"Terrible. Terrible."

"Hey, Kenno, turn on the hockey game. At least we can see some action. This thing stinks."

But one of the women, chain smoking while sipping daiquiris and petting the toy poodle in her lap, stared with fascination at the life-sized three-dimensional images in the corner. "What a build on him," she murmured to the poodle.

In the Midwest the show went on an hour later.

Eleven ministers of various denominations stared incredulously at Rita Yearling and immediately began planning sermons for Sunday on the topic of the shamelessness of modern women. They watched the show to the very end.

The cast and crew of "As You Like It" caught the show during a rehearsal at the Guthrie Theatre in Minneapolis. They decided they didn't like it at all and asked their director to pen an open letter to Titanic Productions, demanding a public apology to William Shakespeare.

The science fiction classes at the University of Kansas— eleven hundred strong—watched the show in the University's Gunn Amphitheater. After the first six minutes, no one could hear the dialogue because of the laughing, catcalls and boos from the sophisticated undergraduates and grad students. The professor who held the Harrison Chair and therefore directed the science fiction curriculum decided that not hearing the dialogue was a mercy.

The six-man police force of Cisco, Texas, voted Rita Yearling "The Most Arresting Three-Dee Personality."

The Hookers Convention in Reno voted Francois Dulaq "Neatest Trick of the Year."

The entire state of Utah somehow got the impression that the end of the world had come a step closer.

In Los Angeles, the cadaverous young man wrote television criticism for the *Free Press-News-Times* smiled as he turned on his voice recorder. Ron Gabriel had stolen three starlets from him in the past year. Now was the moment of his revenge.

He even felt justified.

The editor-in-chief of the venerable *TV Guide,* in his Las Vegas office, shook his head in despair. "How in the world am I going to put a good face on this piece of junk?" he asked a deaf heaven.

In Oakland, the staff of the most influential science fiction newsletter watched the show to its inane end—where Dulaq (playing Rom, or Romeo) improvises a giant syringe from one of his starship's rocket tubes and kills the space-roving Giant Amoeba with a thousand-liter shot of penicillin.

Charles Brown III heaved a mighty sigh. The junior editors, copyreaders and collators sitting at his feet held their breath, waiting for his pronouncement.

"Stinks," he said simply.

High on a mountainside in the Cascade Range, not far from Glacier Park, a bearded writer clicked off his three-dee set and sat in the darkness of his mist-enshrouded chalet. For many minutes he simply sat and thought.

Then he snapped his fingers and his voice recorder came rolling out of its slot on smoothly oiled little trunions.

"Take a letter," he said to the simple-minded robot and its red ON light winked with electrical pleasure. "No, make it a telegram. To Ron Gabriel. The 'puter has his address in its memory. Dear Ron: Have plenty of room up here in the hills if you need to get away from the flak. Come on up. The air's clean and the women are dirty. What more can I say? Signed, Herb. Make it collect."

And in Bernard Finger's home in the exclusive Watts section of Greater Los Angeles, doctors shuttled in and out, like substitute players for the Honolulu Pineapples, manfully struggling to save the mogul of Titanic Productions from what appeared to be—from the symptoms—the world's first case of manic convulsive paranoid cardiac insufficiency, with lockjaw on the side.

: : : : : :

BARD SPINS AS "STARCROSSED" DRAGS
Variety

NEW THREE-DEE TECHNIQUE IS ONLY SOLID
FEATURE OF "STARCROSSED"
NY Times-Herald-Voice

CAPSULE REVIEW
By Gerrold Saul

"The Starcrossed," which premiered last night on nation-wide network three-dee, is undoubtedly the worst piece of alleged drama ever foisted on the viewers.

Despite the gorgeous good looks of Rita Yearling and the stubborn handsomeness of hockey star Frankie Dulake, the show has little to offer. Ron Gabriel's script—even disguised under a whimsical penname—has all the life and bounce of the proverbial lead dirigible. While the sets were adequate and the costumes arresting, the story made no sense whatsoever. And the acting was non-existent. Stalwart though he may be in the hockey rink, Dulake's idea of drama is to peer into the cameras and grimace.

The technical feat of producing really solid three-dimensional images was impressive. Titantic Productions' new technique will probably be copied by all the other studios, because it makes everything else look pale and wan by comparison.

If only the script had been equal to the electronics!

LA Free Press-News-Times

TV GUIDE
America's Oldest and Most Respected Television Magazine

Contents

"The Starcrossed:" Can a Science Fiction Show Succeed by Spoofing Science Fiction?
Technical Corner: New Three-Dee Projection Technique Heralds End of "Blinking Blues"
The New Lineups: Networks Unveil "Third Season" Shows, and Prepare for "Fourth Season" in Seven Weeks
A Psychologist Warns: Portraying Love in Three-Dee Could Confuse Teenagers
Nielson Reports: "Mongo's Mayhem" and "Shoot-Out" Still Lead in Popularity

MITCH WESTERLY, MYSTERY MAN OF TELEVISION

Playperson

WHY RITA YEARLING CRIED WHEN SHE FLEW TO TORONTO

TV Love Stars

DULAQ NOT SCORING, CANADIAN MAPLE STARS NOT WINNING

Sporting News

CAN A GAY PORTRAY A STRAIGHT ON TV? AND IF SO, WHY?

Liberty

NEW THREE-DEE PROJECTION SYSTEM
FULLY SUCCESSFUL
Scintillation-Free Images Result from
Picosecond Control Units Developed by
Oxnard Laboratory in California

: : : : : :

Dr. Oxnard Claims System Can Be
Adapted to 'Animate' Still Photos;
Obviate Need for Actors in TV

Electronics News

17: THE OUTCOME

Bill Oxnard grimaced with concentration as he maneuvered his new Electric TR into Ron Gabriel's driveway. Ordinarily it would have been an easy task, but the late winter rainstorm made visibility practically nil and there was a fair-sized van parked at the curb directly in front of the driveway.

The front door of the house was open and a couple of burly men in coveralls were taking out the long sectional sofa that had curled around Gabriel's living room. They grunted and swore under their breaths as they swung their burden around the Electric TR. The sofa was so big that if they had dropped it on the sportscar, they would have flattened it.

Brenda looked upset as she got out of the righthand seat. "They're taking his *furniture!*" She dashed into the house.

Oxnard was a step behind her. It only took three long strides to get inside the foyer, but the rain was hard enough to soak him, even so.

There were no lights on inside the house. The furniture movers had left a hand torch glowing in the living room. Oxnard watched them reenter the house, trailing muddy footprints and dripping water, to grab the other chairs in the living room.

Brenda said, "Bill! And they've turned off his electricity!" She was very upset and Oxnard found himself feeling pleased with her concern, rather than jealous over it. *She's really a marvelous person,* he told himself.

They looked around the darkened house for a few minutes and finally found Ron Gabriel sitting alone in the kitchen, in candlelight.

"Ron, why didn't you tell us?" Brenda blurted.

Gabriel looked surprised and, in the flickering light of the lone candle, a bit annoyed.

"Tell you what?"

"We would have helped you, wouldn't we, Bill?"

"Of course," Oxnard said. "If you're broke, Ron, or run out of credit. . . ."

"What're you talking about?" Gabriel pushed himself up from the table. He was wearing his old Bruce Lee robe.

"We've been following the reviews of 'The Starcrossed,' " said Brenda. "We saw what a panning the scripts took. They're blaming you for everything. . . ."

"And when we saw them taking away your furniture. . . ."

"And no electricity. . . ."

A lithe young girl walked uncertainly into the kitchen, dressed in a robe identical to Gabriel's. The candlelight threw coppery glints from her hair, which flowed like a cascade of molten red-gold over her slim shoulders.

With a *you guys are crazy* look, Gabriel introduced, "Cindy Steele, this is Brenda Impanema and Bill Oxnard, two of my loony friends."

"Hello," said Cindy, in a tiny little voice.

Brenda smiled at her and Oxnard nodded.

"We *were* going to have a quiet little candlelight dinner," Gabriel said, "just the two of us. Before the Ding-Dong Furniture Company came in with my new gravity-defying float-chair. And the Salvation Army came by to pick up my old living room furniture, which I donated to them. And my friends started going spastic for fear that I was broke and starving."

"Is that what. . . ." Brenda didn't quite believe it.

But Oxnard did. He started laughing. "I guess we jumped to the wrong conclusion. Come on," he held out a hand to Brenda, "we've got a candlelight dinner of our own to see to."

Gabriel's eyebrows shot up. "Yeah? Really?" He came around the table and looked at the two of them closely. "Son of a gun." He grinned.

They walked out to the foyer together, the four of them, Gabriel between Oxnard and Brenda, Cindy trailing slightly behind, twirling a curl of hair in one finger.

"Hey look," Gabriel said. "Come on back after dinner. For dessert. Got a lot to tell you."

"Oh, I don't think. . . ." Brenda began.

"We'll be back in a couple of hours," Oxnard said. "We've got a lot to tell you, too."

"Great. Bring back some pie or something."

"And give us at least three hours," Cindy said, smiling and walking the fingers of one hand across the back of Gabriel's shoulders. "I'm a slow cooker."

It was just after midnight when Gabriel, Brenda and Oxnard tried out the new floatchairs. They were like an arrangement of airfoam cushions out of the Arabian Nights, except that they floated a dozen centimeters above coppery disks that rested on the floor.

"It's like sitting on a cloud!" Brenda said, snuggling down on the cushions as they adjusted to fit her form.

"Takes a lot of electricity to maintain the field, doesn't it?" Oxnard asked.

"You bet," snapped Gabriel. "And you clowns thought they'd turned off my power."

"Where's Cindy?" asked Brenda.

Gabriel gave a tiny shrug. "Probably fell asleep in the whirlpool bath. She does that, sometimes. Nice kid, but not too bright."

"So what's your news?" Oxnard asked, anxious to tell his own.

Leaning back in his cushions, Gabriel said, "You know all the flak they've been throwing at me about the scripts for 'The Starcrossed'? Well my *original* script—the one that little creepy censor and Earnest tore to shreds—its going to get the Screen Writer's award next month as the best dramatic script of the year."

"Ron, that's great!"

Gabriel crowed, "And the Guild is asking the Canadian Department of Labor to sue Badger for using child labor —the high school kids who wrote scripts without getting paid!"

"Can they do that?"

Nodding, Gabriel said, "The lawyers claim they can and they're naming Gregory Earnest as a codefendant, along with Badger Studios."

"The suit won't affect Titantic, will it?" Brenda asked, looking around.

"Can't. It's limited to Canadian law."

"That's good; B.F.'s had enough trouble over 'The Starcrossed.' "

"Nothing he didn't earn, sweetie," Gabriel said.

"Maybe so," Brenda said. "But enough is enough. He'll be getting out of the hospital next week and I don't want him hurt anymore."

Gabriel shook his head. "You're damned protective of that louse."

Oxnard glanced at Brenda. She controlled herself perfectly. He knew what was going through her mind: *He may be a louse, but he's the only louse in the world who's my father.*

"Has the show been cancelled yet?" Gabriel asked.

"No," Brenda said. "Its being renewed for the remainder of the season."

"What?"

Oxnard said, "Same reaction I had. Wait'll you hear why."

"What's going on?" Gabriel asked, suddenly a-quiver with interest.

"Lots," Brenda said. "Titanic is receiving about a thousand letters a week from the viewers. Most of them are science fiction fans complaining about the show; but they have to *watch* it to complain about it. The Nielson ratings have been so-so, but there's been a good number of letters asking for pictures of Rita and personal mail for her. She's become the center of a new Earth Mother cult—most of the letters are from pubescent boys."

"My god," Gabriel moaned.

"Goddess," corrected Oxnard.

"Also," Brenda went on, "Rita's apparently got her talons into Keith Connors, the TNT man. So the show's assured of a sponsor for the rest of the season. She's got him signing commitments 'til his head's spinning."

With a rueful nod, Gabriel admitted, "She can do that."

"The New York bankers seem pleased. The show is making money. The critics hate it, of course, but it's bringing in some money."

"I'll be damned," Gabriel said.

"Never overestimate the taste of the American public," Brenda said.

Oxnard added, "And the show's bringing money into my lab, as well. People are seeing how good the new system is and they're showering us with orders. We're working three shifts now and I'm expanding the staff and adding more floor space for production."

Gabriel gave an impressed grunt.

"What Bill doesn't seem to realize," Brenda said, "is that it's really his holographic system that's created so much interest in 'The Starcrossed.' Nobody'd stare at Rita Yearling for long if she didn't look so solid."

"I dont know about that," Oxnard protested.

"It's true," Brenda said. "All the networks and production companies have placed orders for the new system. Everybody'll have it by next season."

"Then there goes Titanic's edge over the competition," Gabriel said, sounding satisfied with the idea.

"Not quite," Oxnard said.

"What do you mean?"

How to phrase this? he wondered. Carefully, Oxnard said, "Well . . . I made a slip of the tongue to a reporter from an electronics newspaper, about computerizing the system so you can animate still photos. . . ."

"You mean that thing about getting rid of the actors?"

"Somehow B.F. heard about it while he was recuperating from his seizure," Brenda took over, "and made Bill an offer to develop the system for Titanic."

"So I'm going to work with him on it," Oxnard concluded.

Gabriel's face froze in a scowl. "Why? Why do anything for that lying bastard?"

Oxnard shot a glance at Brenda, then replied, "He was sick. Those New York bankers were pressuring him. So I agreed to work with him on it. It impressed the bankers, helped make them happier with a small return on 'The Starcrossed.'" *Call it a present to a prospective father-in-law,* he added silently.

"You oughtta have your head examined," Gabriel said. "He'll just try to screw you again."

"I suppose so," Oxnard agreed cheerfully.

But Gabriel chuckled. "I think I'm going to drop a little hint about this to some of my acting friends. They've got a guild, too. . . ."

Brenda said, "Do me a favor, Ron? Wait a month . . . until he's strong enough to fight back."

"Why should I?"

"For me," she said.

He stared at her. "For you?"

"Please."

He didn't like it, that was clear. But he muttered, "Okay. One month. But no longer than that."

Brenda gave him her best smile. "Thanks, Ron. I knew you were just a pussycat at heart."

Gabriel shook his head. "It's just not *fair!* Dammit, Finger goes around screwing everybody in sight and comes up smelling like orchids. Every goddamned time! He works you to death, Brenda, sticks you with all the shit jobs. . . ."

"That's true," she admitted.

"Leaves me high and dry. . . ."

"You got your award," Oxnard said.

"Can't eat awards. I need work! There's nothing coming in except a few little royalties and residuals. And your mother-humping B.F. has spread the word all over town that I'm too cranky to work with."

Oxnard broke in, "Come to work with me, Ron."

Gabriel's eyes widened. "What?"

"Sure," Oxnard said. "Listen to me, both of you. Why should you have to put up with all this lunacy and nonsense? Ron, how long can you stand to be trampled by idiots like Earnest and that Canadian censor? Come to work with me! I need a good writer to direct our advertising and public relations staffs. You can be a consultant . . . work one day a week at the lab and spend the rest of the time free to write the books you've always wanted to write."

Before Gabriel could answer, Oxnard turned to Brenda. "And you too. You're a top-flight administrator, Brenda. Come to work with me. Why should you give yourself ulcers and high blood pressure over some dumb TV show? We can be a team, a real team—the three of us."

She looked shocked.

Oxnard turned back to Gabriel. "I mean it, Ron. You'd enjoy the work, I know." He looked back and forth, from Gabriel to Brenda and back again. "Well? How about it? Will you both come to work at Oxnard Labs?"

In unison they replied, "What? And quit show business?"

856 6954

are you missing out on some great Pyramid books?

You can have any title in print at Pyramid delivered right to your door! To receive your Pyramid Paperback Catalog, fill in the label below (use a ball point pen please) and mail to Pyramid . . .